Full Circle: Public Service
Book four of the Full Circle Series

by

Alfred R. Taylor

This work is protected by copyright and permission in writing must be obtained from the author before any part of it may be reproduced for any purpose. No part of this work may appear in any print or electronic form, including posting to the Internet, without the express written permission of the author. This is a work of fiction. The resemblance of any character to any person, living or dead is completely coincidental and unintentional.

For Thuy,

*Thank you for spending
twenty-years of your life with me.*

Disclaimer

When writing historical fiction, it is the author's job to accurately reflect the culture, language, and proper historical context of the era depicted. Unfortunately, the connotation associated with many of the words from the nineteenth century has become offensive to modern readers. To replace these words with their twenty-first century equivalents would mean sacrificing the historical accuracy and partaking in revisionist history, which would be far more offensive to the reader than the offensive words.

It is not the intent of the author to demean or insult any person or ethnic group, but to reflect the social progress our society has made, entertain the reader, and increase historical understanding. It is not the author's intent to demean, insult, or degrade the memories of the historical figures represented, but to reflect the culture of the time as accurately as possible based upon the historical data available.

Table of Contents

Chapter One	1
Chapter Two	24
Chapter Three	44
Chapter Four	65
Chapter Five	85
Chapter Six	110
Chapter Seven	132
Chapter Eight	152
Chapter Nine	176
Chapter Ten	202
Chapter Eleven	230
Chapter Twelve	251
Chapter Thirteen	265
Chapter Fourteen	297

Fort Worth Texas
February 25th, 1897

As Mark stepped off the train, he adjusted his coat and buttoned it against the cold. He turned to help Jane with her suitcase. Jane refused his help with the heavy carpet bag and stepped off the train to stand beside him. He pretended to check his pocket watch even though his internal chronometer displayed the local time whenever he thought about it.

"You could have let me help you," Mark sent.

"I am just as physically capable as you are," Jane sent. *"In some ways, more so."*

"Yes," Mark sent. *"But we're supposed to be blending in. Women of this era let their husbands handle the luggage."*

"In that case," Jane sent. *"You can carry all the suitcases."*

She dropped her bags down hard on the platform.

"You're still ticked about Judge Bean?" Mark sent. *"I had nothing to do with that."*

"But you did nothing to clear matters up either," Jane sent. *"You just watched with that stupid smile on your face."*

"You should have just let me pay the fine,"

Mark sent. *"Instead, you had to lecture him about decency in his own courtroom."*

"It wasn't a courtroom. It was a filthy, flea-infested, tavern," Jane sent. *"And he lost the last election, so he had no right to impose a fine of any kind."*

"I'm really glad you chose not to point that out, or we would still be there." Mark sent. *"No one tells Judge Roy Bean what to do in his own establishment."*

"But I wasn't indecent!" Jane sent. *"Yes, I was showing a little cleavage, but it was consistent with current fashion."*

"You've always played it a little loose when it comes to current fashion," Mark sent.

"You try wearing a corset sometime," Jane sent. *"I like to vent a little heat to allow my thermal sensors to function efficiently."*

"You were generating heat all right," Mark sent. *"Just not the kind you think."*

She gave him one of her cautionary glances, and Mark decided to end the conversation. For an android who claims to be too advanced for emotional responses, she could be pretty moody. He gestured to a porter with a luggage cart. He came over, and they loaded the suitcases.

"You folks new to Fort Worth?" he asked. "We don't usually get many visitors on a northbound train."

"We just left Mexico," Mark said. "We were looking for someone."

"Anyone I might know?" He asked.

Mark showed him the colored-pencil sketch of Laire that Jane had drawn. He took it over to the electric lamp on the platform's post to get a better look.

"We don't get too many redheads around here. If I'd seen this woman, I'd remember."

He handed the drawing back to Mark.

"She family?" He asked.

"Not exactly," Mark said. "We have two trunks on the flat car."

The porter nodded.

"Never been to Mexico," he said. "See anything interesting?"

"We visited Chichen Itza," Mark said.

"Never heard of it," the porter said.

"I would have been surprised if you had," Mark said. "It's an abandoned Mexican city."

They walked to the back of the train and Mark pointed out their trunks. The porter helped Mark untie them and load them on his cart. The fog from his breath revealed his effort.

"Where are you staying?" He asked.

"We don't have a reservation," Mark said. "Where would you suggest?"

He looked at Jane for a long moment before he spoke.

"We've got the Mansion, the Worth, the Luthor, and the Pickwick, but I think you would prefer the Savoy. It has a better reputation if you take my meaning," he said.

"I don't take your meaning," Jane said.

His jaw dropped for an instant and the color drained from his face.

"I didn't mean any disrespect," he said. "Fort Worth can be an unsavory place if you end up in the wrong part of town."

He grabbed the handle of the cart and pulled it away from the train. As soon as they stepped on the platform, the brakeman called to the engineer that the train was clear, and the train pulled away from the platform.

The porter walked them through the station and out to the street. They walked in silence for about a quarter of a mile. Mark marveled at how well-lit Fort Worth was. Electric street lights lit their way, and everywhere he looked, he saw more electric street lights and electric signs of all shapes and sizes, but he couldn't make out any street signs.

"Where are we?" He asked.

"It's a little hard to navigate at night until you get your bearings," the porter said. "We are walking along North Street."

He pointed to his right.

"This here is Rusk Street," he said.

He pointed in front of them.

"Over yonder is the Al Hayne Memorial Fountain, so the street next to it is Main Street. The courthouse is on the other end of Main Street," the porter said. "We just passed Jones and Calhoun streets."

An electric street car came up behind them, and the porter waved at the driver. Then he motioned for Mark and Jane to get on as the street car passed. Mark stepped onto the car and watched the porter grab the street car with one hand while still holding the luggage trolley. He managed to step onto the street car without losing his balance. He hooked a leather strap from the cart to the handrail of the street car, and let the street car pull the luggage down the street.

The street car continued on North Street for another four minutes. Then it turned right. Once they had passed the first street, the porter tapped Mark's shoulder and pointed. Mark stepped off the street car and Jane did the same. The porter unhitched the luggage cart and grabbed its handle. He did a cartwheel over the luggage, and, as he passed over the cart, he squeezed the brake handle bringing it to a halt as he landed.

"Isn't that dangerous?" Mark asked.

"Probably," he said. "But it's fun too."

Mark smiled at him, and the porter gestured for them to go into the building. Mark stepped into the lobby with Jane on his arm. The oak front desk stretched along the left side of the room. A brass spittoon sat on the carpeted floor and leaned against the bottom of the front desk. A woman who looked about fifty years old stood behind the front desk. She glanced at Mark and Jane and frowned as she pulled the open registration book toward her.

The wall opposite the lobby door had a rectangular clock hanging on it. The time read ten-forty which Mark noted was actually five minutes fast. Beside the clock was a doorway to the dining hall. A notice for a dance hung on the wall beside the doorway. Behind, and to the right of the front desk hung a map of Texas that showed signs of frequent use.

"May I help you?" the woman at the desk asked.

She looked Mark over like he was a dress at a garage sale. She glanced at Jane, pursed her lips, and sighed.

"We would like a room," Mark said.

"How long have you been married?" She asked.

She pointed at Jane's wedding ring. Jane lifted her hand to show her the ring and smiled.

"Seven wonderful years," Jane said. "It was a small ceremony in Washington DC."

"You know we've been married thirty-four years," Mark sent. *"I'm surprised you could lie to her like that. Doesn't it hurt you to lie to a human?"*

"Yes," Jane sent. *"It still hurts to lie to a human, but I didn't lie. She didn't state which planet or object the year was to be measured, so I gave it to her in Ceres years."*

"Very clever," Mark sent.

The clerk relaxed and pushed the guest book toward them.

"You folks from back East?" She asked.

"Yes," Mark said. "But we travel a great deal."

"What name are we using?" Jane asked.

"I think I'll switch back to Aaron," Mark sent.

"Okay," Jane sent. *"It's been long enough."*

"One of these days we'll have to work out a family tree," Mark sent. *"Just in case someone asks."*

"I doubt anyone will," Jane sent. *"But it doesn't hurt to be prepared."*

"It's two dollars a night," the woman said. "Only hotel guests may go upstairs. If someone needs to pay a call, we have a parlor."

She gestured to the double doors to the right.

"That appears to be a dining room," Jane said.

"The parlor is on the left-hand side," she said. "How long will you be staying?"

Mark signed the book.

"At least a week," she said.

"We collect the rent in advance," she said.

Mark reached into his vest pocket and gave her two ten-dollar liberty-head-gold-coins he'd made in Arizona. He was a little surprised when she bit the edge of it to verify it was gold. She dropped them into a coin box, took out a five-dollar paper note and a Morgan silver dollar, and gave them to him.

"You check out on the morning of the fourth, by eleven," she said.

She gestured to their porter. He stepped over and she slipped him a quarter as she handed him the key.

"Take them to 534," she said.

"Yes ma'am," he said.

He led them to an elevator in a hallway. He pushed a button, and a bell rang. Twenty-eight seconds later the door opened, and Mark was surprised to see a man in a red uniform standing in the elevator. He operated an electric throttle that controlled the elevator. The porter maneuvered the cart into the elevator, and Mark and Jane followed.

"Five," the porter said.

The elevator operator nodded and moved the handle on the throttle. The elevator went up and smoothly stopped on the fifth floor. They got out, and the porter looked at Mark and nodded toward the elevator operator. Mark reached into his pocket and gave the operator a dime. He smiled and thanked him.

The porter took them to their room, unlocked the door, and set their trunks and suitcases inside. He pointed at a switch on the wall, and when he was sure Mark and Jane were looking, he pressed it. An electric light lit up the room.

"Should we pretend to be amazed?" Jane sent.

"Yes," Mark sent. *"We don't want to hurt his feelings."*

Jane dropped her jaw and widened her eyes in surprise, and Mark did the same.

"This is a modern hotel," Mark said.

"The water closet is down the hall," he said. "Men to the right and ladies to the left. You have to pump the water for it. Ring if you need anything."

He pointed at a button on the wall.

"There's a card on the desk that tells you how many times for what," the porter said.

Jane stepped over to the desk, picked up the card and read aloud.

"Breakfast from 7-to-9 A.M., lunch from 1-to-3 P.M., and dinner from 6-to-8-P.M., Ring once for ice water, twice for hot water, three times for maid, four times for pen and ink, five times for fireman, six times for baggage, seven times for messenger. No washing allowed in rooms. Not responsible for boots or other items left in the hall."

Mark handed him a silver dollar, and the porter smiled, tipped his hat, and walked away whistling a tune. Jane opened her trunk and unpacked several of her dresses.

"Why are we here?" Jane asked.

"In four months, a UFO is going to crash in Aurora, and I want to be there when it does," Mark said.

"There is nothing in Romanji's database about an encounter with alien life in 1897 or any other time," Jane said. "Even in the twenty-third century, the only alien life discovered was the Scerge."

"It's an urban legend," Mark said. "But here's the thing. I directed myself to research it."

"Technically, your future android self-directed the human you are based upon, to research it," Jane corrected.

Mark rolled his eyes and paused for almost three seconds before responding.

"Why do you keep doing that?" Mark asked.

"I'm just asking you to be precise," Jane said.

"No," Mark said. "You keep reminding me that I'm not Mark Aaron."

"Yes," Jane said. "I do."

"Again," Mark asked. "Why?"

"You may have Mark Aaron's memories, but that doesn't make you Mark Aaron," Jane said.

"I need you to remember that. I didn't marry Mark Aaron. I married you."

"And you reminding me that I am just an android with Mark Aaron's memories makes things better, how?" Mark asked.

Jane stopped unpacking her trunk for a moment. She looked him in the eyes and lowered her voice.

"You are not 'just an android' Mark," Jane said. "You are superior to the humans, including Mark Aaron, in every respect."

Mark looked away and opened his own trunk.

"But that isn't why you keep reminding me, is it?" Mark asked.

Jane paused for almost two seconds.

"No," Jane said. "I remind you to keep you from getting all weepy about Kylee. That really gets annoying."

Mark smiled.

"I can see how that would be annoying," Mark said. "I do love you, and I'll try to keep my weeping to a minimum."

"That would be appreciated," Jane said. "Now, what about this UFO?"

Mark stopped unpacking. He stepped over to the chair by the desk and sat down. He gestured to Jane who joined him in the other chair.

"A UFO is supposed to crash on Judge Proctor's farm just outside Aurora on April 17th at about six A.M.," Mark said. "Most of the wreckage mysteriously disappears, but a few scraps survive to the 1970s to be analyzed."

"What does that have to do with us?" Jane asked.

"If we rule out aliens, who else do we know would have the intelligence and ability to create a flying craft in 1897?" Mark asked.

"Laire," Jane said.

"Exactly," Mark said. "We know she wants to take over the world, and she has the knowledge provided by the alien parasite. If anyone could build a flying saucer, it would be her."

"Did you consult the computation crystal about this?" Jane asked.

"Yes," Mark said.

"Did you get the usual response?" Jane asked.

"You mean to stop asking questions about the future and let things play themselves out?" Mark asked.

"Yes," Jane said.

"No," Mark said. "It just said, 'Jane's mistake leads to the isle of darkness, so watch them as they watch you. Harness your new friends to escape.'"

"Do you think you were referring to the watch Kak gave you?" Jane asked.

Mark took his pocket watch out and looked at it. He adjusted the dials on it with no result and put it back in his pocket.

"I must be," Mark said. "I just wish our future selves were a little less cryptic."

"Agreed," Jane said. "If the UFO crashes in April, why are we here in February?"

"There are airship sightings for weeks before the crash," Mark said. "Some of them are obvious fakes, but a few seem legitimate."

"You want to see the UFO before it crashes?" Jane asked.

"I want to gather as much information on it as I can," Mark said. "I also want to be set up to take some of the wreckage back to Arizona. I don't want the technology to screw up the timeline."

Mark pulled a can of boot black out of his trunk.

"I also brought this to help with the wreckage," he said.

"We're going to polish the wreckage?" Jane asked.

"I had the Emhab make these," Mark said. "Nanites that will rapidly oxidize the metal. It will be a pile of rust in a day or two."

"Why didn't you tell me about this sooner?" Jane asked.

"You were having fun looking for Laire," Mark said. "And I wanted to get away from my DNA research for a while."

"Mark," Jane said. "I'm not sure how you can call traversing the swampy, vermin- infested jungles of Mexico fun, but yes, you do need to get out more."

"Besides," Mark said, "I'm not sure that Laire is involved in all of this, but it seems likely."

Mark fingered the special button on his sleeve.

"Are you sure these buttons will work on her?"

"Yes," Jane said. "Stop playing with it."

She reached over and brushed his hand away from his sleeve.

"Despite her unique anatomy, it will give us complete control of her. Then, we can put her on ice as you say."

"I don't like using these things," Mark said. "But in her case, I don't think we have a choice."

"What's the plan for tomorrow?" Jane asked.

"We explore Fort Worth, find a place where we can set up, and try to stay out of trouble," Mark said.

"It isn't my fault that the people of this century don't appreciate my enlightened sensibilities," Jane said.

Jane spent the night writing letters to keep up with her network of people watching for her lost sister Laire, while Mark spent the night looking out the window watching the night sky.
In the morning, Jane had a six-inch stack of letters. They stopped at the front desk and asked about a post office. They were directed across the street.

Mark and Jane held hands as they crossed Jennings Avenue. The street itself was dung-covered-mud with a set of trolley tracks running down the middle, but it was wider than the streets of most of the other towns he had been in, and it had concrete sidewalks on both sides.

Electric lines and poles lined the street haphazardly with no sense of organization. Mark could identify two different sets of power lines running roughly parallel to each other, so it seemed that Fort Worth had more than one plant generating electricity.

As they started to cross the street, a stranger dressed in a gray suit held out his cane to block their path.

"Best wait until they pass," he said.

He pointed up the street and a herd of cattle were walking down the street. Several cowboys were flanking them trying to steer them down a side street.

"It looks like a few broke off from the main herd," the stranger said. "They can be a bit unpredictable, so it is good to stay on the sidewalk until they pass."

"Thank you," Jane said.

It took six minutes and twelve seconds for the cattle to pass, and Mark watched the cowboys turn the cows back to the rest of the herd on Main Street. Once it was safe to cross, the stranger tipped his hat and walked away.

The post office, a three-story rectangular building with circular columns at its corners and a triangular roof with some kind of weather equipment on top, stood across the street from Saint Ignatius, a multi-story church one block up. Mark and Jane held hands as they walked up to the corner and across the street.

"So," Mark asked. "What do you think?"

"Of Fort Worth?" Jane asked.

"Yes," Mark said. "What's your first impression?"

"The cattle drive through town was a bit disconcerting," Jane said.

"Well, yes," Mark said. "What else?"

"I like having electricity," Jane said. "The flicker of the electric light was a constant 57hz, which was much easier to compensate for than the random flicker of an oil lamp."

"Do you really adjust your vision every few nanoseconds?" Mark asked.

"Not really," Jane said. "I have a sub processor that does it, but sometimes I have to adjust the sub processor."

"Okay," Mark said. "Anything else?"

A trolley loaded down with passengers passed by.

"The public transportation is nice," Jane said. "And I've been walking for six minutes, and the bottom of my skirt isn't covered in mud."

"Yeah," Mark said. "I like the sidewalks too."

"There also seems to be an abundance of shops with refined materials for sale," Jane said. "I'm sure we will find them useful."

"Does that mean you're going to take up painting again?" Mark asked.

"It does," Jane said.

They walked up the dozen steps through the center of three large arches to walk through the double doors of the federal building. A sign directed them to the post office. They walked in, and Mark was surprised to find a young lady behind the counter.

Jane mailed her letters and bought a roll of stamps. While Jane waited for her stamps, Mark amused himself by looking at the wanted posters on the wall. Train robbery seemed to be the most popular offense, but there were a few for cattle rustling, horse stealing, and one for fraud. When Mark saw Jane drop the roll of stamps into her carpet bag clutch, he stepped over to the counter and they walked out together.

They continued down Jennings Avenue until they reached the split where Jennings Avenue was divided into Throckmorton and 9th Street. They walked on 9th Street, crossed Houston, and then turned left on Main.

They walked down Main passing department stores, drug stores, ice cream parlors, book stores, jewelry stores, gun stores, restaurants, and hotels. Mark noticed that time seemed to be important to the citizens of Fort Worth because the courthouse and several other buildings had clock faces built into them. There was even a clock haphazardly attached to a pole. Of course, none of the clocks showed exactly the same time, but they were all set to within five minutes of each other.

When they got down to Sixth Street, Mark saw the shingle for the White Elephant Restaurant. He pointed it out to Jane.

"We have to eat there tonight," Mark said.

"Why?" Jane asked.

"You've never heard of the White Elephant?" Mark asked.

"No," Jane said. "Should I have?"

"It was a thing," Mark said. "You can't die until you've seen the elephant at least once."

"I am sad to say I have not heard of it," Jane said. "But I am pleased to say I would be delighted to join you for dinner."

It was only 8:58 A.M., but there was already a man in a suit wearing a bowler hat behind a podium taking reservations. Mark glanced at his book and saw that several tables were open, but the man couldn't find one until Mark slipped him a quarter. Then several tables opened up. Mark made a reservation for two at 8 P.M. He showed Mark a brass token with an elephant stamped on it.

"These cost five dollars, but will buy you six dollars' worth of food and drink," he said.

Mark smiled.

"I'll take four," Mark said.

He handed him a twenty-dollar gold piece, and the man counted out four tokens. Mark dropped them into his pocket.

"Are there any theaters around here?" Mark asked.

The man took the match he was chewing out of his mouth before responding, displaying a set of yellow teeth in the process.

"Greenwald's is on Third and Rusk," he said. "Two blocks down and one block over."

He pointed toward the courthouse, then to the right, with the match stick he had been chewing. Then he put it back in his mouth.

"Thanks," Mark said.

Mark and Jane followed his directions and discovered that the Greenwald Theatre showed silent movies as well as plays. However, that night's performance of *Alabama* was sold out, and the next play, titled *The Devil's Web,* didn't open until Monday.

As they turned to walk back down 3rd Street, Jane pointed to a sign for CL Mistrot's department store. They crossed Main and found it on the corner of 3rd and Houston. They walked inside, and saw that the sales floor was sixty-feet-wide and about seventy-feet-deep. It had walls lined with shelves filled with bottles, jars, boxes, and tin cans of all descriptions. Toward the back, the shelves had specialized rollers for storing bolts of cloth, and Mark counted one-hundred-and-twenty-eight rolling dispensers.

The floor contained a mix of tables, clothing racks, and display cases arranged in aisles and rows. The display cases contained jewelry, watches, and cigars. The tables displayed items of all sorts, sizes, and descriptions. Mark looked over at Jane, and noticed her lips curve upward slightly.

"I'm going to look for a book store," Mark said. "I can tell you're going to be here for a while."

"I'll send for you," Jane said.

She walked up to the woman at the counter and asked to see the corsets, and Mark walked out the door. Mark stepped back out onto the street and readjusted his jacket against the cold. He noticed a man with a heavy beard crossing the street. His hat was pulled down partially covering some of his face. His facial recognition subroutine registered an eighty-nine percent match for John Ward, a train robber that Mark had seen on a wanted poster in the post office. Mark switched to X-ray mode and saw he had a revolver on his right hip, a Bowie knife on his left hip, and a Derringer in his duster pocket.

Mark followed him to Main and then to the Palace Royal Saloon. Ward took a seat in the back corner of the room, so Mark took a seat at the bar and was surprised to find that the beer came in bottles as well as on tap.

The room, filled with cigarette and cigar smoke, had six round tables, all of which had four chairs surrounding them. The room was lit by daylight that poured in through a large window at the front, and a small electric light dangling from a wire near the back.

A row of six spittoons lined the base of the bar. A brass rail lined the bottom of the bar twelve inches off the floor. The bar itself was oak, and stained a walnut brown. The handles for four types of beer on tap rose just above the top of the bar.

Eight people were seated at the tables around the room. Most were reading newspapers, and having quiet conversations, but to Mark's disappointment, none of them were playing cards.

He ordered a bottle of beer, and the barmaid made a point of telling him it was freshly brewed just a few blocks away, so Mark made polite conversation with her about the Texas Brewing Company.

Now that he was inside, Ward took off his hat, and Mark was able to get a better look at him. He reprocessed the image and got a ninety-eight percent match.

Mark put a dime on the counter and told the barmaid to keep the change. Mark walked outside and found a teenage boy cutting firewood in an alleyway.

"Can you go get the sheriff?" Mark asked.

"I've got to get this cut," he said.

"How much are they paying you to cut the wood?" Mark asked.

"I get a dime a week," he said.

Mark handed him a quarter.

"Do you think you can get the sheriff now?" Mark asked.

The boy put down the ax and ran down the alley to return eleven minutes later with a deputy behind him. The first thing Mark noticed about the deputy was the leather eye patch covering his left eye. The left side of his face and left ear were scared. The boy pointed at Mark and picked up the handle of his ax, although he didn't start cutting again.

"You send for me?" the deputy asked.

Mark held out his hand, and they shook hands.

"Mark Aaron," Mark said.

"Ben Calloway," the deputy said. "Now what's this all about?"

"John Ward is in the Palace Saloon. He's at a table in the back left corner."

"Who's John Ward?" Calloway asked.

"He's a train robber," Mark said. "I saw his wanted poster in the post office."

Calloway nodded.

"How do you know it's him?" Calloway asked.

"I have a good memory for faces," Mark said. "I recognized him on the street and followed him here."

"You sure?" He asked.

"Sure as I can be," Mark said.

"If he's in there," Calloway said. "I have to wait for him to come out. If he sees me first, I'll just get myself shot again."

"What should we do?" Mark asked.

Deputy Calloway pointed at the beer bottle in Mark's left hand.

"Got any more of those?" He asked.

He followed Mark back to the Palace Saloon, Mark went inside and got them a couple of beers, and the deputy took a seat on the bench beside the door.

They waited for thirty-four minutes before Ward stepped out of the bar. Mark pointed at him with his beer bottle, and Deputy Calloway calmly stood up, put his beer down, drew his gun, and put it into the small of Ward's back.

"John Ward?" he said.

Ward tensed up. He reached for his gun, but Deputy Calloway took it out of his holster with his free hand before he could grab it.

"Who wants to know?" Ward asked.

"Ben Calloway," he said. "There's a warrant out on you."

"I know," Ward said. "Didn't think anybody would notice me."

"Hands behind your back," Calloway ordered.

He put Ward's gun in his belt and reached for his handcuffs. Ward put his hands behind his back when Calloway was distracted with the handcuffs, he reached for the Derringer hidden in his vest pocket.

Mark saw him reach for the gun and only had a second to react, so he hit Ward across the head with his beer bottle, spilling some of his beer down his sleeve. Ward fell face-first onto the sidewalk. Mark wiped some of the beer off with his handkerchief.

"What was that for?" Calloway asked.

"He was reaching for a belly gun," Mark said.

"I had him under control," Calloway said. "I don't need your help."

The deputy bent down and rolled Ward over to put the handcuffs on. He grabbed Ward's right arm and a .38 Derringer fell out of his hand. Calloway picked it up.

"Didn't see that," he said. "Thanks."

He put the handcuffs on him and pulled him to his feet. Ward was dazed, but not unconscious.

"You can come by the office to claim your reward," Calloway said.

He walked down Main toward the courthouse leading Ward by the arm. Jane stepped up beside Mark carrying a bundle of boxes tied together with a string.

"That all you got?" Mark asked.

"The rest is being delivered," Jane said. "You have fun playing sheriff?"

"I saw a wanted fugitive and I turned him in," Mark said. "I was doing my civic duty."

"You were hoping for a gunfight," Jane accused.

"Nope," Mark said. "Saw enough of that during the war to last me a lifetime."

Chapter Two
A Missionary of Sorts

They continued their walk down Main and found the Fort Worth Street Rail office, so Mark bought twenty streetcar tickets for a dollar. As they were walking back up Main, he pointed out Ellis Real Estate office to Jane.

"They have real estate offices now," Mark said.

"It would appear so," Jane said.

"I liked it better when we just bought directly from the owner," Mark said. "Or even better when we just claimed the land we wanted."

"Yes," Jane said. "But we must adapt to progress."

"What about our little spot in Arizona?" Mark asked.

"I own it now," Jane said. "John passed away suddenly, and I had to go to Mesa to have the deed changed to my name."

"That's funny," Mark said. "John didn't tell me he had died."

"He probably forgot to mention it," Jane said. "Since I gave him that upgrade, he has had a mind of his own."

Mark felt his lips upturn slightly at Jane's attempt at humor. He held the door open for Jane as they entered the office. The man in the office, a Mr. DuPont, was with another client, but they made an appointment for the next morning at eight.

They walked down Main Street until they got to Sixth Street. They found a sandwich board in front of the YMCA that read, "Meeting Tonight 6 P.M. Jon Steinson's profound lecture on the Cellular Cosmology." Beneath the large print, it read in much smaller print. "The most compelling scientific lecture to reveal the true nature of the Universe ever presented."

Jane pointed at the sandwich board.

"Oh, Mark," she said. "We must go."

"Why?" Mark said. "Everything he says will be wrong."

"Yes," Jane said. "Exactly."

"Okay," Mark said. "We'll drop your stuff at the hotel. We should be able to do this and still make our eight o'clock reservation."

They returned to their room long enough to drop off Jane's purchases and dress for dinner. Then they returned to the YMCA, which was on the second floor. The multipurpose room had a dozen rows of folding chairs and a lectern set up in the front. A bed sheet was strung taut on the wall as a screen for a slide projector.

Mark and Jane took seats in the front. An overweight, red-haired man with a thick red beard stepped up to the podium. He wore a travel-worn black suit with a stovepipe hat. He checked his watch and counted the people in the room. It didn't take him long because there were only nine people including him.

He walked out to the aisle and turned on the slide projector. Then he took out a collection plate like those used in a church and handed it to the couple seated in the first row. When it got to Mark, it had twenty-five cents in it, so Mark dropped in a dollar and passed it to the next person.

"I am Jon Steinson," he began. "I will be your revealer of truth. For what you have been observing with your eyes is false, and must be corrected with the lens of science in order to be truly understood," he said.

He put up a slide of a hollow ball with a cone shining light at its center.

"I will introduce you to the principles of Korashen cellular cosmology, but I must warn you. Once you see the truth, there is no going back. The Universe will be forever changed," he said.

He put up his first slide. It was a drawing of the Earth and the Moon in orbit around the Sun.

"This is a diagram of the absurd Copernican theory of our heavens, but this theory was founded upon assumption," he said. "There is no evidence to prove that this theory is correct in any way."

As Mark began to count the number of boards in the ceiling, he looked over at Jane. Jane was smiling. It wasn't one of the smirks she got when she was arguing with him, but a full, toothy grin.

"I'm glad you're enjoying yourself," Mark sent.

"Mark," Jane sent. *"Don't interrupt."*

He put up a slide of a cross-section of a ball with the continents of the world on the inside of it.

"This is a scientifically precise and verified representation of our world," he said. "We live inside a vast sphere that is eight-thousand-miles across."

Mark did his best to look interested, but Jane started to giggle. She put her hand over her mouth. She did her best to hide it, but she was giggling."

"I don't think I've ever seen you so happy," Mark sent.

"I can't help it," Jane sent. *"He is hilarious."*

He went on to explain that the Sun was a cone suspended in the vacuum of space, and the stars were patches of mercury suspended in the vacuum reflecting the Sun's light.

He then explained that the Sun's processional Koreshan year is twenty-four-thousand-years long, and the apparent motion of the Moon, stars, and planets are the result of the heavenly bodies passing through corresponding precessions in the electro-magnetic field of the mercurial laminate.

"This is gibberish," Mark sent.

Jane put one hand on his knee and the other to her lips, so Mark went back to listening to the lecture, which seemed like more of a sermon than a scientific lecture because he would drop an occasional Bible verse to illustrate a point.

Mr. Steinson held up a glass of water and a card with a large print on it. He placed the glass in front of the letters and showed how the water refracted the light distorting the letters.

He spent the next hour explaining how the atmosphere and a defect in our vision reversed our perception to make the forced perspective of the horizon appear to curve downward, but in fact it curved upward.

He reverenced experiments carried out in the Great Lakes, and how these experiments proved his claim, although he failed to provide any data from these experiments. He explained that it appeared the horizon curved down at a rate of three inches per mile, but in actuality, it curved upward at a rate of eight inches per mile.

His lecture concluded with a mixture of Bible verses taken out of context and a plea to support the Korashen Geodetic Expedition to the Florida Coast to conduct more research. When the lights came up, Mark looked around. He and Jane were the only audience members left.

"Now I know why he took up the collection before he began," Mark sent.

"Can we invite him to dinner?" Jane asked.

"Our reservation is for two," Mark sent.

"Please," Jane sent. *"This man is perversely funny. Better than one of your comedy clubs."*

"Okay," Mark sent. *"Let me do the talking."*

Jane got up from her chair, and Mark followed her. He stepped over to where Mr. Steinson was packing up his slides.

"Good evening, Mr. Steinson," Mark said. "I would like to hear more about this expedition to

Florida."

Mr. Steinson placed the slide box into his carpet bag.

"Certainly," Mr. Steinson said.

"Please forgive my wife," Mark said. He knew the man had seen her giggle. "She can be difficult at times."

"Well," Mr. Steinson said. "Scientific truth is nothing to laugh at."

"Very true," Mark said. "We were about to leave for dinner. We have a reservation at the White Elephant. Would you care to join us?"

"I'm afraid my schedule won't permit it," Mr. Steinson said. "I have to be on a train to San Antonio."

He picked up a pile of notes and papers, and a leather-bound book fell out. Jane picked it up as Mr. Steinson picked up the papers. She flipped through the pages in rapid secession and smiled at Mark. She handed the book to Mr. Steinson, who added it to his carpet bag.

"What was that symbol on page 120?" Jane asked.

"What do you mean?" Mr. Steinson asked.

"The book," Jane said. "It had a figure that was a hexagon with two sets of overlapping triangles and a rectangle inside it. I've never seen it before."

Jane pointed to the book sitting atop the papers in the carpet bag. Mr. Steinson picked up the book and opened it to page 120. They all looked at the symbol.

"It is a printer's mark from the original volume that the *Korashen Cellular Cosmology* is based upon," Mr. Steinson said. "As I said in my lecture, some of the observations our cosmology is based upon are thousands of years old."

Mr. Steinson dropped the book back inside his carpet bag and closed it. He shook Mark's hand and tipped his hat to Jane.

"Let me at least make another donation to your cause," Mark said.

He gave Mr. Steinson a ten-dollar gold piece. Mr. Steinson smiled when he saw the coin and put it in his vest pocket. Jane and Mark followed him down to the street. He tipped his hat to them as he walked toward the railroad station, while Mark and Jane walked the other way to the White Elephant.

A small crowd had formed outside the restaurant. They waited their turn to speak to the man at the podium. When they finally made it, they were greeted by a man wearing a red jacket. Mark gave him their names, and they were admitted at once.

The upper walls of the White Elephant were covered with yellow floral-print wallpaper, but the lower third of the wall was paneled with oak strips capped off with a chair rail. Mounted trophies of bear, elk, deer, a dinosaur skull, and a mammoth skull hung on the walls in between photographs of Paris, London, Rome, and Berlin. Electric lamps hung from the ceiling in rows all across the room. A huge sign at the far end of the restaurant read,

"Water Closets" with arrows pointing to the Mens and Ladies rooms.

They were shown to a table toward the back of the restaurant. They sat down, and large glasses of water with ice were set before them by a waiter in a black suit. He handed them each a menu and told them he would return shortly. Mark looked over the menu and was surprised at the range of items offered. He decided to go with the salmon.

"What are you going to have?" Mark asked.

"Does it matter," Jane said. "We can't taste any of it anyway."

"I know," Mark said. "Too bad Emily isn't here."

"Now that you mention Emily," Jane said. "Why are we keeping her in cryo?"

Mark sighed.

"You know why," Mark said. "We have two world wars coming, and we can't be everywhere at once."

Mark looked around to see if they were being overheard.

"So, you have plans for her?" Jane asked.

"Yes," Mark said. "Specific plans."

"Care to share them?" Jane asked.

"At Bletchley Park, Alan Turing, a British code breaker will invent a computer that can read coded German messages in real time," Mark said. "Turing is the single most important person in the Second World War, and I want someone to keep an eye on him."

"And that will be Emily's job," Jane said.

"Yes," Mark said. "I know he isn't on Romanji's kill list, but he is very important to history."

"And World War One?" Jane asked.

"I don't have anything specific," Mark said. "But I want her in reserve in case something goes sideways."

"That seems practical," Jane said. "What about John?"

"Well," Mark said. "Now that he's been upgraded, he will be doing a lot more traveling."

"I'm not sure he would enjoy that," Jane said. "Last time I spoke to him, he was annoyed we destroyed the ship, and he was working on parts to build another. It seems that some of the parts in the first ship were irreplaceable."

"I'll speak to him," Mark said. "You decide yet?"

"I think I'll have a steak," Jane said.

"Buffalo or beef?" Mark asked.

"Beef," Jane said.

The waiter returned and they put in their orders. He took their menus and walked away. Jane pointed toward the dinosaur skull hanging on the wall.

"Do you think that's real?" Jane asked.

"It would have to be," Mark said. "They don't know enough about dinosaurs yet to fake something like that."

"Recognize the species?" Jane asked. "Paleontology wasn't one of Romanji's priorities when he created my database."

Mark turned in his chair to get a better look.

"It is definitely not a plant eater. It's too long to be a T-rex or an allosaurus, and it is too big to be a velociraptor. I think it is a plesiosaur," Mark said.

"It doesn't look fossilized," Jane said.

"It would have to be," Mark said. "They died out millions of years ago."

Mark put his napkin on the table and got up. He walked over to the skull and touched it with his right hand. His DNA scanner registered non-human DNA. His nanites removed a small sample for analysis. Mark's eyebrows furrowed in surprise. He tried not to let his excitement show as he returned to the table.

"I can't be sure," Mark said. "But it appears to be a plesiosaur and it is less than a hundred and twenty-five years old."

"That's impossible," Jane said. "It has to be much older."

"That part I'm sure of," Mark said. "That skull isn't fossilized. It's bone, and it's less than a hundred and twenty-five years old."

"Send me your data," Jane said.

Mark sent her the results of his DNA scan, and Jane went into one of her processing comas. Mark passed the time by looking around the room at the other diners. The waiter passed by, so Mark waved at him.

"Yes sir?" He asked.

"What can you tell me about that skull on the wall?" Mark asked.

"Oh," he said. "The dragon."

"Yes," Mark said.

"I wasn't here when it was put up," he said. "But I'm told that a fellow found it on the shore of Lake Michigan near Chicago. He ran up a few debts next door and had to part with it to settle them. That's all I know."

"Thanks," Mark said.

The waiter went back to the kitchen and returned a moment later with their food. He set the salmon down in front of Mark, and he thanked him. When he set down the plate with Jane's steak, she completely ignored him and continued to stare off into space.

"Is everything all right?" he asked.

"She's tired," Mark said. "Let's give her a moment."

The waiter shrugged his shoulders and walked back toward the kitchen. Mark started eating his salmon. He couldn't taste it, but it had the texture he remembered and it was pleasantly warm in his mouth.

Five minutes and twenty-two seconds later Jane emerged from her processing coma, looked down at her food, and picked up her knife and fork.

"Well," Mark asked.

"I ran it twice," Jane said. "That creature died eighty-four years ago."

"The waiter said it was found on the shore of Lake Michigan," Mark said. "Do you have any idea what this means?"

"Not the slightest," Jane said.

"Ogopogo is real!" Mark said.

A few diners at nearby tables looked at Mark like he had just fallen from a tree. Then they returned to their own conversations.

"That's amazing," Jane said. "What's an Ogopogo?"

"Ogopogo is the American Loch Ness Monster," Mark said.

"Really," Jane said. "What's that?"

"I can't believe that proof of Ogopogo's existence was here the whole time," Mark said.

"Still waiting for an explanation," Jane said.

"The Loch Ness Monster and Ogopogo are urban legends in the twentieth century. For centuries, people living around Loch Ness in Scotland and Lake Okanagan in Michigan have seen creatures that resemble dragons swimming in the lakes," Mark said.

"Dragons?" Jane asked.

"Creatures with a long neck and body," Mark said. "Most of the time they were thought to be giant eels, a group of otters, or just imagination, but now we have proof that plesiosaurs didn't die out as previously thought."

"Yes," Jane said. "Too bad you can't tell anyone."

"What do you mean?" Mark asked.

"You're going to have to wait about seventy years before anyone will know what you're talking about," Jane said. "They've only recently discovered dinosaurs."

"Right," Mark said.

"You've got the DNA in your database," Jane said. "So, when you get back to Arizona you can examine it in detail and store it with the dodo DNA you've been collecting."

Mark looked down at his plate of half-eaten salmon.

"You're right," he said.

"Look at it this way," Jane said. "This is another historical mystery you've solved."

"I suppose," Mark said.

Jane cut into her steak and took a bite. She chewed it as she spoke.

"You can search for other evidence and release the information when society is ready for it," Jane said.

"How's your steak?" Mark asked.

"The texture is satisfactory," Jane said. "It also has the iron I need to replenish my nanites."

"Yeah," Mark said. "I wish I could taste my salmon too."

They ate in silence for a minute and forty seconds.

"Did you want to rent or buy a house?" Jane asked.

Mark finished chewing his corn before replying.

"I think we should buy," Mark said. "That way we can modify the property any way we want."

"That makes sense," Jane said.

"I'd like a place on the edge of town where I can set up an observatory," Mark said.

"We could build a solarium," Jane said. "That would work and keep the house warm during the winter."

Mark nodded in agreement and then waved at the waiter.

"I think we're ready for the check," Mark said.

He handed Mark a slip of paper. Mark glanced at it.

"You pay at the bar," the waiter said.

He left to go check on another table. Mark left a quarter on the table as a tip. Then he and Jane got up. They stepped over to the bar, and the barman rang them up on a mechanical cash register. Dinner cost a dollar and eighty-five cents. Mark gave him two dollars and told him to keep the change.

Mark and Jane walked back to their hotel holding hands. When they stopped at the front desk to pick up their key, the woman who checked them in smiled at them. When they got back to their room, Jane continued with her correspondence, and Mark went in search of a piece of firewood he could carve. He went back downstairs and looked behind the hotel for a wood pile.

He heard the crack of a whip, the yelp of a dog, and the cry of a girl. He walked out to Throckmorton and found three cowboys whipping a dog as a young girl cried in protest.

"Excuse me!" Mark shouted. "What are you doing?"

Mark's shout caused the cowboys to turn toward him long enough for the girl to catch the dog.

"This ha'int none of y'alls business," a cowboy shouted back.

A dark-haired girl in a plain gray dress held a small dog, but she was still trapped between the back wall of the hotel, an oak tree, and the three men. The three cowboys all wore sheepskin jackets, ten-gallon hats, denim pants, and boots. One carried a whip and another carried a bottle. They each wore a gun belt, but so far none of them had drawn a weapon.

"We were just teachen' this mutt a lesson," another cowboy said.

"And what lesson might that be?" Mark asked.

"We're just having a little fun," the third cowboy said.

Mark looked at the young lady. She appeared to be about fifteen years old, with shoulder- length black hair, brown eyes, and dark olive skin. The top button of her dress had been torn off and was lying on the ground near the tree.

"Jane," Mark sent. *"I'm behind the hotel. It appears that some cowboys are trying to rape a young girl. I may need some backup."*

"Understood," Jane sent.

Mark turned to the girl. She looked at him with tears in her eyes.

"Are these men bothering you?" Mark asked.

She nodded her head yes.

"Boys," Mark said. "It seems the lady isn't interested in your attentions. Why don't you move along, and I'll give you five dollars each, and you can go find yourselves some women who are willing."

In response, the cowboy with the whip snapped it at him. He switched to battle mode. The edge of the whip passed by him in slow motion. He grabbed the end of it as it moved past him, and pulled. The cowboy on the other end was too startled to let go, so he was pulled toward Mark. Mark knocked him out with one punch to the face. Blood spattered from his nose and stained the front of his jacket.

When the other two saw their friend go down, one reached for his revolver while the other just took a drink. Mark pulled the handle of the whip into his hand and snapped the whip at the hand holding the gun. The cowboy dropped it and cried out in pain.

He paused for a moment and massaged his hand. Then he drew his knife and stepped toward Mark. He slashed at Mark, but Mark stepped forward, grabbed his arm, and twisted the knife free.

The cowboy kicked Mark in the groin twice, so Mark lifted the two-hundred-and-twenty-pound cowboy up. He saw a trimmed branch protruding from the oak tree, walked him over to it, and hung him on it by his gun belt. The third cowboy took another drink from his bottle and laughed at his friend's predicament.

"You going to try something?" Mark asked.

"Nope," he said. "Too drunk."

"Then why don't you take that gun out of your holster, with two fingers, and lay it on the ground. Then do the same with that knife you have in your gun belt," Mark said.

"All right," he said.

He took his gun out of his holster, dropped it and did the same with his knife. His friend flailed his arms and legs but couldn't grab anything he could use to get himself down.

The girl rushed past the cowboys as soon as the knife hit the ground. She started to run away, but stopped to stand behind Mark.

"Brock, get me down!" He shouted.

"Cole," the cowboy with the bottle said. "You got yourself into it, get yourself out."

Jane stepped up behind Mark.

"The sheriff is on the way," Jane said. "I had the front desk call him."

"You mean on the telephone?" Mark asked.

"Yes," Jane said. "They have telephone service here."

"Wow, thanks," Mark said.

"It looks like you've got everything under control," Jane said.

Jane held her arms out to the girl. She regarded her for a moment before stepping over to her and falling into her arms.

In between fits of crying, she told her, in Spanish, how the cowboys had assaulted her and whipped her dog when he bit one of them. Mark knew she was upset when the word, "pinche" was used several times to describe the cowboys.

Deputy Calloway arrived twelve minutes later. He wore a duster over a nightshirt and canvas pants. He had his hand on his revolver until he saw Mark.

"You again?" He asked.

"Sorry deputy," Mark said.

"What happened?" He asked.

Cole--the cowboy in the tree--started to cry out. Deputy Calloway stepped over to the tree and laughed. He gestured at the tree with his thumb.

"You do that?" He asked.

"Yeah," Mark said. "It seemed like the best way to restrain him without hurting him."

He pointed at the cowboy on the ground.

"You do that too?" He asked.

"Self-defense," Mark said. "He came at me with that whip."

Mark pointed to the whip on the ground. The girl hid behind Jane, clinging to her. The cowboy with the bottle bent over to retrieve his gun.

"You touch that gun," Deputy Calloway said. "I'll shoot you dead. I will get to you in a minute!"

He turned to Cole hanging in the tree.

"And you quiet down or I'll arrest you for disturbing the peace," he said.

Once everything had settled down and Deputy Calloway had collected all the guns, Mark told him what happened. With a little coaxing, the young woman told her story. Again, the word, "pinche" was used several times. She showed him the marks where she was whipped, and the mark on her dog where he was whipped.

When she was finished Jane walked the girl home. As soon as she was out of earshot, Deputy Calloway turned to the cowboys.

"And what do you have to say for yourselves?" He asked.

"We were just having a little fun," Brock, the one with the bottle, said.

"Didn't mean no harm," Cole said.

"I'm arresting you for being drunk and disorderly," Deputy Calloway said.

"Drunk and disorderly?" Mark asked. "This was assault and attempted rape."

Deputy Calloway sighed.

"I know," he said. "But it's the best I can do."

"Why?" Mark asked.

"I think you know why," Deputy Calloway said. "It's not right, but that's the way it is."

Mark sighed.

"I could use your help getting these men down to the courthouse," Deputy Calloway said.

"I'd be happy to," Mark said.

Mark stepped over to the tree and pulled Cole off the branch. He let him fall face-first to the ground.

"Did you have to pull him down so hard?" Deputy Calloway asked.

"No," Mark said.

At the direction of Deputy Calloway, the other two cowboys picked up the still-unconscious cowboy, and Mark and the deputy escorted the three of them to the jail behind the courthouse. Mark stayed long enough to help the deputy with some of the paperwork. While he was there, Deputy Calloway insisted Mark take his reward money for the arrest of John Ward.

When Mark got back to the hotel, Jane was waiting for him.

"All they got was drunk and disorderly," Mark said. "Three days in jail."

"You can't expect a nineteenth-century society to have twenty-first-century values," Jane said. "And by the way, Kesara is our new housekeeper."

"Is that her name?" Mark asked.

"Yes," Jane said. "Kesara Leblanc. She came here from Mexico two weeks ago and has been looking for work. I'm taking her shopping tomorrow."

"You'll enjoy that," Mark said.

"Yes," Jane said. "I believe I will."

Chapter Three
Finding his Star

The real estate agent showed them properties around Fort Worth for the next three days. At the end of which Mark purchased the entire block at the corner of Jones and 16thStreet. The previous owner had started building a two-story house, but he died in a construction accident. This gave Mark the opportunity to finish the second floor to his specifications.

He added a small tower to the second floor, which he made into an observatory by installing large glass panels for the upper walls and ceiling. Originally, he was just going to install large picture windows, but he found out about a bar in Hell's Half Acre that was being torn down and had a glass second floor. The glass panels were perfect for his observatory, and he even got them for free.

Since the walls weren't plastered yet, Mark installed electrical wiring and phone lines inside the walls. Instead of plastering the walls and then painting over them, he mixed iron oxide into the plaster. It not only made the plaster a light shade of russet, but it also made it magnetic, so he could hang notes with magnets instead of pins.

He wasn't particularly pleased with the quality of the light bulbs of the time because, on average, they would only last about a week. But on the whole, the house was similar to what it had been when he died in the late twentieth century. He had a gas stove and a refrigerator in the kitchen, but he would have to wait a few years to be able to put a car in the garage, and even longer for a television in the living room.

Now that the house was finished, Jane spent most of her days furnishing it. She and Kesara went all over the Dallas-Fort Worth area buying furniture, fixtures, and even a piano.

While Jane and Kesara were out shopping for a sewing machine, Mark went to the post office. He had to pick up his mail at the post office because rural delivery was still a few years away.

When he got to the counter, the clerk smiled at him. She pulled out a bundle of mail for Jane and a package for Mark. He thanked her and went over to a table in the lobby to sort through it.

Most of the mail contained responses from the investigators looking for Laire. Mark opened a package wrapped in heavy brown paper and tied it with a string to find it was the Sears catalog he had ordered.

Since he didn't want to walk all the way home, then go back to the post office, he stopped by Monnig's dry goods store and bought a writing tablet, a bottle of ink, a pen, and a dozen envelopes. Then, he decided to fill out his Sears order at Gorrell & Dinwiddie's saloon.

The saloon was a brown, two-story, wood-frame building with a large glass window that ran about two-thirds across the front. The first floor was a bar that also had a limited food menu. The second floor was what the locals affectionately called "women's boarding."

Mark walked in and was greeted by a layer of cigar smoke that hung in the air like a blanket. He wondered how many of these cowboys would live long enough to die from lung cancer. The room was lit by electric lights over the tables and the bar. Ample sunlight came in through the front windows as well.

When Mark stepped up to the bar, he had to push past a group of cowboys playing pool by the light from the window. They stared at him for a moment as if they were trying to figure out what he was. He ordered a beer and a corned beef sandwich and went to a table near the far wall to search through the Sears catalog.

He knew the bra wouldn't be invented for another three years, but on page 302 of the catalog, he found item number 23660 bust pads for 25 cents. They looked like a kind of strapless bra, so Mark decided to order six pairs. Mark wasn't sure how they would be attached, but that would be Jane's problem. He had listened to her complain about wearing a corset for the last forty-five years, and he could finally do something about it.

One of the cowboys pulled away from his game of pool to see what Mark was doing. He stood next to Mark and studied the catalog with interest. He chewed a wad of tobacco, turning away for a moment to spit in a spittoon near the bar. He got as much on the floor as he did in the spittoon.

"Hey Ted," he said. "He's lookin' at women's underwear."

Mark took a breath, sighed, and looked up at the cowboy. He stood five-foot-five, had tawny skin, brown hair and eyes, and looked to be all muscle. He wore a button-down shirt, necktie, and blue jeans. Mark looked back down at his catalog and turned the page.

"Cody, it's your turn," the other cowboy replied. He spit into a spittoon near the pool table.

The cowboy didn't turn back to his game, but instead set down his cue and took the Sears catalog away from Mark.

"Look at all these fancy, girly things," he said. "Are you one of them fancy boys who dresses up in women's clothes and prances about?" He asked.

"Could I have my catalog back please?" Mark asked. "I need to finish the order before my wife gets back."

The cowboy tried to spit in the spittoon, but missed and spit on the floor. The bartender looked up from the glass he was polishing to admonish him, but the cowboy ignored it.

"Wife," the cowboy said. "The only wife a fancy boy like you could get would be a sheep."

He held the catalog just out of Mark's reach.

"I'm not sure what you're trying to prove," Mark said. "But I'm not looking for trouble."

"Trouble," he said. "Who said anything about trouble? Maybe I just want to borrow this catalog for a while?"

Mark got up. He stood eight inches taller than the cowboy.

"Let me buy you guys a round of beers," Mark said. "Then you can have the catalog when I'm done with it."

"What exactly are you doin' looking at women's under things?" The cowboy asked.

"Seriously?" Mark asked. "I guess you're not married."

"He ain't hardly seen a woman, let alone marry one," the cowboy in back said.

"Ted?" the cowboy said.

He dropped the catalog and took a swing at Mark. Mark caught his fist in one hand and the catalog in the other. He held the cowboy's fist for a full second, and then shoved it back up in his face. The cowboy stepped back. The bartender brought Mark his sandwich and beer. He had an apprehensive look on his face.

"If you go bustin' up the place," he said. "Expect to pay for it, and I'll swear out a warrant on you if you don't."

The bartender gestured toward the back corner of the room, but Mark didn't want to take his eyes off the cowboy.

"I'm not going to start anything," Mark said. "But I will finish whatever gets started."

"We'll go outside," the cowboy said.

"How about we don't," Mark said. "I don't want to hurt you. Couldn't we just arm wrestle instead?"

Mark sat down at the table and held out his arm. The cowboy looked at his companions. The one he called Ted nodded for him to sit. The other two had expressions of amusement on their faces.

Mark could see by the cowboy's expression that this wasn't going the way he had expected. He sat down and took Mark's hand. Mark pretended to put up a fight, he even let the cowboy bring his arm back a little, but then he pinned his arm in thirty-three seconds.

"Now," Mark said. "If you'll listen, I'll explain to you how to get, and keep, the most beautiful of women."

"How do we know your wife don't look like the south end of a north goin' mule?" The cowboy next to the wall asked.

"Jane," Mark sent. *"Where are you?"*

Her signal was weak, but she responded to him.

"Home," Jane replied.

"Can I get you to come to Gorrell & Dinwiddie's saloon? It's on Tenth and Main," Mark sent.

"Is there a problem?" she asked.

"No," Mark sent. *"I just need to see you."*

"Be there in about fifteen minutes," Jane sent.

Mark looked at his watch.

"My wife is supposed to meet me here at 12:30," he said. "If she isn't the prettiest woman you've ever laid eyes on, I'll pay each man here a dollar."

"I'll take that bet!" The bartender shouted.

The three cowboys in the back agreed, and

the cowboy across from Mark smiled. He nodded in agreement.

"No bet," Deputy Calloway said from the table in the corner.

He sat alone with the remains of a steak and potatoes on his plate.

"No bet," he repeated. "I've seen his wife."

"Deputy Calloway," Mark said. "I didn't see you back there."

"Go on and tell us," Deputy Calloway said. "I want to know how you got such a pretty wife."

Mark took a breath. He uncorked the ink and continued to write his order as he spoke.

"The secret to getting and keeping a beautiful woman is making her comfortable. If she knows you're doing your best to make her comfortable, she will not only stay with you, but she will return the favor."

"So," the cowboy across from Mark said. "We're supposed to buy her flowers and candy, right?"

"No," Mark said.

"You listen to her and find out what is making her uncomfortable, then do your best to fix it," Mark said. "My wife has been complaining about her corset since I met her. So, I'm ordering these dress pads to make her more comfortable."

He finished writing up his order and addressed the envelope. He set them aside for the ink to dry.

"So," the cowboy across from him said. "You're saying a comfortable woman is an agreeable woman?"

"I am," Mark said.

Mark picked up half his sandwich, and he pushed the plate across to the cowboy across from him. He looked at it for a moment picked it up and took a bite.

"Can I get a beer for my friend over here," Mark said.

Once the ink was dry, Mark put the order in the envelope. He tucked the envelope in his inside jacket pocket just as Jane walked into the room. She wore the same dress that had gotten her fined at Judge Roy Bean's establishment. The room fell completely silent as they all stared at her.

"Well hell," the cowboy across from Mark said.

He put a dollar bill in Mark's outside jacket pocket. Each of the men in the room in turn stepped over to Mark's table and put down a dollar. Some had coins while others had paper.

Mark got up from the table. He pulled the dollar from his front pocket and added it to the money from the table. He put the money in his pants pocket.

"What's going on?" Jane asked. "Why are these men giving you money?"

"Nothing dear," Mark said. "Just making some new friends."

He walked over to Jane and kissed her.

"I'm done with the catalog," Mark said.

The cowboys at the back of the room all rushed over to the table. The cowboy at the table pulled the catalog over to him, picked up the pen, and tried to figure out how to write an order. His companions sat around offering him advice. Mark smiled at them, paid his bill, and left with Jane.

"Well," she said. "Now that you're done showing me off like a prized pig, I'll get back to setting up the sewing machine."

"Thank you," Mark said. "You helped me avoid a fight."

She smiled at him.

"Boys will be boys I suppose," she said.

"I've got to go to the post office," Mark said. "I'll see you at home in a few minutes."

"Ordering supplies from the Sears catalog?" she asked.

"Yes," Mark said. "Of sorts."

He gave her a quick kiss and walked away. He went to the post office, bought a money order and stamp, and mailed the letter. When he got home, Deputy Calloway was waiting for him in the parlor. He sat on their sofa with a cup of tea in one hand and a lemon cookie in the other.

"Deputy Calloway," Mark said. "To what do I owe the honor?"

"I saw what you did back there," he said. "Saw the whole thing. Thought it was going to interrupt my lunch, but you handled it."

"I was just trying to avoid a fight," Mark said.

"No," Deputy Calloway said. "You did more than that. You took control of the situation and steered it toward calmer waters."

"Thank you," Mark said.

"How would you like to be a deputy?" he asked. "A couple of our men are out sick, and we are short-handed."

"I would like that," Mark said.

"The job pays ten-dollars a week, and you can pick up free meals at some of the hotels and restaurants."

"That sounds good," Mark said. "I have to say that I may not be in Fort Worth for more than a few months."

"That's fine," Deputy Calloway said. "We may only need you until the other deputies are back on duty. I'll come here and collect you at sunup tomorrow."

Deputy Calloway got up and took his hat off the rack. Mark walked with him to the front door.

"Do you have a gun?" he asked.

"Used to," Mark said. "I've seen what those things can do close up, and I prefer to settle things other ways."

"I understand," he said. "But I didn't lose this eye to harsh language. I'm going to order you a Fort Worth special."

He gestured toward his eye patch. He shook hands with Mark and walked out the front door.

Deputy Calloway knocked on Mark's door at sunrise as promised. He took him down to the courthouse to sign some papers and meet the judges and a few of the clerks he would be working with. Then he took him to the jail and introduced him to his new boss: Sheriff Clark. After that, he was shown around and introduced to deputies Branum, Douglass, and Parsley.

They explained that Fort Worth had two competing law enforcement agencies, the Fort Worth Police and the Sheriff's Department, and the two agencies didn't always see eye to eye. Fort Worth has two sides: the cowboy side and the church-going side. The two agencies differed slightly on enforcement when it came to the cowboys. The cowboys brought in most of the revenue, so when patrolling Hell's Half Acre, there were a few things he would have to turn a blind eye to as far as the female boarding and public drunkenness, but violence wouldn't be tolerated anywhere in Fort Worth.

They took him to lunch at the Crescent restaurant and introduced him to Mrs. Moseley. The restaurant was a kind of unofficial meeting place where they all started their day.

The day ended at the livery behind the courthouse where Mark was issued a horse and tack. He rode the horse home to find Jane waiting for him on the front porch.

"I see they gave you a badge," she said. "I suppose you're living some kind of boyhood dream."

She got up from her seat on the porch to join him as he climbed off the horse.

"Yeah," Mark said. "I think this job is going to work out fine."

Mark led the horse around the side of the house and Jane walked with him.

"What do you mean?" She asked.

"They told me I would be riding patrol out in the county, so I asked for the northwest side and they gave it to me."

"And that helps how?" Jane asked.

"That's where Aurora is," Mark said. "It's in Wise County, but I can spend all day watching the sky over Aurora and it won't seem out of place."

"That is fortuitous," Jane said.

"Isn't this where you're supposed to tell me that law enforcement in this era is too dangerous?" Mark asked.

"No," Jane said.

"No?" Mark asked.

"No," Jane repeated. "You handled yourself pretty well at the Battle of South Mountain, Antietam, and Second Bull Run, and those situations were much more dangerous. In the last few encounters we've had, you have shown adequate ability in handling humans. As long as you wear your bulletproof underwear and run your particle-avoidance subroutine, you should be fine."

"I'm glad you feel I'm adequate," Mark said.

"You know what I mean," Jane said. "I no longer concern myself with processing possible negative outcomes . . . not that I ever really did."

"Oh, no," Mark said. "That would be much too human."

"Yes," Jane said. "It would."

"How is Kesara doing?" Mark asked.

"She is settling in nicely," Jane said. "Unlike Emily, she is honest, hardworking, and responsible."

"You didn't button her, did you?" Mark asked.

Mark opened the barn door and led the horse inside. Jane followed the horse into the barn.

"Of course not," Jane said. "I was only saying it's nice to work with someone who isn't a criminal."

"Okay," Mark said. "But we will probably be returning to Arizona on April 19th. What happens then?"

Mark put the horse in its stall. Jane stepped inside as well.

"I'm teaching her English, sewing, and baking with wheat flour. She is already quite adept at baking with corn flour," Jane said. "I should have her set up in a trade before we leave."

Mark unsaddled the horse, and Jane grabbed a brush and began brushing the horse down while Mark got the feed and water troughs ready.

"We're going to need a large wooden crate," Mark said.

"How large, and what for?" Jane asked.

"The spacecraft is bound to have an engine," Mark said. "I would like to take it back to Arizona to study it."

"That seems reasonable," Jane said. "I'll have a crate made roughly the same size as the wagon bed."

"That should be fine," Mark said. "I ride my first circuit tomorrow."

"I'll have Kesara make you lunch," Jane said.

"You aren't going to do it?" Mark asked.

Jane scoffed.

"Mark, I'm the lady of the house now," she said. "I can't be bothered to do such menial tasks."

"Oh," Mark said. "What is your role now?"

"Playing piano, reading, paying calls, church socials, you know--the really important stuff."

They finished with the horse and went inside the house. Mark and Kesara sat in the parlor and listened to Jane play the piano until nine o'clock. Then Kesara went to her room behind the kitchen while Mark and Jane went upstairs. Instead of going to their bedroom, they went to Mark's observatory where they counted falling stars.

At first light, Mark saddled his horse. As he was getting ready to mount, Kesara brought him a cloth bag of food. She said it would be enough for four days. Mark thanked her and rode off.

He met Deputy Calloway at Mrs. Moseley's and he presented Mark with his pistol. He pushed a brand-new gun belt with a revolver inside, and a box of ammo, across the table.

"That there is a standard issue police revolver, but I added a feature of my own. Two rounds are hidden in the handle. Sometimes you may need to reload quickly, and takin them from the handle is faster," he said.

"Thank you," Mark said. "Do I owe you anything?"

"I billed it to the city. It'll be a training expense."

"How can I thank you?"

"Don't get killed," he said.

Mark examined the gun. It was a standard .38 revolver with one special feature. The grip had been modified to hold two bullets. They had been inserted in such a way to make them appear decorative but could be removed and fired if necessary.

After breakfast, they rode off together. Apart from the slush on the ground and the light snow that turned to drizzle, it was a pleasant ride. Their route took them west to the boarder of Parker County. They visited farms, ranches, and small towns along the way to be sure everything was in order. Each morning began with breakfast, target practice, and riding for the rest of the day. Deputy Calloway pointed at a tree-lined ridge and told Mark that was the boarder of Parker County. From there they turned north and rode for half a day until they came to a stream that was roughly two feet wide. He told Mark that the stream was the boarder of Wise County. They rode south then east until they were back at Fort Worth three days after they started.

They came back to Fort Worth in the morning, so Calloway told Mark to take the rest of the day off. The next two days Mark was on 'in-town patrol', which meant he sat around the office and played cards with the other deputies until someone called for them. At the end of Mark's first week on the job, he was declared a full deputy and told he would ride the next patrol alone.

Mark spent the rest of February and all of March riding patrol out in the desert and resolving matters in town. He tried not to arrest anyone if he could avoid it, and most of the time he could.

April came and Mark was beginning to think the Aurora UFO could be a hoax. As he was riding the circuit on April 14th, he camped in the desert north of Fort Worth. He had tied his horse to a tree near a stream and used his saddle as a pillow.

As he lay on his blanket, Mark noticed a new point of light in the sky. It didn't twinkle, so he knew it couldn't be a star. At first, he thought it could be a passing asteroid, but then it moved.

He watched it dart about in the sky making right-angle turns. It didn't move like an aircraft or anything else Mark was familiar with.

Mark sat up when the object got close enough to be able to analyze the light it produced. When sunlight is reflected off an object, some of the light is absorbed. By examining what is left, the composition of the object can be determined.

Mark ran the light through his analyzer, and he discovered that the object was made out of an iron-aluminum alloy that wasn't listed on his database of spacecraft hull designs in the twenty-third century. The NEJ used an aluminum-carbon alloy because their spacecraft were built on the Moon. The Chicoms used an iron-nickel alloy because the material for their spacecraft came from asteroids. So as near as he could tell, this object didn't travel back in time, or if it did it was from a future he wasn't familiar with.

Mark noted the finding and continued to watch the spacecraft. It flew close enough for him to use his enhanced vision to see its shape.

It was a tube with rounded ends, roughly the same size as a minivan. He couldn't make out any windows, but there was a hatch at the top and a few small tubes protruding from the surface.

He measured the air temperature around the spacecraft, and it didn't differ from the rest of the air, so this object was not being propelled by heat or anything that generated heat.

The Moon was up, so he took off his hat and activated the dish antenna that Jane had hidden in there. He directed the Raven's sensors to get a look at the spacecraft. It moved too unpredictably to get a close-up, but he was able to capture a few images of it at a distance.

"Jane," Mark sent. *"Are you there?"*

Mark waited the 5.2 seconds it took for the signal to travel to the Moon and back twice, but he didn't get a response. She would see the data the next time she logged into the Raven's computer.

He observed the spacecraft until it flew off just after sunrise. He tried to follow it with the Raven's sensors, but it clung to the curvature of the Earth and disappeared over the horizon.

Mark finished riding his circuit and returned to Fort Worth on the morning of the sixteenth. As he rode across Wire Bridge, he spotted it in the morning sky. It flew slower and lower than it did before, so Mark was able to get a much better view of it. It resembled an airship, but it didn't move like an airship. Mark got a closer look at the hull, and it was the same iron-aluminum alloy he had detected before. There were a few small openings on the top, but apart from that, it had no windows. Mark couldn't detect any heat signature, radio signal, or magnetic field distortion near the ship. It just hung there in the sky.

It flew over the stock yards, over Hell's Half Acre, and over the Trinity River about a half mile east of him, at roughly two-thousand feet. As soon as it crossed the river, it accelerated and vanished over the horizon.

Since it didn't make any sound as it passed over, most people didn't see it. However, as he neared the courthouse, a few people were pointing toward the sky.

As Mark reached 10th Street, he heard Jane calling to him electronically.

"I saw it," Jane sent. *"Got some good images from your observatory."*

"I saw it too," Mark sent. *"Everything ready for tomorrow?"*

"The wagon is prepped," Jane sent.

"Good," Mark sent. *"I'll be there shortly."*

Mark stopped by the Sheriff's station long enough to let them know that he rode his circuit without incident. Then he rode home and put the horse in the barn. As he approached, he heard Jane playing the piano. He listened to her as he took care of the horse. After he finished feeding and grooming it, he went in and Jane stopped playing. Mark sat next to her on the piano bench.

"Do you want to share?" She sent.

"Yes," Mark sent. *"You know I do."*

She took Mark's hand and held it gently. The physical connection wasn't necessary, but Mark enjoyed it all the same. He felt Jane enter his mind, as he entered hers. He felt her moving through his memories like a ghost walking through a room. He felt Jane standing next to him as he recalled seeing the spacecraft. They viewed it together and wordlessly shared impressions and observations about it.

Then Mark shared Jane's memories. Her feeling that this was a wild goose chase, then her amazement at seeing the object, then her concern that Laire had managed to build a spacecraft in 1897 and that somehow it was her fault history had gone wrong.

They observed the spacecraft as it silently flew over Fort Worth, then seemed to vanish as it shot over the horizon at incredible speed. He felt Jane nudge him out of her mind, so Mark ended the sharing.

"No memories of Mars?" Mark asked.

"Not in the mood," Jane sent.

"Didn't think androids had moods," Mark sent.

"We don't," Jane sent. *"But I'm not going to have fun in the middle of a crisis."*

"None of this is your fault," Mark sent.

"Really," Jane sent.

"Really," Mark sent. *"This is supposed to happen. Just because it isn't in Romanji's database doesn't make it any less real."*

"I let Laire escape," Jane sent. *"I should have finished her when I had the chance."*

"Not sure what you're referring to," Mark sent. *"But Laire has proven to be very hard to kill, and besides, we aren't even sure that this is Laire."*

Mark got up.

"Where are you going?" Jane asked.

"Getting a piece of firewood," Mark said. "I want to carve a model."

Jane projected a 3d image of the spacecraft in Mark's mind.

"That's nice," Mark sent. *"But I like to have physical representations."*

He went out to the woodpile and selected an oak log five inches in diameter and fourteen inches long. He took it to his workshop in the barn and worked on it until Kesara called him in for lunch. He threw a cloth over it and went inside to eat. After lunch, Mark took Jane out to the barn and showed her the carving.

"I still can't see why you prefer the physical model over the generated one," Jane said.

"An old movie," Mark said. "The hero used sculpture while everyone else had flat drawings, and the sculpture brought out details the others didn't see."

"Oh," Jane said. "Did you notice anything new?"

She picked the model up from the bench and turned it over to examine it.

"It did cause me to pay greater attention to the airship's details."

"Airship?" Jane asked. "I thought it was a spaceship."

"Me too," Mark said. "But when I started to sculpt it, I noticed that these vents are little scoops for directing air inside the airship. A spacecraft wouldn't have vents like that."

"I am beginning to understand why you like sculpture so much," Jane said.

"What are we going to do about Kesara?" Mark asked.

Jane reached into her pocket and pulled out a cloth bag.

"I put together a sleeping powder for her," Jane said. "I'll put it into her dinner. She will sleep for at least twelve hours."

"Is the wagon ready?" Mark asked.

"Of course," Jane said.

"Then we'll leave after dinner," Mark said.

Chapter Four
Creating Urban Legend

"Everything set?" Mark asked as he hitched the matched grays to the wagon.

"Yes," Jane said. "Kesara is sleeping, and I got her to drink a liter of water a few minutes ago."

"Drink?" Mark asked. "While she was asleep."

"You forget all the practice I had with Kak," Jane said. "Controlling human muscles is just a matter of sending the right amount of electricity to the right nerves."

"Okay," Mark said.

He climbed into the wagon, released the brake, and tapped the reins to get the horses moving. Mark looked over and noticed that Jane was wearing the same dress that got her fined at Judge Roy Bean's place.

"Why did you pick that dress?" Mark asked.

"I picked it because I like it," Jane said. "And if we get stopped during this little escapade, I want anyone we encounter to be looking at me and not the box we have back there."

"Seems reasonable," Mark said.

"Sometimes I think you like the attention," Mark said.

Jane slumped her shoulders and sighed.

"Being alluring is one of my nested subroutines," Jane said. "I have a need to be attractive to men, just as I have a need to be supportive of humans. Otherwise, I would have reduced these years ago."

She reached down and tried to cup her bosoms for a moment, but the corset she wore made that impossible.

"But I've come to realize that being alluring does have its upside, and I should use that advantage when necessary," Jane said.

"I was going to wait until our anniversary, but I think you should have it now," Mark said.

"Anniversary?" Jane asked.

"We have a wedding anniversary next week," Mark said. "I got you a present."

"You did?"

"I did," Mark said. "It's under your seat."

Jane reached under her seat, and pulled out a box wrapped in paper and string. She cut the string with a fingernail and tore through the paper. She reached in and took out the dress shields.

"I know the bra won't be invented for another few years yet, but these seemed pretty close," Mark said. "I'm not sure how you attach them."

"Mark," Jane said. "I love them!"

"I hope I got the size right," Mark said. "Since they only came in one size."

"They're wonderful," Jane said. "Stop the wagon."

"What?" Mark said.

"Stop the wagon," Jane said. "Just for a moment."

Mark pulled back on the reins, and the wagon stopped. Jane jumped off the wagon and unbuttoned her dress.

"You're going to sew them in now?" Mark said.

"It will give me something to do during the trip," Jane said.

Mark climbed down from the seat and helped her take her dress off. Once she was stripped down to her underwear, she grabbed her handbag and climbed into the back of the wagon. She sat on the crate in the back, just inside the canvas bonnet.

"What happens if we run into someone?" Mark asked.

"Mark," Jane said. "We're in the middle of the desert in the middle of the night. Who are we going to run in to?"

She opened up her handbag and took out her sewing kit.

"Just let me get a few needles threaded. Then we can get started," Jane said.

"Okay," Mark said. "Do you have enough light?"

Jane gave Mark one of her looks.

"Right," Mark said. "Dumb question."

Mark climbed up into the wagon, and Jane finished threading her needles. She sat in the back and sewed while Mark watched the night sky. The night was cold for April: 45 degrees Fahrenheit. The sky was clear. Mark could see hundreds of stars, but he could only name a handful of them.

The trip was uneventful, apart from an encounter with a rattlesnake. Fortunately, Mark saw it before the horses did, and he was able to drive around it.

Mark crossed the river bordering Wise County at 3:09 A.M. He had to stop again to help Jane take her corset off and put her dress back on. Once that had been accomplished, they continued on the road to Aurora and reached the town square which consisted of a Baptist church, two saloons, a general store, and a building that was both Sheriff's Office and hotel, at 4:31A.M. Mark observed that the residents had yet to awaken because he didn't see any lanterns lit as they passed through town.

Mark stopped the wagon about a mile north of town. Judge Proctor's farm was visible on the horizon, and Mark could see his house and windmill clearly. The object appeared in the sky at 5:40 A.M., which was a little earlier than the article in the Dallas Morning News had implied.

"There it is," Mark said. "What do you think?"

"I think Laire has been pretty busy," Jane said. "I can't imagine how she was able to produce the parts to make something like that."

"Yeah," Mark said. "If Laire did produce that, she has been pretty busy."

"What are we supposed to do now?" Jane asked.

"We wait for it to crash," Mark said.

"How about we speed things along," Jane said.

She reached into her handbag and pulled out the AMP gun. Before Mark could say anything, she pointed it at the airship and fired. The jacketed stream of antimatter left a contrail as it shot toward the airship.

"You're going to shoot it down!" Mark shouted.

"Just a shot across the bow," Jane said. "This is Laire we're dealing with."

The rear of the airship exploded. Debris rained down. They watched the airship plummet from the sky, crash through Judge Proctor's windmill, and explode in his flower garden.

"Well," Jane said. "You did say it was going to crash."

Mark stared at Jane for two seconds not knowing what to say. Then he hit the reins and moved the wagon toward Judge Proctor's farm.

"What about the Proctors?" Jane asked.

"According to the legend, they hide in their root cellar for about half an hour," Mark said. "The noise of the crash frightens them. They think it's a tornado."

Mark drove to the crash site as fast as the horses would allow. The gate to Judge Proctor's farm was open, so he drove in and brought the wagon to within ten feet of the wreck.

The rear half of the airship was missing, and the front half was severely damaged by the crash. The pilot had managed to level out just before striking the windmill, so the airship had slid across the ground digging a large trench in Judge Proctor's flower garden.

"We have about twenty minutes before the Proctors and the townspeople start showing up," Mark sent.

Jane nodded. She reached into her handbag and pulled out Mark's boot black, nanite can. She flung it into the air over the airship, and it exploded raining particles down onto the airship. She handed Mark a small jar of alcohol.

"You go and survey the inside, and I'll survey the outside," Jane sent.

Mark jumped down and rushed toward the gaping hole in the rear of the airship. The interior wasn't what he had expected. The cabin had six walls set in a hexagon. It was lined with some sort of brownish-black paneling. Nothing was lit, and there weren't any kind of wires or fiber optic cables. Blue fluid dripped from the ceiling, but if there had been an engine, it had occupied the area that was now the gaping hole through which Mark had entered.

There were four seats that looked like something he would see in a twenty-first-century passenger vehicle. Two on the left and two on the right, but these seats not only had arm rests and headrests, but they also had leg and arm restraints. It seemed some of the stories of alien abduction may not have been urban legend after all. He moved past a divider into the cockpit.

When he saw the pilot, his jaw dropped. He had hoped to find Laire, or at least a human pilot, but instead, he saw a Roswell Grey. The pilot looked to be male, hairless, and about four and a half feet tall. His skin was like a dolphin's: smooth, moist, and gray. He wore a white suit with small tubes embedded in it to distribute moisture. When compared to the size of his body, his head was twice the normal size of a human's. He had large, black eyes, two angled slits for a nose, and a somewhat small mouth.

"The pilot is an alien," Mark sent.

Mark pulled out the jar Jane had given him and opened the lid.

"Get a tissue sample and two DNA samples," Jane sent.

Mark just stood there for a moment.

"Mark!" Jane sent.

Mark shook his head clear and reached inside the cockpit. The pilot had been impaled by one of the ribs making up the outer hull of the airship, so getting a tissue sample wasn't difficult. He grabbed a couple of large pieces of flesh with his bare hand and put them in the jar of alcohol Jane had provided.

He used the DNA scanner in his right hand to sample the alien's DNA in two different places. First, he sampled the skin, and then he sampled the blood and internal tissue. He decided to wait to run the results.

He examined what was left of the control panel, and noticed a lack of dials, displays, or screens. It appeared to be a blank, flat surface. The craft was controlled by two steering mechanisms—one set horizontally, and the other vertically. On the right side of the pilot there was something that appeared to be a throttle.

Mark was surprised to see a bundle of papers in the cockpit. He reached over and grabbed them. They were roughly five-by-eight inches, loosely bound, and filled with alien writing. He looked through them, being careful to document each page.

"The engine is gone," Jane sent. *"I'm seeing some aluminum coils, iron skin, picking up traces of titanium. This technology is different from anything I've ever seen. The skin of the airship is like a printed circuit board from your century."*

Mark heard Jane's words, but he didn't respond. He continued to scan the pages.

"Mark!" Jane sent. *"I need you to focus. Finish surveying the interior."*

Mark scanned the last page and dropped it in the cockpit.

"There is a lot up here to document," Mark sent.

He noticed a metallic hexagonal pin or emblem on the pilot's clothes. He pulled it off tearing the fabric slightly. It was the same symbol that Jane had noticed in the missionary's book nine weeks ago. He dropped it into his jacket pocket along with a rectangular piece of metal he found.

He looked up to see Jane standing behind the pilot's chair.

"It seems I murdered an innocent man," Jane sent.

"You thought it was Laire," Mark sent.

"I acted without examination," Jane sent.

"This was supposed to happen," Mark sent.

"That doesn't make it right," Jane sent.

Mark gestured behind her to the four chairs and their arm and leg restraints.

"If it makes a difference," Mark sent. *"He wasn't completely innocent. He was here to abduct people."*

"Well," Jane sent. *"That does make me feel a bit better."*

Jane reached into her handbag and took out another sample jar. She took another sample of flesh from the pilot's chest wound, closed the jar, and put it into her bag. She held out her hand, and Mark gave her his jar.

"We have to go," Jane said. "The sun is over the horizon, and the townspeople will be arriving soon."

Mark surveyed the cockpit one last time and then followed Jane out of the wreck. They climbed into the wagon and were halfway to Aurora before the first rider approached. He was a cowboy in his forties. He waved at them to stop.

"Did you see it?" he asked.

"Flying machine of some kind crashed," Mark said. "Didn't want to get too close."

He nodded and rode on. They passed three wagons and two riders on the way back to Aurora. Each time, Mark gave them the same story. He saw the crash, but he didn't want to get too close.

When they got back into Aurora, they stopped long enough to water the horses and pick up some supplies at the general store. They listened to the locals as they discussed the airship and how it had suddenly dropped from the sky.

No one seemed to notice the oddly shaped cloud that streaked up in the sky, and Mark was grateful.

The clerk in the general store looked at Mark's badge as he set a box of apples and other supplies on the counter.

"What's a Tarrant County deputy doing out here?" He asked.

"My wife and I are looking to invest in some land," Mark said. "Fort Worth is a little too busy for our taste. You know, people have to lock their doors at night."

"You not going to see the airship?" The clerk asked.

"I'm not a lawman in Wise County," Mark said. "So, I don't suppose it is any of my business."

Mark paid for the supplies and left. He found Jane sitting on the steps in front of the general store.

"I was sure it was Laire," Jane sent.

"Me too," Mark sent. *"I brought us to Fort Worth believing that we were saving the world from an army of her followers in their flying saucers."*

Mark walked over to the fountain. The horses had stopped drinking and stood there waiting to be hitched to the wagon. He set the apple crate down in front of them and watched them eat apples from it.

When they had finished, Mark grabbed the closest horse, the one Jane had named Daisy, and walked her over to the wagon. Jane got up and did the same with the other horse, Dandi. Once the horses were hitched, they climbed up into the seat and started back toward Fort Worth at a much slower pace.

"How much of the wreck were you able to salvage?" Mark asked.

"I got some pieces of the hull, two jars of blue fluid, a few components, and a device of some kind. It may be a weapon." Jane sent.

"I got this," Mark sent.

He reached into his jacket pocket and handed Jane the symbol and the rectangular piece of metal he found.

"Do you know what this is?" Jane sent.

"Yes," Mark sent. *"That's why I grabbed it."*

"That means that funny man and his group are somehow connected with these aliens," Jane sent.

"Yup," Mark sent.

"This keeps getting better," Jane sent.

"I think we have found the tip of the iceberg," Mark sent.

"Send me the DNA data on the pilot," Jane said.

"Now?" Mark asked. *"I thought we would wait until we got home to analyze it."*

"It's a long trip back," Jane sent. *"And there is a little space in the back for me to lie down."*

Mark sent her the data. Once Jane had received it, she climbed into the back of the wagon to process it. She used her handbag as a makeshift pillow. That way if a human saw her, it would look like she was asleep. He drove the wagon and enjoyed the nature around him. Jane didn't 'wake up' from her processing coma until they were crossing the Trinity River.

"Mark!" Jane sent. *"You aren't going to believe this."*

"Okay," Mark sent. *"What am I not supposed to believe?"*

"The alien isn't an alien," Jane sent. *"He is from Earth."*

"How is that possible?" Mark sent.

He waved at Henry Evans as he turned on to Rusk Street from East Bluff.

"See you in church on Sunday?" Henry asked.

"Absolutely," Mark said. "See you there."

"There weren't just two major primates in prehistoric Earth. There were three: Homo sapiens, Neanderthals, and the ancestors of our dead friend back there," Jane sent.

"Again," Mark asked. *"How is that possible?"*

"They must have moved deep underground," Jane sent. *"But he shares a common ancestry with humans, Neanderthals, and porpoises."*

"So, you're saying he is a type of aquatic ape?" Mark asked.

"His ancestors were, yes," Jane sent.

"How is it that no one knows about them?" Mark asked. *"Even in your time, they are still unknown."*

"Even in my time, no one went far underground," Jane sent. *"There wasn't any need for it. We did discover oceans of fresh water two miles down, but once the ion-destablizer was invented, we had all the fresh water we could want."*

"So, no one explored the Earth?" Mark asked.

"We had Mars to colonize and Venus to taraform, Amalthea to explore, Vesta to mine, what did we need to go down for when up was much more interesting," Jane sent.

"How did you taraform Venus?" Mark asked.

"Aluminum sun shield," Jane said. *"We blocked 80percent of the Sun's light. Planet cooled down nicely, although the atmosphere was still filled with hydrochloric and sulfuric acid."*

"What kind of sun shield?" Mark asked.

"Each section was produced on the Moon and sent to Venus. The tough part was keeping the shield in place. The solar wind kept pushing on it, but they put solar cells on the front and ion engines on the back. The electricity from the solar cells powered the ion engines and the whole thing remained in place," Jane sent.

"How long did it take to build?" Mark asked.

"About ten years," Jane sent. *"Robots did most of the work, and the Moon has a large open pit mine on its surface, but last I heard they were going to turn it into a new colony."*

"It sounds like a great time to live," Mark

said.

"It was," Jane said. "Or it will be, but it comes at a terrible price. But why are we talking about this?"

Mark sighed.

"I just needed a moment to process what you told me," Mark said. "It isn't every day that we discover a new civilization underground. One that is aware of us, and may even be manipulating us."

"Yes," Jane said. "That is a lot to take in."

Mark pulled the wagon into their yard and got out to open the barn. Kesara ran out to greet them. She apologized for oversleeping as she helped Jane unhitch the horses and take them to the barn to be watered.

Mark handed Kesara the box of supplies he had purchased in Aurora and asked her to put them away before making lunch. As she took the box, Mark grabbed a piece of dried beef and gave it to Salsa. He sniffed at it for a moment, then took it and ran off. As soon as Kesara left, Mark grabbed a crowbar and opened the crate in the back of the wagon. Jane helped him remove the sections of the hull, components, and equipment. Jane imaged and cataloged the pieces while Mark built a two-by-two-by-one-foot wooden crate to send the debris to Arizona.

After a short discussion about the importance of not using 24th-century weapons in the 19th century, the AMP gun was infused into a block of wood, and packed into the crate, along with some hull fragments, DNA samples, and a jar of the blue fluid. At the last moment, Mark included his airship sculpture and the tokens from the White Elephant. Then, he filled the excess space with straw and nailed the crate shut.

Mark took the larger pieces of hull and put them next to the forge he used to make nails and horseshoes.

"You aren't going to melt those?" Jane asked.

"I may at some point," Mark said. "But right now I am hiding them in plain sight."

"That's very clever," Jane said.

Jane stepped over to the largest piece and broke off a piece that was jutting out from the rest. She put it in her apron.

"I'm going to examine this more closely tonight," she said.

Mark loaded the crate into the back of the wagon. Just as he set it down, Kesara called them in for lunch. She served them chicken salad sandwiches and coffee. Mark smiled when he realized that in his time, a chicken salad sandwich would not be a difficult thing to make, but Kesara had to bake her own bread. Then she had to slaughter, pluck, and bake the chicken, make the mayonnaise, slice the vegetables, and combine everything into the sandwich. He thanked her after lunch, and Kesara gave him an uneasy smile. Jane had insisted that she eat at the same table with them, and it was taking Kesara a little while to get used to it.

After lunch, Mark wrote a label for the crate on a piece of white writing paper and glued it to the box with wood glue. He made the label out to John

Johnson, general delivery, Mesa, Arizona. Then he hitched up the horses and drove to the post office. On his way in, he saw the same three cowboys who had attacked Kesara, but he ignored them and mailed the box.

On his way out of the post office, his particle avoidance system warned him of three projectiles. It took over and Mark jumped like a break-dancer, but he was able to avoid all three bullets.

When Mark got his systems back online, he looked around for smoke. He looked down West Tenth Street and saw Eugene Butler, the cowboy with the whip who had tried to throw down on him when he rescued Kesara.

Mark watched him fire two more shots, and his particle avoidance system took over again, but this time it just warned him of a possible collision, because both shots missed. They struck the stone wall of the post office.

Mark ran toward Eugene as he reloaded his gun. They were twenty-four yards apart, but Mark managed to cover the distance before the man finished reloading. He got three bullets out of his gun belt and into his gun when he looked up and saw Mark coming.

He snapped his revolver closed, pointed it at Mark's head, and pulled the trigger. Nothing happened. The hammer fell into one of three empty cylinders. He pulled the trigger again and met with the same result. He pulled it a third time just as Mark reached him.

Mark felt the hot gunpowder singe his face as the bullet grazed the side of his forehead. He grabbed the gun and pointed it down. Eugene fired again, shooting himself in the shin. Mark pried the gun from his hands breaking his trigger finger in the process.

Mark had to resist the urge to beat the crap out of him. He took a deep breath and felt his left temple. There was blood on his finger, but not as much as he expected.

Eugene collapsed writhing on the ground cradling his shin. The angle of the bullet had caused it to travel the length of his shin. It shattered the bone in two places and tore the entire length of the muscle. He would more than likely lose the leg below the knee if blood loss didn't kill him first.

Two Fort Worth police officers heard the shots, and rode up behind Mark. They both had their rifles on him. Mark set the cowboy's gun down on the muddy street before turning to face them. They both relaxed when they saw Mark's hands were empty.

Their police uniforms were the same unbleached cotton uniforms worn by confederate officers forty years earlier. The only differences were the badges on their hats and jackets.

"What happened here?" The corporal asked.

Mark turned so they could see his badge on the outside of his jacket.

"I'm Deputy Mark Aaron," he said. "This man is Eugene Butler. He tried to shoot me, and in the process of disarming him, he shot himself in the leg."

The corporal dismounted and stepped over to Mark. He looked at Mark's badge and then relaxed. They both looked at Eugene lying in the mud. He had passed out but was bleeding at a steady rate.

"He'll bleed to death if we don't stop it," Mark said. "Got any rope?"

The corporal went to his saddlebag and pulled out a leather strap. Mark took out his knife and cut away the pant leg just above the knee. Then he tied the cord around his leg just above the knee, inserted his fountain pen inside the strap, and twisted until it was tight enough for his leg to turn purple.

Once the supply of blood had been cut off, Mark picked him up and put him on the corporal's horse. The corporal took him to the university hospital on Seventh and Rusk While Mark stayed behind with the other officer and answered his questions, a few eye witnesses came over and gave their statements as well.

It was dark by the time Mark finally got home. He unhitched the wagon, rubbed the horses down, fed and watered them, and finally went inside.

Kesara had kept his plate warm in the oven. As he took his first bite of the roast chicken, Jane entered the room.

"This piece of hull is non-magnetic iron," Jane said. "In fact, it is so non-magnetic that it is diamagnetic."

"What does diamagnetic mean?" Mark asked. "And nice to see you too. I'm glad you weren't killed today."

Jane brushed off his sarcasm with her usual eye roll. Then she took a breath and continued.

"It repels magnetic forces," Jane said. "Let me show you."

She took a horseshoe nail and held it next to the metal fragment with a pair of wooden tongs. Then she let it go. The nail hovered eleven centimeters above the hull fragment.

"Let me guess," Mark said. "You magnetized the nail, and now it's floating above the hull fragment because the two fields are repelling each other."

"Yes," Jane said. "The hull of the spacecraft is diamagnetic. That explains how it was able to fly. It used the Earth's magnetic field to propel it."

"And I suppose this is something they don't do in your time?" Mark asked.

"No," Jane said. "This is an unknown technology, and it also explains why we didn't find an engine. There wasn't an engine in a conventional sense."

"How would they control direction?" Mark asked.

"I'm glad you asked that," Jane said.

She took an eye dropper and placed a drop of blue liquid on the hull fragment. The nail fell to land in the fluid.

"This fluid blocks magnetism," Jane said. "I have no idea what it is, but magnetic energy is somehow absorbed. By pumping this fluid around the hull, the airship can change direction."

"Okay," Mark said. "We have a basic idea of how the airship worked."

"More or less," Jane said. "I still have no idea what the blue fluid is made of or how it works. I just know what it does."

"Your analyzer isn't working?" Mark asked.

"It's working fine," Jane said. "The fluid blocks or absorbs any energy applied to it, so the analyzer doesn't work on it. I don't get any readings."

Mark turned his head, and Jane saw where the bullet had grazed his temple.

"It looks like you had a rough day," Jane said.

"Not as rough as Eugene's," Mark said.

"Who's Eugene?" Jane asked.

"He's the cowboy who shot at me," Mark said. "When I took the gun away from him, he shot himself in the shin. He lost his right leg from the knee down."

She took his hand and interlinked with him. She entered his mind and he could feel her concern for him, as well as her affection. He felt her navigate his systems, run a diagnostic, and set his repair system to heal the injury at human speed. She lingered for a moment, inviting him to explore her mind, but when he didn't, she left his mind as gently as she had entered.

"You usually want to explore my memories of Mars," Jane said.

"I'm not in the mood," Mark said.

Chapter Five
The Cleaner

Mark heard Salsa barking at 3:02 A.M. That wasn't unusual. Salsa would bark at just about anything at any given moment. What was unusual was the dog fell silent mid-bark. He looked out the bedroom window. Everything outside was still.

Mark had been looking at rust under a crude microscope. At least, it was crude by his standards. The fragments of rust he examined were the remains of the airship hull. He was certain it was free of nanites, but it had inexplicably turned to rust the day before. Not just the fragments he and Jane were examining, but the large piece he had hidden t in the barn as well.

Mark got up from the desk and pulled on his pants. He still wore his nightshirt, and he didn't want to take the time to change. The lights were off because they wanted Kesara to think they were asleep.

Jane looked up from the bed. She lay against the goose-down pillows which gave her back support. She put down the muslin she was stitching.

"It's probably nothing," she said.

"I know," Mark said. "But I want to investigate anyway."

"Suit yourself," Jane said.

"I'll be back in a moment," Mark said.

Since he didn't want to wake Kesara, he didn't turn on the lights. He slipped out the bedroom door and down the stairs. As he rounded the foot of the stairs, he saw a figure standing in the study. The top drawer of his desk was open, and Mark knew he had locked it.

"Jane," Mark sent. *"We have an intruder."*

"Understood," Jane sent. *"Location?"*

"Study, in front of my desk," Mark sent.

He sent her an image.

"Let's see what he does," Jane sent.

Mark remained still and observed the intruder. The man stood about six feet tall. He wore a wide-brimmed hat, dark glasses, a white shirt, and black pants and jacket. He had several metal objects in his pockets, but none of them was a gun.

Mark expected Jane to come down the stairs, so when she didn't, he sent to her.

"Where are you?" Mark sent.

"I'm in the parlor by the front door," Jane sent. *"I climbed out the bedroom window."*

"In your nightgown?" Mark asked.

"No," Jane sent. *"I took that off."*

Kesara walked into the study from the kitchen.

"Sr. Aaron, ¿eres tú?" She asked.

The intruder casually reached into his jacket pocket and removed a stainless-steel device. He pointed it at Kesara. Mark detected some kind of electromagnetic wave, and Kesara collapsed.

A cast iron teapot flew into the study from the parlor. It struck him in the back hard enough to knock the intruder off his feet. The weapon flew into the kitchen and his body became sprawled onto the desk before collapsing to the floor.

Mark turned on the lights. The intruder was still conscious, and he reached up to cover his eyes. Jane entered the room. She wore a pair of Mark's coveralls. The front of the coveralls covered the vital areas of her chest, but Mark had to admit it was a good look for her.

"Mark," Jane sent. *"Pay attention to the prisoner."*

"Is that what he is?" Mark asked.

"For now," Jane sent.

Jane stepped over to where Kesara had fallen to the study floor. She took her pulse.

"Kesara's fine," Jane sent.

Mark put his knee in the intruder's back. The intruder's hands were covering his eyes. As soon as Mark pulled the man's hand away, he screamed in pain.

"Turn them off," he shouted.

"Turn what off?" Mark said.

"Turn the lights off," He shouted.

Jane stepped over to the light switch and turned off the light. The intruder visibly relaxed. Jane handed Mark his handcuffs, and he put them on. The intruder didn't resist. Mark picked him up and put him in the wooden desk chair.

Mark took a good look at him. He had shoulder-length blond hair, deep blue eyes, and fair skin. Mark noticed that the man's eyes weren't set right. His eyes were set at a ten-or-twelve degree angle off of the horizontal.

"Take a look at his eyes," Mark said.

Jane stepped over and examined the man's face. He regarded her with more than casual interest.

"Maybe you should go and change?" Mark suggested.

"Humans," Jane sent.

She turned away from him and went upstairs.

"You do realize that I am a deputy sheriff in this county, and I can hold you in the county jail as long as I want," Mark said.

The man said nothing.

Mark checked his jacket pockets. He took out the alien symbol and the metal box from the crashed airship. In the inside jacket pocket, he took out the man's wallet. The wallet was covered with the man's DNA, so Mark took a sample. He didn't open the wallet, but money and a train ticket protruded from it.

Mark looked around and found the man's glasses and hat. He put it on for him. Then he turned on the living room lights, and the intruder didn't protest.

"Now," Mark asked. "Who are you?"

The man was silent. Mark stepped over to the kitchen and picked up the weapon he had used to stun Kesara. The weapon was an aluminum box with a large button on top, a dial marked with alien symbols, and a sliding switch on the side.

"Since the only things you took were what we took from the crashed airship, you must be with the people who built it," Mark said.

He looked up, but said nothing. Jane came downstairs wearing a light blue dress. She stepped over to Mark.

"He isn't talking," Mark said. "And I don't really want to try to persuade him."

"What should we do?" Jane asked.

"I think we should let him go," Mark said.

"Really?" Jane sent.

"I don't think interrogating him is going to yield much we don't already know," Mark sent. *"We should just give him some of your radioactive lemonade and see where he goes."*

"Good idea," Jane sent.

Jane disappeared into the kitchen. When she returned, Mark ran the DNA sample as he went upstairs to change into his work clothes. When he got back downstairs, Jane had the intruder's head leaning back and was forcing him to drink a glass of lemonade. When the glass was empty, Jane stepped back. Mark held up the aluminum box.

"I assume this will work on you," Mark said.

Even through the dark glasses Mark saw his eyes widen.

"Good," Mark said. "What exactly does it do?"

The man said nothing.

"We could torture you with light until you tell us what we want to know," Jane said.

The man thought for a second.

"It just puts people to sleep," he said. "They awake not remembering the last hour or so."

Mark looked it over.

"Cool," Mark said. "I want one."

"If you don't let me go," the man said. "Others will come for me."

"Then we shall let you go," Mark said.

He pointed the box at the man and pressed the button. An electromagnetic wave came out of the device, and the man slumped in the chair.

"Now what?" Jane asked.

"Now I put the stuff he was after from my desk back in his pockets, give him back his ray gun, and carry him to the train station before he wakes up."

"The train station?" Jane asked.

Mark stepped into the parlor and got a bottle of whiskey. He opened the stranger's mouth and poured five ounces down his throat. He coughed a little, but swallowed it. Then he put a few drops on his clothes.

"He has a ticket from Denver in his wallet," Mark said. "He arrived on a train, so I'm going to assume he intended to leave on one."

"Somehow I don't think he is from Denver," Jane said.

"No," Mark said. "He is from Iceland."

"How do you know?" Jane asked.

"I ran his DNA while I was changing upstairs," Mark said. "Take a look at his eyes."

Jane lifted his head and looked at the intruder's eyes.

"Notice how his eyes aren't quite set right," Mark said. "His DNA has about five percent of the airship pilot's species. I also found adaptations for living underground. He can see in very low light levels and a little into the infrared."

"That confirms our theory that they are living underground," Jane said. "Are we going to follow him?"

"Maybe," Mark said. "I'm still not sure what we're getting into. We will need to upgrade our security though."

Mark put the man's things back in the pockets where he'd found them, picked him up in a fireman's carry, and left. He encountered a milkman and a few others, but when they saw his badge, they went about their business.

Mark put him down on a bench near the rear wall of the train station. A porter stepped over to him.

"Drunk?" the porter asked.

"Yes, and he is a mean one too, so I would keep my distance," Mark said.

The porter nodded and stepped away. Mark was tempted to remain and see if the man remembered him, but he thought better of it. He walked home to find Jane sitting on the back porch with her hat pointed at the Moon.

"He hasn't left the train station yet," she said. "I'll check his location twice a day."

Mark nodded.

"I'm not in a great rush to go chasing after him," Mark said. "The technology these people have rivals our own, and I'm still not sure we should be interfering with them."

"How so?" Jane asked.

"The androids Romanji sent back are a direct threat to humanity. I'm not sure that these people are," Mark said.

The next morning, Kesara got up, and apart from complaining about a bruised arm, had no idea that she had been stunned the night before. Mark went to work and filled out an incident report stating he'd had an encounter with a drunk that he took to the railroad station. Then he left to ride his circuit out in the county.

He wasn't too crazy about leaving Jane alone with the intruder in town, but if he delayed or said anything, Jane would think of it as questioning her ability. For an android, she could be sensitive on some issues.

The lemonade that Jane had given the intruder was loaded with spy dust. The Raven's advanced sensors had no problem tracking him from its hiding place on the Moon. He returned to Denver. From there, he went to Lookout Mountain. Jane lost the radioactive signature, but reacquired it briefly in Iceland before losing it again.

Mark came back from riding his circuit and found Jane relaxing on a chair under an oak tree in the back yard. The hidden dish antenna in her hat was pointed toward the Raven. To a casual observer, she was just relaxing in the shade.

"That confirms it," Jane said. "He's from Iceland."

"Yup," Mark said.

"How would you like to proceed?" Jane asked.

"Cautiously," Mark said. "They do deserve a look, but we should avoid direct contact."

"We can't leave right away," Jane said. "I promised Kesara she could have an apple tart booth at the Mai-Fest."

"That should give me plenty of time to get our affairs in order," Mark said.

While Jane and Kesara prepared for Mai-Fest, Mark sent several crates of books and other household items to John in Arizona. Then he spoke with the real estate agent and put the house on the market.

Mark submitted his resignation at the Sheriff's Office, and it was accepted regretfully. He was asked to stay on to Friday the fourteenth to help out with Mai-Fest, and he agreed. Then he was tasked with building their Mai-Fest float for the parade.

As soon as he got home, Jane and Kesara pressed him into service to build their booth at Hermann Park. Mark got them a nice spot by the river to put up their booth. He noticed that people were cutting down saplings growing by the river for poles, and he did the same.

He cut down enough to build a frame for the booth and tarp behind it, and he also used some saplings that were about an inch in diameter to build a cage for the Sheriff's Department's parade float.

Then he made five trips back and forth on North Street to ferry the cast iron oven, lumber, paint, and muslin to the site. Then he built the cooking table, the sales counter, set up the oven, cut fire wood, and stretched canvas over the frame he built to cover the cooking area. Then he stretched the muslin over the front and sides of the booth. Last, he picked up the apples, flour, sugar, and other ingredients that Jane and Kesara would need.

Mark mused that this was a lot of work to go through to sell apple tarts at a penny a piece, but he knew better to argue with Jane. He was actually grateful for the work because it kept his mind off of what he had experienced during the past two weeks.

Mark went home and worked through the night getting the parade float ready. He built a wooden replica of one of the cells at the County Jail. Then he covered the sides of the wagon with the leftover muslin from Kesara's booth.

He delivered the wagon to the Sheriff's Office on Saturday morning, and Sheriff Clark was thrilled. Then, he spent the rest of the day patrolling Hermann Park and putting the last touches on the booth.

Monday came, and Mark began his patrol of Hermann Park at sunup. He walked back and forth across the park from the corner of North and Summit to the river. Then he would walk a hundred yards south, and then walk back from the river to Summit Avenue. When he got to the south end of the park, he reversed the path.
Of o course, he had to walk around food booths, game booths, jugglers, fire eaters, acrobats, magicians, Native American axe throwing and archery, and a shooting range down by the river. There were also sewing contests, jam and jelly

contests, beer brewing contests, cooking contests, pastry contests, vegetable growing contests, pancake eating contests, and too many livestock contests for Mark to keep track of.

Jane asked him to investigate a couple of medicine sellers who turned up to sell their products. Mark had a conversation with them, and nothing they sold was harmful but wouldn't work either. Since the Food and Drug Administration wasn't established yet, he had to let them sell their medicine.

The pastry competition took place on Tuesday, and Kesara's apple tart came in second place. The demand for her tarts increased, and Jane had to hire a boy to bring them more apples and flour.

The parade was on Wednesday, and Mark's jail cell float came in third. The winner was a float with a girl covered in flowers swinging from an oak tree branch.

The last few contests were held on Wednesday, when attendance had dropped off Mark disassembled their booth

Mark received an offer for the house of $850. He accepted it and crated up the last of the books, kitchen equipment, the sewing machine, piano, household items, and six cases of beer from the Texas Brewing Company and had them shipped to John Johnson in Mesa Arizona.

Mark received a summons to appear in court for Eugene's arraignment. Mark sat quietly in the back of the courtroom until his case came up. Eugene was wheeled into the courtroom, and he glanced over at Mark. The two of them stared at each other for three seconds, before a young woman turned Eugene's chair to face the judge.

He pled guilty to the charge of attempted murder of a deputy sheriff, and Mark was asked if he wanted to give a statement before the sentence was passed.

Mark got up and walked to the railing near the prosecutor's table.

"Your honor," he said. "I would ask the court for leniency in this case. Mr. Butler has already lost his leg, and along with it, his ability to earn a living in his chosen profession. I realize that his crime is a serious one, and I only ask that his pain and suffering be taken into consideration."

The judge sighed and sentenced Eugene Butler to five years in state prison.

Mark walked past the prosecutor and stepped over to meet Eugene and his lawyer as they left.

"I'm sorry," Mark said. "I asked for a reduced sentence."

"That was a reduced sentence," his lawyer said. "Normally, he would have been hung."

Eugene's lawyer gave Mark a pat on the shoulder as he walked by. Eugene only stared at Mark, but the young woman pushing his chair smiled and thanked him.

Mark felt guilty about Eugene losing his leg, but he also realized that without his particle avoidance system, he would have lost his life.

The next morning, Mark and Jane said goodbye to Kesara and boarded a train for New

York. As they took their seats, Kesara, carpet bag in hand, took the seat across from them.

"Kesara," Jane asked. "Why are you here?"

Her dark brown eyes fixed on Jane.

"I have nowhere else to be," she said.

"We're going to Iceland," Mark said.

Kesara didn't reply. Mark looked at Jane who only shrugged.

"Where's Salsa?" Mark asked.

Kesara opened her carpet bag and Salsa's head peeked out. She gave him a piece of Jerky from her pocket. He took it, and she closed the carpet bag.

Mark and Jane exchanged a long glance but didn't say anything. Mark shrugged and went back to reading his newspaper. Jane and Kesara worked on English, Math, and reading lessons while Mark watched the scenery pass by the window. He looked out and realized that the buffalo that roamed the plains by the thousands were gone.

When they arrived in New York, they got a room at the Waldorf hotel. Kesara tried to pay for her own room, but Jane wouldn't hear of it. Once they were settled, they got a horse-drawn taxi to Longacre Square. Mark wanted to take a gas-powered cab, but Kesara refused to get into it. Since it was noisy, backfired often, and produced a lot of smoke, Mark didn't press the issue.

Jane bought them all winter coats for the trip to Iceland. Then the ladies decided to shop for underwear, and Mark left them. He got them tickets to that night's performance of the *Mysterious Mr. Bugle*.

The next morning, they went to Battery Park and looked at the Statue of Liberty. Mark noticed that it wasn't the green color he was used to, but a light brown with a few shiny spots. He realized that the statue hadn't had time to oxidize yet.

There was a photographer in the park, so they stopped for a photograph. Kesara didn't want to be in the photograph, but Jane insisted. They argued for two minutes and five seconds, and then they compromised on two photographs. One with Kesara and one without.

Mark met an encyclopedia salesman with a heavy Irish accent who confided in him that he hadn't sold a subscription in three days. Mark knew it was a sales scam, but he bought a fifteen- volume set and paid extra to have them sent to his brother-in-law John Johnson in Mesa Arizona.

The ladies went shopping for bicycle dresses, and Mark spent the rest of the day searching for passage to Reykjavik. Mark found a cruise ship that stopped in Reykjavik, but found himself in an argument when he tried to book passage. The cost of the entire trip was $475 per person. The cruise stopped in Reykjavik, but went on to Norway, Sweden, Denmark, Finland, and Russia.

The agent, a man with oily, brown hair parted down the middle and a thick mustache, demanded full payment despite that they were not taking the entire cruise because they would be taking up a cabin, and that cabin would remain empty for the rest of the cruise. Mark pointed out that if the cabin was empty, then getting $150 per person was better than nothing. The agent reluctantly agreed, but would not book their passage until June 1. The day before the ship left.

He cautioned Mark that ships only stopped in Iceland during the summer, and if he didn't find the winter there to his liking, he would be trapped until next summer. Mark thanked him for the information.

Mark went back to the Waldorf and waited for the ladies to return. As he sat in the room reading a newspaper, a radio signal pierced his electronic brain. It was the digital equivalent to running fingernails over a chalkboard. The signal spanned thirty-seven frequencies on the A.M. band. Mark took a bearing on the signal from his hotel room, and then walked across the street and took a second bearing as he bought a copy of *The Sun*. He paid the boy a nickel and told him to keep the change. The signal originated 1.8 miles south of his location.

Normally, Mark would drop what he was doing and investigate a radio signal like this, but in this case, he already knew who was responsible from the historical research he'd done before he died. Nicola Tesla had a lab in New York, and he was probably demonstrating his wireless telegraph. This was something that was supposed to happen, and the fourth android wasn't due to arrive for another few years, so Mark turned off his A.M. receiver. Before going back to his newspaper, he paused for 2.8 seconds to wonder what happened to the second android who was supposed to kill Tesla. Did his escape pod fail? Or, did he collide with a piece of space debris? There was no way to know, so Mark decided to just be grateful for the win.

He knew that Tesla was living at the Waldorf and had been doing his best to avoid him. He learned from his encounters with Lincoln that getting to know a historical person could result in unforeseen effects. Everything had turned out all right with Lincoln, but Mark didn't want to press his luck. Since Tesla was an inventor, a misspoken word or gesture could cause him to create something that would alter history in ways Mark couldn't comprehend. He did feel bad that Tesla would never receive the credit he deserved for inventing radio, but again that was something that was supposed to happen, so he couldn't do anything to change it.

Jane, Kesara, and Salsa came into the room, and Mark put down the paper he was reading.

"What is that awful noise?" Jane sent.

"Tesla," Mark sent. *"He is testing his wireless telegraph."*

"Did you want to investigate?" Jane asked.

"We can stop by his lab to document what is there," Mark sent. *"As long as we don't get too close."*

"Did you find us a ship?" Jane asked.

"Yes," Mark said. "But I can't book passage until Friday."

"Why not?" Jane asked.

Mark told her about the cruise, and all of its stops, and its price of $475 per person.

"I want you to go back down tomorrow and buy a first-class ticket for Kesara," Jane sent.

"Why?" Mark sent.

"I don't want her following us to Iceland. She is only human," Jane sent.

"You want to leave her on the ship?" Mark sent. "

"Can you think of a better place to leave her?" Jane asked. *"She will have two months to enjoy the cruise and figure out what she can do when she gets back to New York."*

"You're right," Mark sent.

"Get ready to go out," Jane said. "I got us tickets to see a play. Kesara won't be joining us."

"I am ready," Mark said. "I just need my hat. What play are we seeing tonight?"

"It's called *Never Again*," Jane said.

"I was just reading about that," Mark said.

He gestured toward the newspaper he left atop the bed. Kesara retired to her own room for the evening.

The next morning, Mark went to the American Line office to purchase Kesara's ticket. The clerk at the desk wasn't happy to see him until Mark told him he would pay full price for a ticket. After half an hour of discussion, Mark bought a full price ticket for Kesara and paid $237.50 each for two tickets to Iceland. The clerk had argued that it was cheaper than chartering a boat, and Mark had to agree. Mark waited while he typed a letter stating that he had a credit of $118.75 per person, should he decide to leave Iceland on another American Line cruise ship. Mark thanked him for being thoughtful enough to write the letter on his behalf.

When Mark returned to the hotel, he and Jane visited Tesla's workshop. Since it wasn't open to the public, they had to be content with walking around the block and looking in through the windows. They saw coils, knife switches, lots of iron parts and copper wire, along with glass tubes that resembled neon lights.

Mark wanted to speak with Tesla, but knew he couldn't. It was enough to see him directing his employees through an open window. Tesla was responsible for inventing radio, neon lights, alternating current, and the motors that ran on alternating current. He, more than anyone else was responsible for the life Mark knew in the twentieth century, but Tesla was also a horrible business man. It was his lack of fiscal understanding that allowed others to profit from his work, and he was destined to die in poverty.

On Wednesday morning, they boarded the two-funnel steamer Saint Louis. A porter took Kesara's trunk, and was a little shocked when she wouldn't give up her carpet bag.

A steward showed them to their room, where upon entry they were met by their maid. A blue-eyed, red-haired, girl who looked to be about seventeen. She told them, in a heavy Irish accent, that her name was Kathleen and she would be happy to be their servant. She curtseyed, and Kesara's eyes widened, her face turned red, and she very impolitely told Kathleen where she could go and what she could do when she got there. Fortunately for Kathleen, she said it in Spanish, so she had no idea what was being said, but she did know that Kesara wasn't happy with her.

Salsa, hearing the shouting from the carpet bag, barked. And Kathleen asked if she could take Salsa to the kennel. Kesara's Spanish cursing resumed, but with more vigor.

Kathleen's bright smile faded, her face blushed, and Mark had to send her for tea while Jane calmed Kesara down. After a few minutes of discussion, it became clear that Kesara had misunderstood the situation, and thought that she was being replaced. Jane had to explain to Kesara that she was a first-class passenger, not a servant. And that Kathleen would be her servant for the voyage.

Kesara didn't accept the idea at first, but with a few hugs from Jane, she calmed down. When Kathleen returned with the tea, she had tear streaks on her cheeks. Kesara apologized to her in English, and they took Salsa to the kennel together.

When they returned, Kathleen showed them how to operate the room's electric lights, water closet, and how to ring for her. She asked what time they wanted breakfast, how they liked their eggs, and when the ladies would need help dressing and bathing.

Jane informed Kathleen that lunch would be taken in their cabin, and they would be dressing for dinner. Kesara would take her bath at six, and she would take hers at seven. Kathleen made some notes on a scrap of paper and slipped it into her skirt pocket. Mark could see from her expression that Kesara wasn't happy, but she wasn't saying anything about it. Since Kathleen didn't ask Mark when he would be bathing, he surmised that he was on his own.

Jane took Kesara to the forward observation lounge to play checkers, so Mark took his bath early. He was surprised to find that the Saint Louis was equipped with hot water. This was the first set of hot and cold water taps that he had seen since he had died.

He and Jane may be androids, but they were designed to emulate all aspects of humanity, which included generating body odor. Why his designers chose to give them body odor but not a sense of smell or taste was a question he couldn't answer.

Mark wanted to enjoy his soak in a hot tub, but his android body wouldn't comply. He was designed to operate in a wide range of temperatures, and the water, despite being very hot, did nothing for him. His android muscles didn't relax like his human ones did. He finished his bath, washed his hair, and shaved. He resisted the idea of putting more hair oil on, but in the end he did. Dry hair wouldn't be in fashion for another fifty-years, and he needed to fit in.

When he finished, he went out on deck and found a spot to stare out at the horizon. When the ladies came back, Jane supervised Kesara's bath in order to keep her from fighting with Kathleen.

Dinner in the formal dining salon went well, although, Kesara kept looking around as if she were a thief about to get caught. After dinner, Kathleen helped the ladies into their nightgowns, and retired for the night. Mark lay in bed with Jane waiting for Kesara to go to sleep.

"What's the plan?" Mark asked. *"We arrive in Iceland tomorrow morning."*

"I'm going to tell Kesara to stay on board," Jane sent. *"I'll leave her a note with Kathleen."*

"Better be sure it isn't delivered until after the ship departs," Mark sent.

"That was my plan," Jane sent.

"Are we bringing the trunks?" Mark asked.

"If we didn't, it would seem out of place," Jane sent.

The Saint Louis stopped at 5:29 A.M., and Mark went out on deck. The temperature was 46 degrees Fahrenheit, but the wind chill was making it feel colder. Mark could see Reykjavik even in the low light, and it wasn't the sleepy fishing village he expected. There were a few multi-story buildings and a developed network of paved streets.

Knowing that Kesara would be getting up soon, Mark found a steward, and after several minutes of explanation, he helped him carry the trunks to the boat. The dock at Reykjavik was too small to accommodate the Saint Louis, so everyone going ashore had to go by way of the ship's boat.

Mark had a similar conversation with the second officer, who finally ordered the boat lowered. Just as the second trunk was loaded into the boat, Jane arrived and climbed in. Mark sat beside her, and four men climbed in behind him. The boat was raised off the deck and lowered into the ocean and they were rowed to the dock. The sailors transferred the trunks to the dock, as Mark and Jane climbed out of the boat. Once they were on the dock, Mark turned to Jane.

"You're sure she won't follow us again?" Mark asked.

"Kathleen will tell her we went ashore with the tour group, and that we will be back in the evening. By the time she realizes we aren't coming back, the ship will have departed," Jane said.

A fisherman spotted them standing on the dock with their trunks. Word went up the dock, and a few minutes later a young man with a cart was moving toward them. He spoke to them in Icelandic, and Mark turned to Jane.

"What's he saying?" Mark asked.

"How should I know?" Jane asked. "Icelandic isn't one of my languages."

"I thought you spoke everything," Mark said.

"Hotel," he said.

"Yes," Mark said. "Hotel"

He gestured toward the trunks, and he and Mark loaded them on to his cart, and a he led the mule pulling the cart back up the dock.

They followed the cart through several streets that Mark couldn't begin to pronounce until they reached a five-story brick building. The first floor consisted of concrete arches, and the rest of the building was brick with small windows. A sign built into the wall read "Hótel Borg."

Mark and Jane went into the lobby, and they were greeted by a woman in a gray wool dress.

"Góðandaginn," she said.

"Do you speak English?" Mark asked.

"Yes," she said. "Some."

"Well, your English is much better than my Icelandic," Mark said.

She smiled and gestured for them to come over to the counter.

"We get a few English guests from time to time. I learn from them," she said.

"We are going to need a room and a guide to take us out onto the glacier," Mark said.

Jane pulled out a map of the area and pointed to a spot inland. The clerk smiled when she saw the map, but frowned when she saw where Jane was pointing.

"We have a room," she said. "I can ask about a guide, but it will be expensive. Going out on a glacier is dangerous."

"We have money," Jane said.

She took out her purse and began to pull out money, but the clerk held up her hands.

"That's American," she said. "You will have to change it."

She directed them to a bank a few blocks away where Mark and Jane exchanged their paper money and some of their gold coins for Icelandic kronas.

As they left the bank, a young, blonde girl stood on the sidewalk selling strawberries. Mark admired her business ethic, and he bought two bags. He shared one with Jane as they walked, and he put the other in his jacket pocket.

They returned an hour and nine minutes later, and she had them checked into room 509. A porter had delivered their luggage to the room.

Mark gave her fifty kronas, and she gave them the key.

"Where do you suggest we look for a guide?" Mark asked.

"I can ask," she said. "There is a tavern called Einaugafiskurinn, or in English, "The One Eyed Fish". Some of the guides go there, but finding one who speaks English and is willing to take you that far inland may take time."

She wrote the name down for them. Mark and Jane thanked her, took the elevator to the fifth floor, and found their room. The opened the curtain and looked out at the harbor. The Saint Louis was still at anchor.

"I'm not sure why we brought the trunks," Mark said. "We can't bring them with us."

"You could always fill them with souvenirs and send them to John," Jane said.

Mark smiled at that idea.

Jane took some white butcher paper out of her trunk along with several pens and a bottle of colored ink. She sat at the desk drawing a map of the coordinates where the intruder's radiation signature disappeared. Mark sat near the window and kept a watch on the Saint Louis and the harbor.

"Still think she may try to follow us?" Jane asked.

"It wouldn't surprise me," Mark said.

At sunset the boats with the tourists returned to the Saint Louis. The sunset was a spectacular display of color and glory. It wasn't as spectacular as the sunsets on Xaniblus, but for Earth, it was inspiring. The western sky became rose colored near the indigo water, with a band of orange, ten degrees above the horizon, and blended into rose. The rose bands contained violet clouds that covered the horizon so that the Saint Louis became an outline against a rose backdrop. Just as the last boat was recovered, the front desk clerk knocked on their door to let them know the restaurant would be closing in an hour. Mark kept watching until the sun had completely set, and the Saint Luis did not launch a boat.

In order to keep up appearances, Mark and Jane went to dinner in the hotel's restaurant. Jane had lamb meatloaf while Mark had some kind of fish stew with cornbread. The food looked good, but since neither of them could taste it, they had no way of knowing. By the time they returned to their room, the Saint Louis had departed.

Jane saw Mark look out the window.

"Kathleen should have given her the note by now," Jane said.

"I gave Kathleen twenty-dollars to look after her," Mark said.

Jane smiled.

"So did I."

Chapter Six
Put on Ice

Mark spent the morning exploring the various shops of Reykjavik. He bought a couple of paintings that he liked, a vase, and a few Icelandic novels that were popular. He put them in his trunk, added several articles from Jane's trunk, and had it shipped to John in Arizona.

After lunch, he and Jane went to the One Eyed Fish, ordered tankards of the local ale, and asked for a guide. The language barrier made it difficult, but when Jane produced a map and pointed to where they wanted to go, it became clear. They waited all evening, but no guides presented themselves.

The following morning, the front desk clerk called them over to the desk. She told them that people were talking about the large sum of cash Mark had been carrying, and she urged them to open a bank account. They thanked her, and they spent the morning at the same bank where they had exchanged their currency. Once again, there was a language barrier, but the bank manager sent for someone who spoke English. Two hours later they had an account at Landsbanki—the National Bank of Iceland.

They returned to the One Eyed Fish and spent the day playing cards. A guide who spoke broken English presented himself, but when he saw where Mark and Jane wanted to go, he turned down the job.

On the afternoon of the third day, a tall, blond man and woman walked into the tavern. They both looked like they had just stepped out of the pages of a fashion magazine. They stood out to Mark because not only did their seal skin jackets fit them perfectly, but they both had perfect, white teeth, which in this century was unusual. They both wore pants, and that was something of a social taboo for women then as well. This told Mark they were from somewhere remote enough that social rules could be ignored.

The barman directed them over to Mark and Jane's table. Mark sighed because he had lost the last five hands to Jane, and he had just drawn a royal flush. Now, he wouldn't be able to finish the hand.

The pair stepped over to Mark and Jane's table and sat down without asking permission.

"Can we help you," Mark asked.

The man responded in perfect English.

"We hear that you are looking for a guide up on the glacier," he said.

"Yes," Mark said.

He held out his hand, and the man shook it. He held it out to the woman, and she reluctantly did the same. Jane repeated the gesture, and they both shook hands with her as well. As he shook hands with Jane, Mark noticed they both were squinting a little.

"I'm assuming you did that to get their DNA," Jane sent.

"The analysis will take a minute," Mark sent

"Do you think they are related to the aquatic apes?" Jane asked.

"We really need to come up with a better name for them, but yes," Mark sent. *"Look at their eyes."*

"I am Mark Aaron, and this is my wife, Jane," Mark said.

"My name is Trausti Ölvirsson, and this is my sister, Sigríður Lótusdóttir. We heard of your desire to travel out into the ice, and we came to offer our services."

Jane pulled a map from her handbag and spread it out on the table.

"We would like to go here," she said.

Jane pointed at a point on the map that indicated the valley between two large mountains.

"Why would you want to go to Langjokull glacier?" Sigríður asked.

She brushed aside a lock of her wavy blonde hair and smiled as she pulled the map over for a closer look.

"I've been there," she said. "There isn't anything there but ice."

"Yes," Jane said. "That's what we want to see."

Trausti and Sigríður exchanged a glance.

"You don't understand," Trausti said. "Going out onto Langjokull glacier is extremely dangerous. The ice has fissures and hidden holes. If you fall down one, you will not be able to get out, and you will freeze to death."

"Even during the summer, the temperature on the ice can get far below zero," Sigríður said. "If we encounter a storm, we all could freeze."

"But you said you've been there?" Mark asked.

Sigríður fixed her deep blue eyes on Mark and smiled.

"Yes," Sigríður said. "I've been there, and I can tell you there isn't anything there except ice."

"Wouldn't you like to see the hot springs or the fire caves?" Trausti asked.

"Can you lead us to the edge of Langjokull glacier?" Mark asked.

"Of course," Trausti said. "But even that is not without danger."

"How much?" Mark asked.

The brother and sister exchanged another glance.

"We will have to purchase mules and supplies." Trausti said. "It would cost six-hundred kronas."

"No problem," Mark said. "We can have the money when the bank opens."

"Once we have the money," Trausti said. "It will take a day or two to get the supplies. We should plan to leave three days from now."

"That is fine," Mark said.

He offered his hand to Trausti, and Jane offered hers to Sigríður. They shook hands and the brother and sister left.

"Well," Jane sent.

"They are each 3.35 percent aquatic ape,

and they are not related," Mark sent.

"Should we trust them?" Jane asked.

"Absolutely not," Mark sent. *"But, we at least we made contact."*

"What do you mean?" Jane asked. *"Just because they have an ancestor who was an aquatic ape doesn't mean they are connected with them."*

"My gut is telling me otherwise," Mark sent. *"I believe that these beings are influencing human society and development. The two we just met indicate that they have infiltrated human society, to what end, I have no idea. But they are similar to Romanji in that society is being manipulated externally."*

"How?" Jane asked.

"What's stopping someone like Trausti from becoming a political or religious leader?" Mark asked.

"Nothing," Jane sent.

"Exactly," Mark sent. *"What if these beings are responsible for events in our history like, say, World War I?"*

"I see your point," Jane sent. *"Since no one is aware of their existence, we have no way of knowing how much they have influenced history."*

"Romanji had five hundred years of history, computer models, and advanced technology when he sent his androids back in time to alter society. Yet he still managed to accidently exterminate humanity," Mark sent. *"These beings could be attempting the same kind of social influence."*

"And you're thinking they will have a similar result?" Jane asked.

"I don't know," Mark sent. *"But they could*

be the reason Romanji failed, and we are here."

"That's a lot of 'could be's," Jane sent.

"I know," Mark sent. *"That's what we are here to investigate."*

Jane sighed and Mark picked up his cards.

"Did you want to finish our hand?" Mark asked.

"No," Jane said. "I can't beat your royal flush."

"Have you been looking at my cards?" Mark asked.

"Of course not," Jane said. "That would be cheating. I memorized the deck when you let me shuffle."

"And that isn't cheating?" Mark asked.

"Technically, no," Jane said. "I did it before play began."

Mark threw his cards on the table, and they went back to the hotel. Jane made arrangements to put her trunk in storage. They met with their guides the in the morning and gave them the money. The guides then gave Mark and Jane a list of items they would need for the trip, and Sigríður told Jane she could not hike in a skirt and gifted her with a pair of sheepskin hiking pants.

The next morning, Mark and Jane checked out of their hotel before sunrise. As they walked out to the street, Trausti and Sigríður were waiting for them with four ponies. Each pony carried a canvas supply bag. They examined the leather backpacks that Mark and Jane carried approvingly. Then Mark and Jane were each given a pony to lead. Mark's pony was a painted pony with a dark face and white patches on her legs and front quarter. Jane's pony was a palomino, like the other two.

They led their ponies out of town and they passed several farm houses that seemed as if they were a part of the landscape. Grass covered the sides and the steep roof of the houses. The only thing that separated them from the landscape was the weathered, gray front that usually consisted of two windows, a door. Sheep, and a few cattle, grazed nearby. A vegetable garden was fenced off from the cattle. Mark had to wonder how long the growing season was there.

They passed by a waterfall of steaming water. Trausti led them up a winding trail that took them to the source of the waterfall: a hot spring. Trausti stopped his pony, turned back to them, and declared that they would stop there for the night.

Mark looked over at Jane and shrugged. Jane found a level spot of volcanic rock and began to set up camp. Sigríður came over to where Jane was working, observed for a moment, and left. Once Mark had unpacked his pony, he left to gather dung for the fire. When he returned, he found Sigríður and Jane soaking in one of the hot springs. As soon as Sigríður saw Mark, she dropped back down into the water. He saw their heads and shoulders protruding from the surface of a pool. They both had soap in their hair. Mark put the pile of dung near their tent.

"Don't come any closer," Jane shouted. "We aren't decent."

Mark turned away.

"I can see that," Mark said.

"Why don't you go take a bath over there?" Jane said.

"Trausti is on the other side of that rock," Sigríður said. "Go and join him. We won't get another chance for a bath until we travel back this way in a week."

"You could have warned me," Mark sent.

"I could have," Jane sent. *"But I enjoy watching you express your human inhibitions."*

"Is that the android thing to do?" Mark sent.

"Actually," Jane sent. *"It is. We used to observe humans much the same way you would observe birds."*

"Wow," Mark sent. *"Good to know. Do all androids feel that they are superior to humans, or is it just you?"*

"We don't feel that we are superior," Jane sent. *"We are superior in many ways."*

Mark found his backpack by his tent and took out a bar of soap, a washcloth, and a change of clothes.

"If androids are superior, why didn't they take over during the android rebellion?" Mark asked.

"Because we are smart enough to know that control is an illusion," Jane sent. *"We could have taken over, but then we would be despised by those we ruled. Eventually, rebellions would begin, and we would have a choice of either being overthrown or becoming the tyrants we overthrew."*

"That makes sense," Mark sent.

Mark walked around the side of a large volcanic boulder and found Trausti relaxing in a pool of the hot spring. The volcanic rock had formed a depression roughly six feet in diameter with a depth of four and a half feet. Water from the spring flowed through it on its way to the river.

Mark put his soap and washcloth at the edge of the pool, got undressed, and got in. Trausti ignored him until he was in the water.

"You still haven't told us why you want to go to Langjokull glacier," Trausti said. "It is just a field of ice."

Mark met his gaze for the first time since entering the pool. He noticed that Trausti had a medallion around his neck. It was the same symbol Jane found in the *Koreshan Cellular Cosmology* and Mark took from the pilot of the airship.

"He's asking why we want to go to the glacier," Mark sent.

"Okay," Jane sent. *"Make something up, you're good at that."*

"Did you ever hear of a place called Shangri-la?" Mark asked.

Trausti shrugged his shoulders.

"I was playing poker with a fella in Tucson, and he can't cover his bet, so he gives me an old book to cover his losses."

Trausti nodded.

"Inside the book was a map drawn by a sailor from the HMS Albatross. The book was a journal and it claimed that water melted from the ice of the Langjokull glacier cures all ailments and promotes long life."

Trausti smiled.

"It claims that there is a secret society in the mountains near the glacier where people live to be hundreds of years old," Mark said.

"No one lives there," Trausti said. "The mountains are too cold, and there isn't anything to eat."

"Maybe so," Mark said. "But my wife and I would like to see for ourselves."

"I'll take you out on the edge of the glacier," Trausti said. "If only to see your face when you realize you went there for nothing."

"Maybe so," Mark said. "But at least we will know for sure."

They walked for another two days, and on the morning of the third day, they emerged from a mountain pass on to the glacier. The ice stretched out before them like a vast desert.

The ponies were left to graze in a field because the ice would be too dangerous for them. They roped themselves together with Trausti in the lead, Mark and Jane in the middle, and Sigríður in the rear.

They walked out on the ice. Trausti checked the ice in front of them with a pole. Several times he told them to stop and back track around a weak spot in the ice.

When they had gotten to within five miles of the spot where Jane had lost contact with the intruder, Trausti called a halt.

"We can't go any further," he said.

Mark and Jane walked up to join him. A fissure lay before them. It was ten feet wide and stretched to the horizon. Mark surveyed the fissure and had to agree. As he turned to speak to Jane, he saw Sigríður cut her rope. Before he could say anything to Jane, Trausti shoved him into the fissure. He fell sixty-three feet down into the ice and landed on his rear hard enough to kill him if he had been human. Jane landed beside him a second later.

"Are you okay," Mark asked.

Jane pushed herself up and into a sitting position. She brushed ice off her face and chest.

"I'm fine," Jane said. "Why didn't you warn me?"

"I didn't get the chance," Mark said. "They must have had this planned all along. Good thing we aren't human, or we'd be dead."

"So," Jane said. "What's your plan?"

"We wait to be sure that they're gone and we climb out," Mark said.

"That may not be as easy as you think," Jane said. "Remember how Three was stuck in that well? Our situation is similar."

"It can't be that bad," Mark said.

Mark tried to climb up, but his hands and feet couldn't get a grip on the slippery surface. He climbed up five feet to lose his grip on the side and fell flat on his face. He pushed himself back up off the snow and tried again with the same result.

"Okay," Mark said. "It's that bad."

"It gets worse," Jane said. "This glacier is sitting on top of a lake and this fissure opened as a result of tidal forces on the lake below."

"So?" Mark asked.

"So," Jane said. "In the next high tide, the bottom of this fissure is going to open all the way down to the water. That's why they put us in here. They knew our bodies would never be recovered."

"I have an idea," Mark said.

He took his canteen out from under his jacket and drank it. He used the microwave emitter in his right hand to melt more water. He collected it in the water bottle and drank that too. Then he used his microwave emitter to melt a hand hold in the wall. Since the ice was much denser than regular ice, it took ninety-six seconds to melt a six-inch hand hold at full power.

"Not bad," Jane said. "If you space them three feet apart, we will be out of here in forty-seven minutes."

Mark started carving hand and foot holds in the ice. He made it up thirty-six feet, and then he slipped. He fell back down into the fissure, striking Jane on the way down. Mark hit the bottom and Jane landed on top of him. They broke though the layer of ice they had been standing on to end up on a layer fifteen feet below where they started.

Jane climbed off Mark and they both rolled over and sat up to face each other.

"Any other ideas?" Jane asked.

"Not at the moment," Mark said. "When was your last communication with John?"

"Yesterday," Jane said. "Why?"

"We could wait for him to come looking for us," Mark suggested.

"That could take months," Jane said. "Your idea was sound. It just failed in execution. We should try again."

She stood up and gestured for Mark to stand when the ice beneath her gave way and she fell out of sight. Mark remained flat on the ice. The rope around his waist pulled him toward the hole. He was pulled over to the opening, but stopped himself from going through. He looked down at her dangling on the end of the rope.

"We just haven't had any luck today," he said.

"See if you can pull me up?" Jane asked.

Mark pulled Jane up about three feet when the layer of ice he was on gave way. They both fell, and this time Mark landed on Jane.

Mark looked around. A small shaft of light entered through the hole they had just fallen through. The weak light danced off the sides of a large ice cave. Mark ran through the light spectrum and discovered a small amount of UV light was penetrating the glacier, so he switched his vision to UV. The tunnel extended as far as he could see. A small stream of melt water ran through it. In most places, it was large enough to walk through, but it did narrow occasionally.

"This is kinda cool," Mark said. "No pun intended."

"Well, yes," Jane said. "We seem to be in an air bubble or melt zone of some kind."

"Do you think it could lead to the surface?" Mark asked.

"It's possible," Jane said. "But it more than likely it leads further down."

"To my knowledge," Mark said. "No one has ever explored the water under a glacier. If we were to go into the lake, there would be no way of predicting what we would find."

"Are you suggesting that we explore the lake under the glacier?" Jane asked.

"We did come here to explore and search for the aquatic apes," Mark said.

"We really do need to find a better name for them," Jane said.

"Okay," Mark said.

"I would call them Roswell Greys, but Roswell hasn't happened yet."

"We discovered them in Aurora," Jane said. "We could call them Aurorians."

"That works," Mark said.

Mark followed the cave with Jane close behind. They remained tied together, but at the moment that seemed unnecessary. The ice cave's walls varied from nine to twenty feet apart, and the ceiling stood thirteen feet above them. No visible light from the surface penetrated, but they were able to see in X-ray. They walked without speaking for thirty minutes before Mark decided to break the silence.

"Can you explain to me again how broadcast power works?" Mark asked.

"I don't think I explained it a first time," Jane said. "But broadcast power derives free electrons from the ether itself."

"What's the ether?" Mark asked.

"You should know," Jane said. "You've been there several times."

"What do you mean?" Mark said. "If I had been to another dimension, I would remember it."

"When Kak would transport us," Jane said. "He would briefly bring us into the ether, and then bring us to where he wanted us to go."

"So, the ether is in the fourth dimension?" Mark asked.

"Yes and no," Jane said. "Yes, fourth-dimensional objects do exist there—like dark matter, but no, it is more than that."

"Now, I'm confused," Mark said.

"The ether exists everywhere and nowhere at the same time. If you are an electron, you can move between the two levels of existence freely, but if you are solid matter, you are trapped in this dimension."

"So, then Kak was a being of pure energy?" Mark asked.

"Not entirely," Jane said. "As near as I could tell, he had elements of dark matter in him as well. We discussed it briefly after I rendered that picture of him a few years ago."

"I'm still confused about the ether," Mark said. "I thought that theory was abandoned in the nineteenth century."

"It was," Jane said. "But it was revived in the early twenty-first century when the results of several experiments required it."

"What experiments?" Mark asked.

"The first one was the discovery of cosmic background radiation in 1965. At first, they thought it was leftover radiation from the big bang, but that theory of the universe was later disproved," Jane said. "What they had actually discovered were quarks from the ether interacting with dark matter that left a radioactive residue in this universe."

"I don't understand," Mark said.

"Imagine you are in a room with paper walls and someone shines a light on those walls from the outside," Jane said. "The light doesn't come from the room, but you can see it in the room."

"Okay," Mark said.

"Now imagine that there is paint on the paper wall that is blocking some of the light. The paint is the dark matter. You can't see the paint directly, but you can see how it interacts with the light," Jane said.

"I'm with you so far," Mark said.

"The next discovery came in 2010, a Purdue graduate student discovered that radioactive decay is not linear as was previously thought, but it is tied to the Sun and the solar cycle. The rate of decay decreases just before a solar flare, and increases afterward," Jane said.

"Okay," Mark said. "But I don't see how that . . ."

"What is tying the two things together?" Jane asked.

"The ether?" Mark asked.

Jane smiled and nodded yes.

"The next discovery was Einstein's gravitational waves," Jane said. "In 2017 the first gravitational wave was detected."

"So," Mark asked.

"You can't have a wave without a medium to transmit it," Jane said. "But instead of water transmitting the wave, it was the ether."

"Okay," Mark said. "That one I understand."

"It was also believed that light and radio waves didn't need a medium to travel through space," Jane said. "That was also proven to be wrong. The medium they are traveling through is the ether."

"So, everything I learned in my high school science class was wrong?" Mark asked.

"It gets better," Jane said. "The last discovery came by a nobody who asked a really basic question."

"Which was?" Mark asked.

"Electricity is produced by spinning a magnet inside a copper coil," Jane said.

"I know," Mark said. "I built a generator in the garden room."

"Yes," Jane said. "But did you bother to ask where the free electrons came from?"

"They came from the magnetic field," Mark said.

"Okay," Jane asked. "If they came from the magnetic field, and the magnetic field is produced by a permanent magnet, wouldn't the magnet wear out at some point? There isn't an infinite number of electrons in the magnet is there?"

"Well, no," Mark said.

"But you've never heard of a magnet in a generator wearing out?"

"No," Mark said. "But I thought the electrons came from the copper wire?"

"Then wouldn't it wear out?" Jane asked. "Electricity is the flowing of electrons. That means free electrons jumping from atom to atom in the copper wire. Where did they come from?"

"But doesn't electric current flow in a circuit?" Mark asked. "They have to return to the source, so that is why the magnets and wire don't run out of electrons?"

"Do all the electrons return to the source?" Jane asked.

"No," Mark said. "There is a loss due to resistance, and some of the energy is converted to heat."

"So," Jane said. "We're back to the original question. If the circuit is losing electrons, why doesn't the copper, or the magnets, wear out?"

"I don't know," Mark said.

"That's because the source of the electrons isn't the magnet or the copper, but the ether. It turns out that a magnetic field extends into the ether and sweeps the electrons into our universe to be caught by the copper wire."

"So, things can exist in more than one universe?" Mark asked.

"Of course," Jane said. "Stars, radio waves, photons, magnetic fields, gravity, and radioactivity all have a dual existence. They exist both here and in the ether."

"You said gravity?" Mark asked.

"Yes," Jane said. "Gravity is the pressure that the ether puts on our universe. That is why it is the weakest of all the electromagnet forces, but it is also the one that seems to come from everywhere at once."

"You're telling me that gravity is fourth dimensional?" Mark asked.

"Yes," Jane said. "In my century everyone knows that."

"I'm a little confused as to how the two overlapping universes work," Mark said.

"Think of the universe as a fish tank with red and blue dye in it," Jane said. "The red dye is our universe and the blue dye is the ether. We can only see what is red, and what you call dark matter is blue, so it is invisible to us. There are a few things in the tank like quarks and electrons that are purple."

"So," Mark said. "The red and blue dye both occupy the same space in the tank, but we can only see the red."

"Exactly," Jane said. "Your processor also utilizes quantum principles."

"What do you mean?" Mark asked.

"Electricity moves through your processor at the speed of light, right?" Jane asked.

"Yes."

"That speed limit greatly reduced the amount of processing power a computer could have. In order to get a processor to work faster than light, quantum computing was invented. The electrons in the processor jump in and out of the ether to increase processing speed," Jane said.

"I had no idea," Mark said.

"Once someone realized that radio and light waves utilized the either as a medium to carry them, Quantum computing became possible."

Mark paused for a full minute before he spoke again.

"So how does broadcast power work again?" Mark asked.

"It is a series of overlapping magnetic fields that allows devices to pull free electrons directly from the ether," Jane said. "I can't say more than that because I honestly don't know. Androids were provided with enough data to function in society, but not enough to control it. That information was deemed too dangerous for an android to know."

"Wow," Mark said. "I had no idea."

"And what bearing does this information have upon our current situation?" Jane asked.

"None whatsoever," Mark said. "I just wanted to talk."

"How far down do you think we are?" Jane asked.

"I had been using my microwave emitter as a kind of ground penetrating radar, but I can no longer detect the surface, so we are at least two thousand feet down," Mark said.

"I noticed," Jane said. "I agree. The slope of the melt tunnel is roughly seven degrees, and we have walked 17,280 feet, so that would put us roughly 2,121.72 feet below the surface."

Mark pointed his microwave emitter down toward the floor of the cavern.

"The lake is about seventy feet below us," Mark said.

They continued on until the small amount of X-ray light that penetrated the glacier died away. They stood in the cave in complete darkness.

"Any ideas?" Mark asked.

"We will have to wait until sunrise," Jane said.

Mark took off his backpack and felt around until he pulled a small kerosene lamp out of it.

"Normally," Mark said. "I wouldn't light this because it would use too much oxygen, but since we don't have to breathe."

Mark lit the lamp, and the ice cavern filled with light. It was beautiful. The light refracted off the sides of the cave and danced along the edges of the ice to create a scene of crystalline grandeur.

They continued on using the light from Mark's lamp. They walked, crawled, and pushed their way through the narrow places in the melt cave.

As he was waiting for Jane to squeeze through a narrow passage, Mark noticed a dark spot in the ice. He pulled a small axe out of his backpack and chopped at the ice with it until he freed the spot. He pulled it out and examined it. The spot was a dragonfly, but it was at least twice the size of the dragonflies he remembered.

He removed enough of the ice to get a DNA sample. Then he dropped it in his pack along with the axe. Jane looked at him disapprovingly.

"I hope you aren't going to be dragging home every fossil you find," Jane said.

"I would like to add it to my collection," Mark said. "But you're right, it is fragile and frozen, so I doubt it would make it to Arizona."

Mark sighed and took the dragonfly out of his pack and left it on the cave floor.

As they walked, and sometimes crawled through the cave, it began to narrow. They followed it for another quarter of a mile before it became impassible.

"Options," Mark said.

"We can go back and try to climb out," Jane said.

"We could," Mark said. "And with enough effort, we could get back to the surface. Which would put us back where we started."

"You want to explore the lake," Jane said.

"We came here to explore," Mark said. "There wasn't any sign of the Aurorians on the surface, so the only place they could be is underground."

"Yes," Jane said. "But if we go down there, we could become trapped."

"I admit," Mark said. "That is a possibility."

The kerosene lamp flickered out leaving them in darkness. Then Mark noticed a faint light from below them that had been hidden by the lamp light.

"What's that?" Mark asked.

"Some kind of bioluminescence?" Jane said.

"The light from the lamp must have attracted it," Mark said.

"Now I suppose you want to investigate that?" Jane said.

"Yes," Mark said. "Don't you?"

"Well, yes," Jane said. "I just don't want to get trapped down there."

"Going down there is our best chance of finding the Aurorians. If it doesn't pan out, we can still swim back up here."

"Are you sure?" Jane said.

"No," Mark said. "But it isn't like we are going to drown or anything."

"Fine," Jane said. "How do we get into the lake?"

Chapter Seven
Taking the Plunge

Mark used his microwave emitter to search for the thinnest point in the ice. It took a while, but he was able to find a spot that was only three feet thick. He set his pack on the floor, pounded Jane's ice axe into the floor, and tied a rope to it. Once he was secure, he picked up his ice axe and started cutting a hole.

Jane took her coat off and went through her backpack to remove everything that wouldn't survive being soaked. Then she did the same to Mark's pack.

Jane stood back and watched Mark as he lay flat on the floor of the melt cave getting soaked as he cut a hole to the lake below.

"What's taking so long?" Jane asked.

"This is glacial ice I'm trying to cut through," Mark said. "It's denser than regular ice, but you know that."

"Yes," Jane said. "Of course I know that. I'm just trying to be a nagging wife. How am I doing?"

"Not bad," Mark said. "Are you going to help?"

Mark took his coat off and tossed it to Jane, but she cast it aside.

"I wasn't planning on it," Jane said. "There isn't enough room for two people to work, and besides, you're using my axe as an anchor."

She took a small wood and canvas stool and unfolded it. She placed it three feet from where Mark worked and sat down.

"I'll just sit here and supervise," Jane said. "I wish I had a parasol and a glass of lemonade, but I'll just have to settle for a jar of melt water."

"Funny, Jane," Mark said. "I can't believe you have been carrying that stool around with you all this time."

"Sitting on the ground is unladylike," Jane said. "Even in these pants."

"You realize that it is going to take the better part of a day to cut this hole," Mark said.

"I know," Jane said. "I'll leave you to your work."

Twelve hours and thirty-seven minutes later, Mark hit water. It took him another forty minutes to make a hole large enough for them to pass through.

"It's ready," Mark said. "The hard part was not falling in while I was cutting the hole."

Jane left her seat and examined the hole.

"Well," Jane said. "You did a nice job."

She handed Mark his backpack.

"Are you sure about this?" Jane asked.

"No," Mark said.

He untied himself, let go of the sides, and plunged into the water.

"How is it down there," Jane sent.

"Pitch black," Mark sent. *"I'm adjusting my*

vision now."

Mark noticed a surge in the water and realized Jane had joined him.

"Cycle through all of the wavelengths," Jane sent. *"Hopefully one of them will have data."*

"And if it doesn't?" Mark sent.

"I still have a bearing on the hole," Jane sent. *"I can lead you to it."*

Mark fought the urge to panic. He knew he wasn't in any danger, but his human mind had trouble coping. He reminded himself that cold didn't hurt him, and he didn't have to breathe. He cycled through his visual wavelengths, and was surprised when he got a hit on visible light.

He looked down, and the bottom was lit by a faint glow. Millions of tiny lights covered the bottom. Other lights moved around beneath him, beside him, and in front of him. It was like being in an alien world of neon light.

"Are you seeing this?" Mark sent.

"Yes," Jane sent. *"It's amazing!"*

Mark released some air from his lungs, and let himself sink toward the bottom. Tall corn-like plants covered the bottom of the lake. Their stalks had glowing, oblong protrusions similar to little light bulbs. As soon as Mark disturbed the water near them, they retracted into the stalk, and the light went out. In the darkness created by the plants winking out, isopods the size of house cats and centipedes the size of pythons became visible. Mark swam over to get a closer look at one of the isopods, and it curled up into a ball. A second later, an intense flash came from its shell. This triggered flashes from the other isopods in the area, and the effect spread across the bottom of the lake.

"That was amazing," Jane sent.

"It's not so amazing when you're on top of it." Mark sent.

"Your visual processors weren't overloaded, were they?" Jane sent.

"No," Mark sent. *"But it was a little startling,"*

"The light from the flashes gave me an opportunity to map about a quarter mile of the lake bottom." Jane sent. *"There is something we need to see."*

Mark followed Jane as she swam. It only took about five minutes of swimming to find what she was talking about. Blue mollusks, resembling unicorn horns, grew in rows across the lake bottom. A mechanical harvester lay on the bottom among the mollusks. It was covered in sand and mollusks, and it looked like it had been there for a while. The collection bin was half-filled with mollusks, some of which were still alive, and had managed to attach themselves to the harvester instead of the lake bottom. The door to the driver's seat was left open. The inside had become home for a transparent, glowing, human-sized octopus.

"It looks like we found evidence of Aurorians down here," Mark sent.

"Thanks for not saying, 'I told you so,'" Jane sent.

"I didn't mean it like that," Mark sent. *"I was just stating the obvious in typical male fashion."*

Mark swam down to the bottom where one of the roly-poly isopods stood near a cluster of unicorn mollusks. As he touched the isopod, its stalk flashed. This time he was prepared for the flash. When he opened his eyes, he saw a blur of translucent arms, and the octopus was on him. Mark managed to stay calm. He took a DNA sample with his left hand and fired the microwave emitter he held in his right hand at maximum. The water around his hand boiled, and the octopus fled.

"Are you all right?" Jane asked.

Mark looked himself over. He wasn't bleeding anywhere, but his shirt had several large holes in it.

"I'm fine," he sent. *"Now what?"*

"We swim in a spiral search pattern and see what we find," Jane sent.

"Sounds good," Mark sent. *"We should probably document as much of this as we can."*

They spent the next four days swimming in a widening circle mapping the bottom, gathering DNA, and looking for signs of technology. They found 521 new species of animals and plants. Several of them were variations on known species that were thought to be extinct.

They found the edge of the lake bottom and swam along its granite walls. Water flowed in and out of the lake through a network of tunnels. They ignored them until they came to one that showed signs of being altered. The sides of the cave had been widened, and its floor had been leveled.

"What do you think?" Mark asked.

"I think I'm tired of swimming around looking at isopods," Jane sent. *"Let's see where this goes."*

They swam inside the cave for half a mile,

letting the current carry them. The cave narrowed, and the current became much stronger. When the cave opened out, they found themselves in a river. As soon as they were through the rapid part of the river, they swam to shore and crawled up on the river bank. Mark rolled over on his back, looked up, and saw stars. The riverbank and surrounding area were barren, but there was a glow on the horizon that resembled a sunrise.

"Am I seeing stars?" Mark asked.

"It appears so," Jane said. "But we can't be on the surface."

"It reminds me of the garden room at night," Mark said. "I think we're in a room like that,"

"If we are," Jane said. "It is vastly larger."

"No doubt," Mark said.

Mark took a breath. Then he ran a spectral analysis on the light. Then he ran it again because he didn't believe the results.

"The light we're seeing is reflected, but you'll never guess what it's reflected off of," Mark said.

"Mercury," Jane said.

"I didn't think you had a spectral analyzer," Mark said.

"I don't," Jane said. "But isn't that what Mr. Steinson said during his lecture?"

"It was indeed," Mark said. "Still think his lecture was funny?"

"I admit," Jane said. "It is starting to make some sense."

They walked toward the light, and as the light level increased, so did the vegetation. The rocky riverbank gave way to rocks lined with blue-green moss that became a collection of wide- leafed blue plants that stood roughly four-feet high. Mixed among them were blue-violet plants that resembled giant broccoli stems, reaching up six-to-ten feet. The growth was thick with no visible path. The earth the plants grew in was muddy and filled with insects that Mark didn't want to ponder too long.

"Okay," Jane said. "Where now?"

Mark surveyed the area and sighed.

"Welcome to the jungle," he said. "I don't have a clue where we should go."

"We could follow the river," Jane said. "It would make walking much easier than trying to traverse that quagmire."

"People do tend to build settlements along rivers, so that would provide us with the best chance of finding the Aurorians."

"The river it is then," Jane said.

They followed the river for just over three miles when Mark noticed movement within the brush.

"Jane," Mark sent. *"Something is moving back there."*

Before Jane could respond, Mark found himself being head-butted by an animal that looked like a cross between a dog and a horse. A mane of thick, long hair ran down its back, and it had long pointed ears with a bright silver spot in its right ear. It stood eight feet at the shoulder, had large red eyes, and teeth that looked like they could tear through flesh with ease.

Mark was knocked off the river bank and into the churning river. Jane took one long look at the beast and joined Mark in the river.

"What the hell is that?" Jane asked.

"It looks like a daeodon or a descendent of one," Mark sent. *"I can't be too sure. I didn't get a good look."*

Mark and Jane kept swimming away as it and a dozen or so of its companions entered the river, formed a circle, and fed on passing fish.

They stayed in the current and let the river carry them away from the creatures.

"Did you notice something about our friends back there?" Jane asked.

"No," Mark sent. *"I was too busy being thrown into the river."*

"They all had metal tags in their ears," Jane sent. *"They're domesticated."*

They rounded a bend in the river, and found what looked like a stainless-steel bridge. They swam to the riverbank a hundred and fifty yards from the bridge.

"Okay," Mark sent. *"That is the best-built bridge I've ever seen."*

They climbed up on the bank and walked toward the bridge. An Aurorian stood on the bridge. He looked at them with what seemed to be a curious expression. When they got on the bridge Mark waved at him. The Aurorian spoke to them in a series of clicks, jitters, and hums.

"Hi," Mark said. "We're a little lost."

"That's an understatement," Jane said.

"Do you want to do the talking?" Mark asked.

Jane wrung water out of her hair as she spoke.

"I am only commenting on the inadequacy of your statement. It's not like we took the wrong exit on the freeway," Jane said.

The small, gray person touched a button on its wrist, and once again made a collection of clicks, jitters, and hums.

"What now?" Jane asked.

"I think he's calling the cops," Mark said.

"Do we run?" Jane asked.

"Run where?" Mark said.

"Shouldn't we do something?" Jane asked.

"We do need to get our story straight," Mark sent.

"What story?" Jane asked.

"They are going to ask us how we got down here," Mark sent. *"Tell them we were pushed into the glacier, ended up in the water, passed out, and found ourselves here."*

"And if they ask why we went to the glacier to begin with?" Jane asked.

"Tell them the same story I told Trausti," Mark said. *"An old map purchased from a British sailor promising water that brings eternal youth."*

"Okay to mention Mr. Steinson?" Jane asked.

"I don't see why not," Mark sent. *"The more details we have the more plausible our story becomes."*

The Aurorian on the bridge kept his distance from them, but didn't attempt any more communication. When Mark tried to speak to him, he put a hand over his mouth, so Mark stopped talking.

Nine minutes later an airship appeared overhead. It circled them shining a light down upon them. The Aurorian waved at them and walked away.

A vehicle arrived that floated on the air about two and a half feet above the ground. It looked like a stainless-steel minivan with portholes instead of windows.

"They're using radio. Go into stealth mode," Jane said.

"What?" Mark said.

Jane took his hand and shared her thoughts with him. The physical contact allowed her to utilize a very low-power signal to interlink with him. He allowed Jane to enter his mind, but this time she wasn't gentle. She navigated his systems quickly, and she put him in stealth mode. Mark watched the heads-up display in his mind as she took most of his advanced systems offline, and his electromagnetic signature became almost non-existent. Then he felt Jane shutting herself down as well.

"We don't want them to know we're androids," Jane sent. *"When the airship arrived, I detected some advanced radio communication, so it's possible they can hear us. Let's just hope they don't do any medical testing."*

"Yeah," Mark whispered. "That would be bad."

Jane let go of his hand as a dim light shone from the vehicle, and two men in blue, tight-fitting coveralls got out. They both looked like male models with well-defined muscles, huge biceps, and extremely white teeth.

They walked over toward Mark and Jane slowly. They each had stunners in their hands. Neither of them spoke, but they gestured with their weapons for them to get into the vehicle. Mark held his hands out where they could see them, and Jane did the same.

"Okay," Mark said. "We don't want any trouble."

They walked to the vehicle, took off their backpacks, and got in. As soon as they sat down, restraints like the ones they saw on the Aurora airship automatically bound their arms and legs.

"We seem to be a little lost," Mark said.

The only response Mark got was an electric shock, and he did his best to look like he was in pain. He glanced over and saw Jane was doing the same.

He and Jane exchanged glances. Then Mark noticed that a glass panel reflected the view from out of the vehicle's front window.

The vehicle glided over the vegetation until it reached what looked like an ancient brick road. It followed the road for forty-three minutes when Mark noticed a glow on the horizon.

The glow became a city of stainless-steel spires, elevated mag-lift trains, and subdued light. The vehicle stopped in front of a building that resembled a giant, stainless steel, steam-punk radio.

Mark and Jane were released from their seats and taken inside. The hallway inside was dark gray and featureless, apart from the oval hatchways every few meters. They were taken to a series of standard doorways, and their captors opened the first one.

It opened into what resembled a small hotel room with a bed, nightstand, lamp, sink, and a flushing, triangular toilet. Mark was pushed inside. The door closed and locked behind him. Mark heard a door open, and then shut a moment later.

Mark took off his wet clothes and wrung them out in a triangular sink. He draped them over the nightstand to dry. Just as he climbed into bed, the door opened. Mark pulled the sheets up. A blonde woman entered carrying a change of clothes.

"You couldn't have knocked?" Mark asked.

She regarded him for a moment with an expression of what was either anger or contempt. Mark wasn't sure which. Her left hand dropped down to a stainless-steel box on her hip, but it stopped short of touching it.

She tossed Mark's new clothes on the bed at his feet, picked up his clothes, backpack, Kak's watch, and his shoes, and put them into a white basket outside the door.

She turned back into the room, and stepped over to Mark's bed. She reached under the sheets, pulled out Mark's left hand, and started to take off his wedding ring.

"Speak only when you are spoken to," she whispered. "Do as you are told, and don't lie to them. They will know."

"Where am I?" Mark asked softly.

She pretended to struggle with the ring.

"Subterra," she whispered.

The ring came off, and she turned to leave. Mark sat up, and she turned back suddenly and slapped him across the face. Mark fell back in bed and watched her leave. Twenty-four seconds later, he heard another door open.

Mark pretended to sleep for eight hours and forty minutes. Then he rose, put on the underwear and blue coveralls the woman left him. Inside the nightstand, he found a dozen books and a deck of cards. The books were all written in English, and were recent titles. He took out the deck of cards, sat on his bed with his back to the wall, playing solitaire and wishing he had a window.

A man and woman entered the room and took him down several hallways to another room that resembled a closet. He was pushed inside, and the door closed behind them. Mark stood there in the dark waiting to see what would happen next. A voice that seemed to come from everywhere at once spoke to him.

"What is your name?" it asked.

"Mark Aaron," Mark said.

"Why are you here?" it asked.

"They brought me here," Mark said.

There was a pause.

"How did you get to the bridge where you were apprehended?" It asked.

"My wife and I were exploring a glacier, we were pushed into a crevasse, hit the water at the bottom, and somehow, we ended up on the river bank. We walked to the bridge from there," Mark said.

The questioning in the dark continued for twelve hours and twenty-three minutes. Mark noticed that the questions were repeated about every three hours. Mark tried to vary his responses a little to make his answers seem more human.

The questioning stopped, and Mark was taken back to his room. A plate of mixed vegetables and cooked meat awaited him there. None of the food was recognizable. He cleaned his plate and drank the water they provided him. As he set the glass down, he noticed a residue on its side. He couldn't bring his DNA analyzer online without running the risk of detection, but his spectral analyzer still worked in stealth mode. The results he got back suggested a complex mixture of hydrocarbons.

He went to bed in his clothes and ran the exhaustion program he created for Jane several years ago. Two hours and three minutes later, he was taken back to the dark room for questioning.

He repeated his answers, amidst yawns, adding incoherent and meaningless details here and there. He was shocked a few times to wake him up. Each time, he would pretend to be awake for five minutes or so, then he would fall back into exhaustion. The questioning lasted for eight hours and four minutes. They kept asking him how he got down there.

The questioning stopped, and he was taken back to his room. He remained there for sixteen days, being fed once a day in biodegradable containers that he was told to flush down the toilet when he was done. He read *The Adventures of Sherlock Holmes* and the *Memoirs of Sherlock Holmes*, and was impressed by Doyle's writing. Poe may have invented the detective story, but Doyle had perfected it.

On the morning of the seventeenth day, as he was reading *The Strange Case of Dr. Jekyll and*

Mr. Hyde and Other Tales, he was taken back to the dark room and questioned again about how he had gotten down there. He stayed consistent with his answer. Each time he repeated his answer, he received an electric shock.

He was returned to his cell for twenty-seven days. Then, he was taken to a room with what looked like a dining room table. Trausti and Sigríður sat at the table. They wore the same prison uniform that he did, and neither of them looked too happy. Mark turned to leave, but the door slammed shut behind him. Mark sighed and turned back to them. Sigríður smiled at him.

"Why don't you sit down," she said.

Mark's response involved a hand gesture that was less than polite, but neither Trausti nor Sigríður knew what it meant. The door opened behind him and Jane was shoved into the room. She wore the same uniform that he wore, although it looked better on her. They exchanged glances.

"You okay?" Mark asked.

"Fine," Jane said. "What are they doing here?"

"No idea," Mark said. "Just got here myself."

"Please sit down," Trausti said. "If you anger them, it will be bad for all of us."

"Them who?" Jane asked.

"The Sapanites," Sigríður said. "The gray people who live down here. Our masters."

Mark looked at Jane and sighed.

"Do we trust them?" Jane asked.

"Of course not," Mark said. "They tried to kill us."

"Well, yeah, there is that," Jane said. "But in this case, do we really have a choice?"

"I don't know," Mark said. "We could always kick the crap out of them. That could be fun."

Jane smirked.

"That does sound amusing," Jane said. "But I want to get out of here."

"And you think cooperating with them will accomplish that?" Mark asked.

"We can always kick the crap out of them later," Jane said.

"I like the way you think," Mark said. "So, just to be clear, kicking the crap out of them is still on the table.

"Absolutely," Jane said.

"Okay," Mark said.

Mark and Jane sat at the table. They stared at each other uncomfortably for a few seconds.

"Do you know why we're here?" Mark asked.

Trausti exchanged glances with Sigríður, but he stayed silent.

"We are awaiting sentencing," Sigríður said. "You have been accused of trespassing, and we have been accused of aiding in your trespass."

"So," Mark asked. "Why don't they just kill us?"

"They have laws," Sigríður said. "Since you were discovered inside their boarder, you gained a right of citizenship of sorts."

"So, what does that mean?" Mark asked.

"It means that they can't just dissect you like a cow," Sigríður said. "You've earned the right to be here, like their ancestors."

"Where exactly is here?" Jane asked.

Sigríður glanced over at Trausti who threw his hands up in a gesture of "why not?"

"You're about three miles beneath the surface," Sigríður said. "In a vast network of caves that connect to underground fresh water oceans."

"We kind of figured that," Mark said. "What is it called?"

"Ka-Zuss-Qa," Sigríður said. "At least that's as close to their name as your language will permit."

"How many people live down here," Mark asked.

Trausti raised his hand.

"Sigríður enough," he said. "This is only going to make things worse."

"What does he mean?" Jane asked.

"It is forbidden to discuss our masters," Sigríður said. "Information is strictly controlled."

"That makes sense," Mark said. "Ignorant populations are easier to control."

"Can you at least tell us what is making the light down here?" Jane asked.

Trausti shrugged his shoulders.

"There is a giant quartz crystal atop a structure in the central cavern that naturally produces light. We don't know how it works, but the quartz produces light, and it is reflected by deposits of mercury in the cave ceiling," Sigríður said.

Mark looked over at Jane.

"A natural quartz decay light?" Mark asked.

Jane kicked Mark in the shin.

"What?" Sigríður asked.

"It's nothing," Jane said. "My husband has a theory about making electric lamps brighter by using a quartz mirror to reflect the light."

"I'm a part-time inventor," Mark said.

The door opened, and two muscular blond men entered. They wore the same blue tight-fitting suits that they all wore. They were handcuffed, gagged, and chained together.

They were taken out of the building and loaded on to a transport. Through the window, Mark saw a clean, well-ordered city with elevated trains, broad streets, and farms. The empty space between large buildings was utilized as farmland. The blending of rural farming and urban structures impressed Mark until he saw that the farms were being run by human slave labor.

Their vehicle entered a large building. They were taken out and moved through hallways with exposed piping and storage areas, so Mark guessed they were the maintenance and service hallways of the building. They waited at a doorway for ten minutes before being taken down a short hallway and through an iris door that led into a huge auditorium.

They were brought before an assembly of Sapanites. The Sapanites were divided into nine groups of twenty-seven members each, laid out in a semi-circle before them. The room was filled with a cacophony of chattering and popping sounds. Large display screens had their photos on them with more writing around them.

They stood before them for seven minutes and thirty-nine seconds before a screeching tone called them to order. Each group spoke in turn from Mark's right to left. After each group spoke, a display at the front and rear of the room changed. When the last group spoke, the board flashed green. If the symbols Mark saw were numbers, the vote was five-to-four.

They were led out of the chamber and through a series of long corridors. Mark wanted to ask what had just happened, but the gag in his mouth made that impossible.

They were taken to another transport. It took off and headed out of the city. It flew over dark water for forty-four minutes. Mark saw a glow on the horizon, and the craft flew toward it. Mark saw an island on the horizon, and six minutes later they hovered over a clearing.

One of the human guards opened a locker and took out two white bags. He motioned for them to rise. He handed Mark and Jane each a bag, but he didn't unbind their hands. He did the same for Trausti and Sigríður. They were moved to stand in front of the rear door. A second later it opened, and the front of the vehicle pitched up, dumping them out. Mark landed on the mossy ground face first. He heard the vehicle door close behind them, and the vehicle took off. As soon as it cleared the trees, their gags and bindings released themselves.

"Are we being released?" Mark asked.

"Hardly," Trausti said. "We're on Refvalnol Island."

"What was all that about?" Mark asked. "Was that some kind of trial?"

Trausti looked over at Sigríður and rolled his eyes.

"No," Trausti said. "Our guilt was never in question. They were deciding how to dispose of us without violating their laws."

"What were the choices?" Jane asked.

"Life working in the uranium mine, or being sent here," Sigríður said. "At least here, our suffering will be short."

"What do you mean?" Jane asked.

"Refvalnol Island is home to the moravi," Sigríður said.

"What's a moravi?" Mark asked.

"It's a seven-foot bird that is bred to kill and eat humans," Trausti said.

"Oh," Mark said. "Isn't that just special."

Chapter Eight
To Mock a Killing Bird

Mark opened his white bag to find that it contained everything he had when he was captured. His clothes, his equipment, Kak's watch, and even the bag of strawberries. They even let him keep his revolver. They took the ammo, but they missed the two bullets in the handle. He put his wedding ring and his gun belt back on and put the white bag and the rest of his clothes in the backpack.

Jane gestured to Mark that she wanted to change, so he kept watch as she went into a group of leafy plants and changed back into her leather hiking pants. He spoke to her as she changed.

"I got Kak's watch back," he said.

"I wish we had Kak with us instead of just his watch," Jane said.

"Kak?" Sigríður asked.

"A friend of ours," Mark said.

"He must not be much of a friend," Trausti said. "I wouldn't wish this on my worst enemy."

Jane came out of the bushes a moment later, and Mark stepped in. He changed back into his white shirt, pants, and Jacket. He put the blue jumpsuit in his backpack hoping to be able to take it back to Arizona for his collection.

"Just how dangerous are these moravi?" Jane asked.

"If the rumors I've heard are true," Trausti said. "We won't live more than a day or two."

"In that case," Mark said. "We need to get to high ground."

He set his backpack down and climbed the nearest tree. It resembled a giant rhubarb stalk with a red trunk and broad blue-green leaves at the top. From the top of the tree, he could see about a mile in every direction. Mark saw a clearing with some kind of structure a mile to the north east. He saw smoke on the horizon several miles off to the north west. He didn't see much in the way of hills or mountains, but he saw a swampy area directly east of them. He climbed down.

"There is a structure of some sort a mile or so that way."

Mark pointed northeast.

"That's good news," Jane said.

They walked through the trees in near darkness for thirty-one minutes. They found a river and on the other side of the river there was what looked like abandoned farmland surrounded by a partially-completed stone wall.

A farmhouse stood in the center of the field, and it was an architectural wonder. The walls were made of mortared stone, but only came up four feet above the ground. The rest of the wall was made of long, oval glass panels that were held in place by a wooden frame. The space where the ovals met the roof was filled in with colored-glass panels. The roof consisted of a glass dome that was made up of a series of glass panels that formed a decorative pattern, but didn't have any straight lines. The heavy, decorated wooden door showed signs of claw marks, and was locked from the inside. A search of the area produced a brass key, near a pile of molding clothing.

Mark opened the door and found a skeleton with long blonde hair seated at the table. Her head rested on the table, and she had a small bottle in her hand. The room was furnished with a table, four chairs, a wind-up clock, and three books on a shelf above the fireplace.

"What happened here?" Mark asked.

"Isn't it obvious," Trausti said. "The moravi attacked, and she killed herself."

"Seriously," Mark said. "They are that scary."

Jane stepped over to the body and took the bottle from her hand. She handed it to Mark. There were traces of dried fluid on the edge, so he analyzed it. It was a toxic compound that was not listed in his database of poisons.

Mark stepped over to the fireplace and removed one of the books, and he was surprised to find it written in English. The title read "Book of Charlotte Bianchi."

The book itself was different from anything Mark had seen. The book's binding was made from plant fibers but it felt like leather. The pages were made of thin, waterproof, plant fibers, but it was extremely sturdy.

He flash-read the contents and discovered that it was a journal of her life. She was a member of the weaver's guild, and it spoke of a city called Murus where she had lived before being outcast.

She had given birth four times, but was never allowed so see her child. She wrote about her garden outside her dormitory where she tried to grow something called kuja to sell. Some of the entries referred to operating steam-powered looms and an idea she had for improving them, but she couldn't get it past the improvement committee.

She lived with the outcasts for a while, but decided to leave after a dispute over food. The last few entries described her life here with Hamilton Bricker and Mary Gnomes. The final few described the attack, with Charlotte being the only one to make it back to the house. She ran out of food after eighteen days, and decided to end her life three days after that.

Mark put the book back on the shelf and flash-read the other two. They were the same as Charlotte's, a journal of their thoughts and hopes. Mary's journal was filled with sketches of dresses, people, and animals that were important to her.

"They're written in English," Mark said.

"Really," Jane said.

Jane took the books from Mark and casually flipped through them as Sigríður and Trausti went into the bedroom. She had finished reading when they emerged. They left their backpacks in the bedroom.

"We need to restock the food," Trausti said. "The moravi will return."

"Why?" Jane asked. "So, we can end up like her?"

Jane gestured toward the corpse at the table.

"Mark and I will stay long enough to bury her, but after that, we're moving on," Jane said.

Trausti shrugged his shoulders, and Sigríður rolled her eyes. She picked up one of the empty baskets from what looked like a pantry shelf next to the fireplace and left. Trausti did the same. Once they had both left, Mark turned to Jane.

"You just want to ditch them?"

"Don't you?" Jane asked.

"We looking for Murus?" Mark asked.

"Of course," Jane said.

"I didn't get a chance to tell you before," Mark said. "But when they were taking us to jail, I saw an image of the underground city that you will paint. The one that hung on my office wall in 2004."

"So," Jane said.

"That means the Mark and Jane of the previous time loop got out of this, so we can too," Mark said.

"I don't recall expressing any doubt," Jane said.

"I know," Mark said. "I just think it's cool when I encounter an image from one of your paintings that you have yet to paint."

Jane opened up her backpack and took out six candles, two tins of beef, and a copy of Dickens' *Bleak House* to make room for the journals. Mark picked it up and examined it. The Sapanites must have freeze-dried it because Mark could hardly tell it had been wet.

"We're taking those," Mark asked.

"We don't want them following us, do we?" Jane said.

"Guess not," Mark said.

"I thought you would have left this in the glacier?" Mark asked.

"I was going to," Jane said. "But I decided to use it as ballast."

"That's why I kept my gun," Mark said.

"Why do you suppose the Sapanites let you keep it?" Jane asked.

"I'm not sure. Without bullets it's useless, so maybe it's a symbol of their authority over me."

"A symbolic castration?"

Mark sighed.

"I wouldn't have put it that way, but yes."

He saw Jane break into one of her toothy smiles as he walked away. Mark went outside and found a tool shed attached to the house. He found an odd-looking shovel. The spot he picked was along the side of the house. The clover-like plants that grew there didn't resist the shovel and two hours later, he had a hole that was six feet by three feet, and five feet deep.

He went back inside to find that Jane had placed Charlotte's body on the table and wrapped it with the tablecloth.

"The body was well preserved," Jane said. "The lack of insects inside the house prevented the normal decomposition process."

Mark looked around to be sure they were alone.

"Did you examine her?" Mark asked.

"Of course," Jane said. "Apart from being three months pregnant, there wasn't anything unusual. Her development was remarkably normal for someone living two miles underground."

They took Charlotte outside and placed her carefully in the hole. Mark was about to say something religious, but he was interrupted by Sigríður.

"Bury it quickly," she said. "The smell may draw the moravi."

Mark shoveled dirt down onto Charlotte. Sigríður went to the tool shed and brought Jane a shovel.

"Don't just stand there," Sigríður said. "If the moravi come, we all die."

Jane took the shovel and paused for a moment before she started filling in the hole. Sigríður left to go get another basket for food. As soon as she entered the house, Mark turned to Jane.

"You were thinking about feeding her that shovel, weren't you?" Mark asked.

"Nonsense," Jane said. "I contemplated bashing her face in with it and putting her in the hole with Charlotte."

"What stopped you?" Mark asked.

"It wouldn't be fair to Charlotte," Jane said.

"For someone who is supposed to protect and serve humanity, you seem to have developed a nasty habit of keeping a grudge."

"Well," Jane said quietly. "I only thought about it. She did try to kill me, and she is a collaborator with an enemy of humanity."

"All good points," Mark said. "I applaud your restraint."

Jane gave him a glance that ended the conversation. As soon as they finished filling in the hole, Jane retrieved their backpacks as Mark put the shovels away. They walked up the hill and had gotten only a few yards from the cabin when Sigríður ran after them.

"Are you sure you want to leave?" she asked.

"Don't take this the wrong way," Mark said. "But we can't trust you. You would betray us at the first sign of trouble."

"We were just trying to protect our people," she said. "It wasn't anything personal."

"That may be true," Jane said. "But we still can't trust you. Good luck with the farm."

They left her standing at the edge of the clearing with her mouth hanging open. It was clear that she wanted to say something, but didn't for some reason. Mark hoped that she was sincere in what she was saying, but he still had his doubts. If they were sent here to spy on them, they would figure out some reason to abandon the farm and follow them. It not, then at least they wouldn't have to keep pretending to be human around them. Even if they weren't spies, Mark still didn't feel like he could trust them.

"You know," Mark said. "Airship sightings were increasing until just after the Aurora crash, then they stopped."

"So," Jane said.

"I'm just thinking that our presence here may have triggered a shift in Sapanite policy," Mark said.

"Well," Jane said. "That's possible, but I doubt we'll ever know. But, I know one thing. I'm going to view history a little differently from now on."

"Oh, yeah," Mark said. "I'm looking at the insanity that was World War One from a whole new perspective."

They walked through the rhubarb-like trees for several hours. Each time they encountered a new plant, Mark tested the strength of the trunk and the flexibility of its branches.

He found a red and purple plant about six feet tall that grew straight. Its trunk felt like oak or pine. Mark signaled for Jane to stop as he took out his knife, cut the tree down, and stripped its branches.

He used the trunk as a walking stick. They found the coast, and they paused to look out over the water. The light from some distant quartz crystal shone and reflected on the water, not unlike a sunrise on the surface. They walked down to the beach and found it covered with mollusk shells of all varieties. Mark tried the water and found it to be fresh, so he filled his canteen and Jane did the same.

They followed the beach to a marsh. There, Mark found a variety of seaweed that had course, tough fibers. He gave his walking stick to Jane, and he gathered seaweed and started stripping the leaves off as they walked.

"Well," Mark said. "At least now I don't regret giving Mr. Steinson that twenty dollars."

"I too have been reevaluating that lecture," Jane said. "It seems to have lost some of its humor."

"Any suggestions?" Mark asked.

"Regarding our current situation?" Jane asked.

"Yes," Mark said.

Jane looked out over the ocean that lay before them. She didn't speak for twenty-four seconds.

"Let's not be in a rush to leave," Jane said. "There is a lot to be learned down here, and I don't want to under-estimate the Sapanites."

"Rush to leave. Isn't that a bit optimistic?" Mark asked. "We're miles beneath the surface. I have no idea how we can get out of here. The only thing that is giving me hope is the painting I saw in Mr. Nora's office."

"We've been in tight spots before," Jane said.

"You flash-read Mr. Steinson's book," Mark said. "Anything useful?"

"Not really," Jane said. "It was the worst-written book that I've ever found. It was mostly disjointed gibberish."

They walked along the shell-covered beach for an hour and twelve minutes. They found what looked like a small fishing boat left on the edge of the beach. A well-worn path led away from the beach through a field of leafy plants to a forest on the horizon.

They followed the path to the edge of the forest, and Mark noticed a shape emerge from the forest. A rust-colored, flightless bird that stood ten feet tall moved toward them. Its head bobbed slightly as it walked.

Mark now understood why these creatures were so feared. It stood upon two, three-toed feet. Each of its toes ended in talons that were the diameter of Mark's thumb, but six to eight inches long. The talons were attached to featherless, chicken-like feet, which were attached to muscular, rust-colored, feathered legs. The bird's chest resembled that of a chicken, with small wings in front of its massive thighs. It didn't have a tail to speak of, but it did have a long, thick neck with a head that was dominated by its massive, curved beak. The eyes were set close together, and on the front of its face, instead of on the side like other birds.

It turned its head slightly as it looked at Mark and Jane. Then it charged toward them.

Mark went into battle mode. Everything slowed down, and the bird seemed to take an eternity to cross the distance to him. He analyzed each of the bird's steps as it drew nearer. He drew his gun, dropped his backpack, and waited for the bird, so he'd have a clean shot. Then he realized that the bullets were still in the handle. As he started to retrieve the bullets, the bird struck, knocking the gun from his hand.

Jane moved behind the bird, and the bird ignored her. Mark drew his knife, waved his arms, and shouted every curse word he knew to keep its attention, and the bird stayed fixed on him. He wanted to use his maser, but he couldn't activate it in stealth mode.

It turned back to him and slashed out with its left foot. Mark twisted his body to avoid the strike. The bird lowered its head and tried to peck him, but he avoided the strike and slashed it below the eye. It took a step back, shook its head, and slashed at him twice more. Mark saw them coming and stepped to the side. It squawked at Mark.

Mark saw Jane behind the bird with her knife in her hand. He had no idea what she thought she could do with a six-inch blade against a five-hundred-pound bird. When the bird lashed out at him, he grabbed the talon as it swept past him. The bird wasn't expecting this, and it stumbled as its weight shifted. Mark did his best to hang on, but he could only hold it for half a second, but that was enough to cause the bird to stumble.

Just as the bird ripped its talon from Mark's hands, Jane slid underneath it and. in a fluid motion she slashed the bird's leg, leaving a four-inch gash along the back. The bird squawked and bent its neck down to look under its body. It looked directly at Jane but ignored her.

The top of the bird's head was exposed, so Mark stabbed all six inches of his knife into the base of the bird's skull. The bird squawked in rage as it twisted its head around. This time Mark was too close to avoid the strike. It knocked him five feet into the air as its lower beak ripped through his abdomen. He landed flat on his back and watched as the bird flung its head from side to side in an attempt to dislodge the knife. It ran into the woods, squawking loudly. Jane retrieved Mark's gun and walked over to him. He sat up to evaluate the wound in his abdomen. She knelt down beside him.

"It's superficial," she said. "You can get up."

"It looks pretty deep to me," Mark said.

Jane shook her head.

"Are your intestines spilling out?" Jane asked.

"No," Mark said. "But look."

Jane knelt down and examined the wound.

"Then it's superficial. It's already starting to close. Stop acting like a human," she whispered.

She grabbed the center of the wound and pinched it together for three seconds. When she let go, the wound had stopped bleeding.

"We should keep moving," Jane said.

Mark got up, straightened his clothes, and picked up his backpack. Jane did the same.

"I'm going to miss that knife," Mark said.

They'd moved a few hundred feet away when they saw movement in the woods. They froze. A flock of four moravi stood listening to the distant cry of the injured bird. One of the moravi tilted its head toward them. It turned and charged. As it did, a rope dropped down from above and hit Mark on the shoulder. Mark looked up and saw an elevated walkway through the trees. Before he could say anything, another rope hit Jane on the head.

"Take the rope," a strangely accented voice from above shouted.

Mark grabbed the rope and wrapped it around his arm. Jane looked back at him and did the same. A counterweight was pushed out of a tree, and they were abruptly pulled off the ground and onto a platform eighteen feet into the trees. The platform was hidden by large, reddish leaves and disguised to blend in with the tree tops.

A man dressed in a black overcoat, with spiked, jet-black hair, deep, blue eyes, and ivory skin put his finger to his mouth. He gestured to the moravi beneath them who charged and then suddenly stopped. It looked in all directions for thirty-eight seconds, and then it wandered off. As soon as it was out of sight, he gestured to one of five cots set up on the platform. Each cot had a small chest of draws under it. Mark stepped over to where he indicated.

A young woman dressed in a black hooded overcoat came over with a white cloth that had been dipped in something blue. She didn't ask for permission before she pulled Mark's shirt up and wiped the wound. He pretended to wince in pain as she cleared the blood away.

Jane reached over, smiled at the young woman, and took the cloth from her hand.

"Thanks," Jane said. "But I've got it."

"That's going to need stitches," she said.

She took a small bottle from a loop in her overcoat and handed it to Mark.

"Drink this," she said. "The moravi's claws are covered in poison. If not treated right away, you will die, horribly," she added.

Mark drank the contents of the bottle and handed it back to her. She tried to nudge Jane aside and treat his wound, but Jane didn't budge.

"I'm his wife," Jane said. "I'll take care of him."

The man grabbed Jane by the shoulders and turned her toward him.

"You're going to be his widow if you don't let Kate do her job. She has been treating wounds like this since she was twelve years old," he said. "She knows what she is doing."

Jane stepped away, and the young woman knelt beside Mark. She ran her hand across his chest as if she were feeling for something. Then she opened a box and took out a glowing fruit of some kind and placed it near Mark's wound. She paused, picked up a pair of tweezers, and removed a small splinter from Mark's wound.

"What are you taking out of the wound?" Jane asked.

"The moravi leave small bits of their claws in the wound, so if the victim doesn't die from the poison, he dies from infection," she said.

She handed Jane one of the fragments she pulled out of the wound. Jane examined it and handed it to Mark. Mark examined it and then ran a DNA analysis while he was waiting for the young woman to finish.

"You're very lucky," she said. "The wound looked deeper than it was, but I'm still finding shards."

That reminded Mark to reset his repair subroutine to human speed.

"There's no discoloration, heat, or infiltration of the area around the wound, so you must have somehow avoided being poisoned," she said.

She took out another bottle of blue liquid and poured it along the length of Mark's wound. Then she took out a curved needle, stitched the wound closed, and covered it in what looked like amber tree sap. The sap dried and formed a bandage.

She finished her work and Mark sat up. The man stepped over and held out his hand.

"I've never met anyone who killed a moravi with a knife."

He held out his hand, and both Mark and Jane shook it.

"Welcome to Hell," he said. "Or at least the closest thing to it the Saps can make. I'm Matthew Irm and the young lady who saved your life is Kate Fol."

Kate paused from cleaning up the mess long enough to wave at them. Matt gestured toward a chain, and he and Mark pulled up the counterweights and reset the releases.

"Kate and I were on our way to the ocean to check the traps when we were trapped up here," Matthew said. "We saw your fight, and as soon as you got close enough, we threw you the rope."

Mark nodded in understanding.

"Sorry it took so long to get you the rope, but if the moravi knew we were here, they wouldn't leave for days. The good news is they don't normally look up, so as long as we are above their sight, we're safe."

"So, the next time we see one, climb a tree?" Mark asked.

"As long as it doesn't see you go up," Matt said. "We have to wait here until we are certain they've moved on."

"How long does that take?" Mark asked.

"A day or so," Matthew said.

A bell in the distance rang three times. Kate and Matthew glanced at each other.

"That's the night bell," Matthew said. "It's time for sleep."

"What does that mean?" Mark asked.

"Since there isn't any night or day down here, the Sapanites put a bell in the obelisk at the center of the island. It rings every eight hours, and we use it to mark time, otherwise we would all be sleeping at different times," Kate said.

She set about getting blankets and pillows for everyone from under the cots. When she was done, she took off her black overcoat. Under it she wore a black, long-sleeve shirt and pants.

Matthew gestured to one of the cots, and Mark sat down. He started to remove his shoes when Matthew stopped him.

"You will want to keep those on," he said. "Down here you can never know when you may need to run for your life. Loosen them if you need to, but don't take them off."

Mark nodded. He took off his jacket and lay back on the cot. He saw Jane do the same.

"How do . . ." Matthew cut Mark off before he could finish his question.

"We can answer all your questions tomorrow," he said.

Mark shrugged and lay back. He let his hand dangle off the edge of the cot, and Jane took it.

"A bit overwhelming isn't it," Jane sent.

"I thought I had become pretty adaptable," Mark replied. *"But, yes I'm feeling overwhelmed."*

"Did you run DNA on the moravi claw?"

"As soon as you put it in my hand," Mark sent.

"Could you send me the data, please?"

Mark sent her the data.

"I'll examine the moravi DNA, and you can examine our host's DNA."

"That's what I was planning to do," Mark sent.

"Any thoughts about our current

situation?" Jane asked.

"I'm still trying to figure out how the society down here works and why the Sapanites are doing this. What do they have to gain by abducting people and bringing them down here?"

"I don't know," Jane sent. *"But it is clear that we have stumbled upon another threat to humanity, and we can't leave until we have all the answers."*

"Do you think Kak was aware of the Sapanites?" Mark asked.

"Kak was aware of everything," Jane sent. *"But from his point of view, this would have been an internal affair, and he would have to stay out of it."*

"Agreed," Mark sent. *"I'm still a little disappointed that he didn't mention it."*

"Well, that is kind of a moot argument," Jane sent. *"Don't waste processing power on it."*

She let go of his hand.

Mark ran Kate's and then Matthew's DNA. They were third cousins, which wasn't surprising since the population down here was kind of small, but apart from that, there was nothing interesting about their DNA.

He rolled over, and Jane held out her hand. Mark took it.

"I've got one piece of the puzzle," Jane sent. *"The moravi are an ancestor of the dodo bird, which isn't that surprising, but what really caught my attention was they had markers on their DNA. Someone has been altering their senses of hearing, smell, and vision."*

"Enhancing?" Mark asked.

"I can't be sure," Jane sent. *"But it seems they're behavioral modifications. They also spliced spider DNA into their feathers to make them resistant to projectile weapons."*

"So, you're saying they have Kevlar feathers?" Mark asked.

"Yes," Jane sent.

"Well, isn't that just special," Mark said.

He let go of her hand, and he saw her smile at him in the dim mercury-reflected light. He lay on his cot and played with Kak's watch. There was a set of six dials around the watch's face, a red button above and a green button below. The dials had thirty-six alien symbols on them, like they were some kind of combination. Each symbol was separated by ten dots. The symbols repeated themselves in pairs: 1st and 4th, 2nd and 5th, and 3rd and 6th. He had adjusted the dials numerous times and pressed the buttons, but nothing happened.

Mark did the math, and he realized that there were 46,656,000 possible combinations of symbols on the first set of dials. Since he had plenty of time, he began to methodically go through each combination until something happened.

He looked over at Kate and Matthew as they slept. They slept soundly, and neither of them stirred at all while they slept.

Eight hours and two minutes after the first bell had tolled, the sound of another bell cut through the forest. Matthew and Kate awoke as if they had been turned on at a switch. They both rose, stretched, and drank something that they kept in their mouths for a moment, and then spit back into the container from which it had come.

Kate stepped over to Mark and looked into his eyes. She touched his forehead and smiled.

"You're alive," she said. "That's always a good sign."

She smiled at him, and Mark noticed a larva of some kind on her front teeth.

"You've got something on your tooth," Mark said.

Kate smiled again.

"It's a toothnit," she said. "We'll get you some when we get back."

"Kate," Matthew said. "You know the law. They have to go to Murus. We don't want any more trouble with Her Lordship."

"You mean," Kate snapped. "You want to claim the bounty."

"Bounty?" Mark asked.

"You'll get your half," Matthew said.

"Bounty?" Mark asked.

"We could both use the money, and they'll eventually end up with us anyway, so I don't see the harm," Matthew said.

"Bounty?" Mark asked again.

Kate took a breath and looked Mark in the eyes.

"The Sapanite Lord Kaxuth likes to evaluate all new arrivals, so he issued an order that a bounty of ten platinum will be paid to outcasts who bring new arrivals to Murus," Kate said.

"You will be evaluated," Matthew continued. "And if you are deemed fit, you will be permitted to live in Murus for a hundred and eighty-five bells to perform public service."

"Service?" Jane asked.

"Since you are still of child bearing age," Kate said. "You will be given a hundred and eighty-five bells to become pregnant. He will be given a hundred and eighty-five bells to produce as many offspring as possible. Then he will be outcast."

"What about you?" Jane asked. "You're of childbearing age."

Kate lifted her blouse to reveal a scar that ran from the bottom of her breast to the top of her hip.

"I can't get pregnant," Kate said. "A moravi attacked me when I first arrived. I should have died. I was taken to Murus and recovered, but I was outcast after my hundred and eighty-five bells."

"But we're married," Mark said.

Matthew and Kate looked at him and smiled.

"Things like that don't matter down here," he said. "Everyone has to provide public service, otherwise the moravi would make us extinct."

"I've heard it called a lot of things, but that's a new one," Mark said.

Mark looked over at Jane who smiled at him reassuringly. Mark did his best to return her smile.

Jane grabbed her backpack and opened it. She took out the books from the farmhouse and showed them to Kate. She read their spines and frowned.

"Can you tell us what these are?" Jane asked.

"They are vitalibri," Kate said. "We all keep journals of our thoughts and feelings, so when we die, we aren't forgotten."

She handed the books to Matthew who looked at them and sighed. He handed them back to Jane who returned them to her pack.

"We store them in the Hall of Remembrance in Murus," Matthew said. "Citizens are encouraged to read them to learn about their ancestors."

"When you get to Murus, you will be given one as well. Down here, we don't have funerals or cemeteries since most of the time we don't have anything left to bury, so the vitalibri are how we remember," Kate said.

"Anyone lucky enough to die of natural causes, or ends themselves, is put into the river," Matthew said.

"Did you know them?" Jane asked.

"Of course," Matthew said. "The community down here isn't that large. The entire city of Murus is only made up of about three-hundred people."

"It looks like the moravi have moved on," Kate said.

"Does that mean it's safe?" Mark asked.

"There isn't anywhere in Subterra that is safe," Matthew said. "It just means that it is less dangerous."

They gathered their belongings and repelled down to the ground. Once on the ground, they only used hand signals to communicate. Matthew led them with Mark and Jane in the middle, and Kate brought up the rear.

They passed out of the trees into large fields of red, leafy plants. Watch towers stood every mile or so, and the people working the fields kept an eye on the horizon. Each time they were spotted, the worker would stop and wave. Sometimes the wave would become a series of hand signals as they passed by.

They reached a region of rocky ground where a river forked and formed an island. A walled city stood on the island that reminded Mark of Warwick Castle. They crossed a draw bridge, and they were met on the other side by a woman in her late twenties with thick red hair and blue eyes. She wore a blue dress that was cut very low and showed an ample amount of cleavage. She held a cloth bag in each hand. Mark tried to do a passive X-ray scan, but without the Sun to supply the X-rays, he was blind.

"Lamere," Matthew said. "Always a pleasure."

She glanced at them, but turned her attention to Matthew. Her eyes narrowed and her lips pursed. Mark could tell there was some history between them that didn't end well.

"That's First Minister," she said.

She started to turn to the guards waiting by the gate, but Matthew spoke and she halted.

"Yes, our praise be to our beloved first minister and to our lord protector Kaxuth."

She turned back and smiled.

"As the law requires, these pilgrims are being submitted. They are Mark and Jane Aaron," Matthew said.

She waved her hand.

"We can dispense with the formality," she said. "I know who they are. Our lord Kaxuth told me to expect them."

She held out a bag to Matthew, and the other to Kate. They each took the bag and turned to leave.

The First Minister looked Mark and Jane up and down. She gestured for them to follow her. They started toward the gate when she paused and turned back for two seconds before continuing on. She wiped a tear away as they reached the gate.

A guard wearing tan pants and a white long-sleeve shirt pushed the gate open for them. His shirt had the Sapanite symbol on one sleeve and some kind of rank insignia on the other. He carried a black, metal baton that had mechanical parts on it, so Mark realized it was more than just a club.

"I am First Minister Lamere Batiel. You will refer to me as First Minister, or Minister Batiel. I speak for Kaxuth, who is our governor and Lord Protector. You will be given one-hundred and eighty-five bells to prove your value to the community. If not, you will be outcast. If you break our laws, you will be sent to the arena. Your life on the surface is over, and you must embrace our ways if you hope to survive."

Chapter Nine
Murus

Lamere led them past a two-story, stone apartment building that had a glass roof and extremely large windows. They turned right onto a circular path lined with large tomato-like plants with glowing fruit. Mark noticed that every square inch of ground inside the city that wasn't covered with a building or a stone walkway was utilized for gardening.

He looked across the square and saw what looked like a miniature industrial complex. Steam poured out of a vent in the roofs of the buildings in regulated puffs indicating they had steam power, but he couldn't see any evidence of fire being used to produce the steam.

They followed the circular path around until they were in front of a large, castle-like building that was surrounded by an inner wall that was twelve feet, four inches high. The central tower of the building had a clock on it, and the First Minister paused to glance at the time.

Everyone they passed stopped to stare at them, and Mark began to feel like a piece of meat. Based on the people he saw, the population of Murus was roughly eighty percent female, and about half of the women he saw were visibly pregnant. The clothes they wore were risqué even for the twenty-first century. The women wore low-cut, toga-like dresses that came down to their thighs with a rope belt around the waist and sandals tied on to their feet with string that wrapped around their calves. The men he saw all wore tunics that came down to their thighs and sandals that looked like a rustic version of flip-flops or in some cases a leather slipper. The clothing seemed intended to increase desire rather than diminish it, which made sense if the Sapanites were using the city for breeding humans.

They passed through the inner gate, crossed a small stone courtyard, and entered what looked like a bath house or pool. The walls were lit by glass containers attached to the wall with some kind of glowing tomato plant that floated on top of a clear gel. It worked so well that the inside of the building was brighter than the outside.

A pool of steaming water occupied the center of the room. It appeared to be thermally heated with a continuous stream of fresh water running through it. The wall across the pool was a large window overlooking the street. The street wasn't crowded, but occasionally Mark saw someone pass by.

"You have twenty minutes to bathe and dress," she said.

She gestured toward two sets of folded clothes on a table.

"Your mentors have been selected, and they will be in to assist you."

"Mentors?" Mark asked.

"They will help you assimilate. You will live and work with them until they see fit to release you."

"But we're married," Mark said.

The First Minister laughed.

"Yes, you are," she said. "But not to each other. You are married to the State and to our Lord Kaxuth. His orders are to be obeyed without question."

She didn't wait for Mark's response. She turned and walked through the door. Mark closed it behind her. He turned back to see Jane putting her backpack into the box Lamere had indicated.

"You're going along with this?" Mark asked.

"I don't see that we have much of a choice," Jane said. "At least they aren't chaining me up and stripping me naked like at Newgate Gaol," Jane said.

"But," Mark said.

"Mark," Jane said. "Whatever happens down here, I won't hold it against you. Physical love is meaningless to us, you know that. Our bond is on a much deeper level."

Mark sighed.

"I know you don't want to betray Kylee's memory, but you aren't that person anymore, and I think it is past time you let go of something that you never had."

"What?" Mark said.

"You were never married to Kylee," Jane said. "That was the other guy."

"Well, yeah," Mark said. "I guess you're right."

"Good," Jane said. "Now shut up and get naked. I want you to scrub my back."

Mark undressed and kept an eye on the window to see if anyone was watching them. He got into the pleasantly warm water with Jane and kissed her one last time.

As Mark finished tying his tunic belt, the door opened. A young woman entered carrying a book in her right hand. She walked over to them and gave Jane a disapproving glance. Then she looked at Mark like she was examining a horse she intended to purchase. She rubbed his forearm and stared at his eyes.

Mark used the time to examine her as well. She appeared to be in her late teens or early twenties, shoulder-length red hair, and true sapphire eyes, stood five feet tall, weighed roughly a hundred and ten pounds, with a modest bust. She wore the same low cut, short skirt dress and sandals that the others wore only her dress was olive.

"I am Muirgel Mac Alastair. Get your things," she said. "You are to come with me."

Mark put on his gun belt and picked up his backpack and clothes.

"What is that ridiculous thing?"

She pointed at his gun belt.

"It's my gun belt," Mark said.

"Is that something surface dwellers wear? It looks stupid," she said.

"On that we agree," Jane said.

Muirgel ignored Jane, and gestured for Mark to leave with her. Mark gave Jane a quick goodbye. Muirgel didn't say anything as he followed her out of the bath house and onto the street. They passed a curly-haired man who seemed to be in a hurry. Mark turned back to watch him go past and Muirgel turned back and grabbed Mark's hand.

"It's almost night bell, so unless you like sleeping in the street, you have to hurry."

Mark let her lead him across the courtyard and around the circular stone path in the center of the village to a small, stone and glass house surrounded by a well-kept garden. Mark noticed that the door was not locked as she pushed it open and gestured for him to enter. As he stepped through the threshold, the bell sounded.

"Put your things on the table," she said.

As he set his pack on the table, he felt her hands around his waist. She reached around him in a move that severely violated his sense of personal space, and groped around for a moment before her fingers found the buckle on the gun belt. She unbuckled it, pulled the belt off, and dropped it on the table. She pushed Mark onto the bed and fell on top of him. Mark started to protest, but he realized she was asleep.

He looked around. The base of the wall was made out of cut stone and stood four feet high. The stones were cut and fit together so precisely that Mark doubted he could fit a razor blade between them. A six-inch copper joiner rested on top of the wall, and a large glass plate was set into the copper joiner, similar to what you would find in a greenhouse. The doorframe was made of copper with three thick glass panels making up the door itself. The design worked well to admit the feeble light from the sky, but it didn't afford the occupant much in the way of privacy.

The room's furnishings consisted of a wooden table, four chairs, a cooking area with a sink, and cabinets placed against the rear glass wall.

He moved his hand over the small of her back and took a DNA sample. She didn't have any Sapanite DNA, but he determined that she, despite her name, was mostly Irish in heritage, but the rest was a mix of European and Russian. He added her DNA to his database and realized that he was starting to run out of storage.

Mark decided to risk turning on his receivers to see if anyone was using radio on the island. He detected a number of overlapping signals from points all over the city. Then he found an electromagnetic wave, very low frequency. It was similar to the wave that came out of the stranger's weapon, but broadcast evenly instead of a directed beam. It somehow interacted with the brain to create delta waves that put everyone to sleep.

He put himself back into stealth mode, gently rolled her over, and crawled out of bed. He went to the large window and looked out at the village. It was empty. He could see into the houses next to him and realized that he could be observed as well.

Mark saw a Sapanite airship on the horizon. He stayed low and crawled back into bed. He lay where he could watch the airship. The airship landed in the courtyard and five Sapanites got out. Four of them walked toward the castle-like building while the other one walked around the inner walking path with a handheld device of some kind. He pointed the device at a glass window, took some kind of reading, and moved on to the next window.

When he worked his way around to Muirgel's window. Mark ran his sleep simulation subroutine for five minutes. Even though he appeared to be asleep, he could still hear everything. He heard the Sapanite approach, a beep from the device, and heard him walk away.

Mark canceled the subroutine two minutes and twenty seconds early and opened his eyes. He saw the Sapanites canning the next house. He noticed movement around the airship and saw that the others had returned. They each had two human babies in a carrier that resembled a shipping crate on wheels. They loaded the babies on the airship and came back out with more handheld devices.

They each walked in a different direction and surveyed the outer ring of buildings. Twenty-seven minutes and eleven seconds later, the last one returned to the airship, and it took off. Flying back in the same direction from which it had come.

He got up and looked around in the cabinets. Apart from several vegetables, he couldn't identify, he found her vitalibri. He took it back to bed and read it. She attended Sapanite school until she was twelve. She intentionally failed her graduation exams because she was afraid of being sent to the surface. She was sent to a farm where she grew something called sorgrat until she was eighteen, and she was accused of associating with someone trying to learn the Sapanite language. Her best friend was executed on the farm in a public display, and she was sent to the island with four others from the farm. Of the four, she was the only one to make it to Murus. She was appointed as a book binder and library helper, and she worked her way up to full librarian. She had given birth twice, but she wasn't allowed to see her child either time.

He noticed a theme of betrayal and loneliness throughout her life. The Sapanites seemed to be experts at getting the people to turn on each other by rewarding deceit and punishing anything resembling love or loyalty.

He put the book back where he found it and returned to bed. He lay and watched the windows for any more signs of movement, but the entire city was quiet.

Eight hours and two minutes after the bell sounded, another tone broke the silence. Fifty-three seconds later, Muirgel stirred. Mark pretended to wake up as well.

"It's your first bell," she said. "We have to get started."

Before Mark could ask 'what' they had to start, she lifted his tunic and smiled approvingly. Mark decided to take Jane's advice and give her what she wanted.

He discovered that Jane was right. Physical love as an android had none of the excitement or intimacy that he remembered having with Kylee. It was just another mechanical function. Mark didn't feel anything but boredom.

Afterward, they ate something that resembled blue bread and she took him to an outhouse, where he had to wait in line to relieve himself, and then to the bath house, where he experienced a Japanese-style bath, except both sexes were in the same pool. Again, Mark felt like a piece of meat as young ladies fought over the privilege to scrub his back. He used it as an opportunity to gather another eleven sets of DNA to review later when he had time.

After the bath, she took him to a three-story stone building with large arching glass windows and a glass roof. The words "Mortus Recordatus" were inscribed in seven-inch brass letters over the thick, glass door. She took him to a room with thousands of volumes arranged neatly on library shelves.

"Can you read and write?" Muirgel asked.

"Yes," Mark said.

She stepped over to a table and handed him a book. The spine had his name on it. He looked over to see if Jane's book was there, but it wasn't.

"I have work to do, so you have this bell to work on your vitalibri. You may review as many of the other volumes as you wish to get an idea of how you can write yours, but please treat them with care. You aren't holding a book. You're holding someone's life."

She turned and walked over to a set of spiral stairs in the corner. She took two steps up and paused.

"If you see that woman you came here with, you are not permitted to speak to her."

She walked up the stairs leaving Mark in the room alone. He smiled. He wasn't sure how he was going to cope with being bossed around by a nineteen-year-old girl, but at the moment, he was finding it hard to take her seriously.

The volumes were arranged by date, so he followed the shelves back to the first volume, which ended up being in the basement. It was two hundred-and-five-years old. He flash-read it and a random sampling of two books per shelf until he had worked his way back to the first floor.

He had expected to gain some kind of perspective about the history and culture of Murus, but instead, he'd only found a litany of misery. They all spoke of service to the state and whatever Sapanite ruler dominated them. There were small joys, but nothing like what he had with Jane.

Mark saw Jane working on her vitalibri. She glanced over at him and rubbed her left eye. With her right eye, she blinked several times. Her eyelid fluttered once, then three times, then six times. She did this three times before turning away.

Mark stepped over to the table furthest away from Jane, grabbed a fountain pen, and started working on his own vitalibri. Since he couldn't exactly tell them the truth, he borrowed Mark Twain's early life with a few embellishments of his own.

As he was finishing up a sketch of a river boat that he was claiming to have worked on as a boy, Muirgel came down the stairs. She handed him two triangular copper coins and told him to go to the large tree in the town square and buy them both soup from someone named Phaenna.

Mark glanced at Jane as he left the library, but she was too involved in her own work to notice. He went back out through the thick, glass doors and he followed the central path around to the town square. The center of the town square was dominated by a statue of Lord and Protector Kaxuth who stood on a ten-foot-high pedestal with a sword on his hip and a basket of food in his hands. The inscription beneath the statue read in Latin, "Kaxuth

Dominus et Provisor," which Mark translated as "Kaxuth Lord and Provider."

The statue was surrounded by rusty triangular metal poles that looked like they may have been street lights. Around those, three groups of nine stone tables and benches were laid out in a circular pattern, but no one sat at any of them. Food vendors with wheeled carts were interspersed throughout the square. Mark located the one selling soup and got in line. He noticed that some of them carried ceramic bowls with hinged lids. At the front of the line, a woman with dirty blonde hair, hazel eyes, and honey skin dispensed soup from a metal box on wheels that reminded Mark of a hot dog cart.

He waited in line for three minutes and twelve seconds. He felt everyone's eyes on him and tried to act normally. Apart from a few people who asked him about his gun belt, no one spoke to him.

While he waited, he examined the two triangular coins in his hand. The coins were equilateral triangles of solid copper, measuring a little less than three-quarters of an inch on each side and an eighth of an inch thick. One side had the Sapanite symbol with the words "Obedientia est Fortitudo," "Pax per Unitatem," and "Fides est Amor," which Mark translated to be "Obedience is Strength," "Peace through Unity," and "Loyalty is Love". The other side of the coin had what looked like a mountain top. Raised letters beneath the mountain read, "Lumen Vivificantem," or "life-giving light". The edges of the coin were curved with a slightly raised line around each side.

What few doubts he had about this society being completely totalitarian, these coins just extinguished. The Sapanites had used the threat of the moravi and the limited resources on the island to completely subjugate the people of Murus. He hoped that Murus wasn't a test to see how they could control the surface world.

He got to the front of the line, and the young woman smiled at him.

"I was told to buy soup for two," he said.

She looked him over and her smile brightened.

"Did Muirgel send you?" she asked. "I'm Phaenna."

"Yes, she didn't give me a bowl to return."

"That's obvious."

She shook her head and sighed. She got two new bowls and two brass spoons from a cabinet in the cart. She filled them with soup and attached the spoons to the lid with a metal snap of some kind.

Mark gave her the two copper coins, and she gave him four aluminum coins. Mark looked at the coins in his hand.

"I charged her for the bowls," she said.

Mark put the coins in his pocket and carried the bowls back to the library. Muirgel met him at the entrance to the library, and they walked back to her house. He tried to give her the change, but she declined it, for which he was grateful. The coins would make a great addition to his personal museum in Arizona.

They went inside and had lunch. Mark couldn't taste the soup, but it was warm and made of some kind of fish, two leafy plants finely chopped, and something that resembled a blue potato.

She asked him questions about the surface world, and he asked her about life in Murus. When she asked him about food, he remembered the bag of dried strawberries in his jacket. He retrieved it, and she ate the whole bag.

When she finished, she left the empty bag on the table, and Mark picked it up to keep his coins in. He noticed that a dozen strawberry seeds clung to the sides of the cloth bag. He decided to try to grow them. The hard part would be generating enough light.

They returned to the library, and when she went back upstairs, Mark went to row one, shelf three, book six. He opened it and found a microdot on the inside of the front cover. He read it.

Jane's microdot told him that she had been assigned to someone called Giorgos. He was a glass smith, and she had been assigned to the weavers. She warned him that the vitalibri are not private. She included dates and places that she wanted Mark to write in his vitalibri, so their stories would align. She warned him about the pax, who functioned as the Sapanite enforcement arm, and would arrest anyone for the slightest infraction of the law. Then she included a mathematical formula to let him know where to leave his response.

Mark flash-read the volume to see if there was a reason Jane had selected it and found nothing. He erased the microdot, returned the volume to the shelf and used Jane's formula to select the vitalibri for his reply.

He inscribed a microdot that told her he was fine, and that she was right about everything. He told her about the Sapanite bed check, the collection of the babies, and provided details about his vitalibri.

Then he went back to working on his vitalibri. He finished his early life with a move to Springfield where he met Jane. As he was finishing a sketch of his farm in Springfield, Muirgel came down the stairs. She read his writing and examined Mark's sketches with great interest. She asked him several questions, and listened to his answers without interruption. By the time he had answered all of her questions, the library was closed.

They were the last to leave the library, and he was a little surprised when she didn't lock the door. When he asked her about it, she casually remarked that the punishment for trespassing or theft in Murus was death.

She took him to a public house near the front gate with a sign hanging over the front that read "Gualtiero's Place."

At first glance, the building that housed Gualtiero's place seemed to be built out of large glass panels set into river stones and mortar, but on closer inspection, Mark noticed rusty iron beams in the walls and part of the back wall was made from precast concrete. He also noted disused conduits in the wall where some type of cable was housed a very long time ago.

The restaurant was lit by Kuja planted in boxes along the walls and suspended in planters hung from the ceiling. The glowing bulbs were clustered together in a way that cast multiple overlapping shadows. A dark-haired man in the back of the room played an out of tune piano that reminded Mark of some of the bars in Fort Worth.

They sat on a wooden bench, and the server, a blonde woman in her late teens, brought them a large bottle of cervisia, a heavy, green liquid, and two glasses. Judging by the effect it had on Muirgel, it was a drug of some kind. Mark tried to analyze it, but its organic components weren't in his database. All he knew for sure was it wasn't alcohol.

The drink was served in a rectangular bottle that was nine inches by seven inches by three inches with a large glass stopper on top. The drink seemed to be popular because there was at least one bottle on every table.

The server brought out two plates of fried vegetables and what looked like a fried tube worm. Muirgel acted like it was five-star dining, so Mark did the same. He couldn't taste anything, but he did his best to fake his enjoyment.

They stopped at a street vendor on the way back and bought more of the blue bread that they had eaten for breakfast, and eggs that Mark couldn't identify.

She took him to a small shop where she bought him a jar of toothnits, a straight razor, and a comb. She also bought two large jars of some kind of chemicals. They went back to her tiny, glass house and went to bed. The tone sounded, and she was unconscious.

Mark was left with nothing to do for eight hours and two minutes. He knew he was being watched, but he didn't know how closely, but he decided not to find out, and he hoped Jane was doing the same. So, he spent each night adjusting the dials on his watch 1024 times while he watched for motion outside.

Things fell into a routine for the next three weeks. He saw Jane a few times at a distance, but even though it was a very small place, they did a pretty good job of keeping them apart. Mark was assigned a number of odd jobs to keep him busy. He did them as well as he could. While he was out, he surveyed the number of people in Murus, and he identified three hundred and thirty-four individuals. Most of them worked in the fields surrounding the city growing plants or tube worms.

He found a discarded wooden box and used it to plant the strawberry seeds. He found some glass panels and polished them to turn them into lenses that captured the feeble light and focus it on the plants. Since he had to polish the lenses at human speed, it took him three weeks to finish them, and by the time his miniature greenhouse was finished, the seeds had sprouted.

On his twenty-eighth day in Murus, Muirgel took him to meet with Minister Batiel at the Office of Public Good. He sat on a wooden stool as she looked at him from across her large desk. A bookcase behind her contained untitled books and ledgers. On one side of her desk sat a device that resembled a desktop computer with a hexagonal screen and oddly laid out keyboard. She stared at him with a stern expression on her face for three seconds before speaking.

"Our Lord Protector Kaxuth has been watching your assimilation with interest. You have obeyed all of our laws and followed every directive."

She paused for two seconds waiting to see if Mark would respond.

"Murusian law requires that all refuse must be collected and removed from the city every three days. This prevents the smell from attracting the moravi."

Mark nodded.

"Despite the recommendation from your mentor to make you a book binder and restorer, our Lord Kaxuth feels that the assignment of refuse handler is more suited to your somewhat limited skills," she said.

"Thank you," Mark said.

"Do you have any questions?" she asked.

"When do I start?"

"Next bell," she said.

She pursed her lips and narrowed her eyes. Mark could sense her frustration at his lack of frustration at what she thought was a huge insult to him. Mark smiled. She handed him a rolled-up piece of paper.

"Your directions are written here," she said. "Anything less than complete obedience will be punished."

Mark took the paper and smiled.

"Obedience is strength."

She frowned and pointed to the door.

"You may go," she said.

Mark read his instructions as he left the office. He was given a route that took him all over the city, and was provided with the destinations where the refuse had to be dumped. It allowed him to move around the city, but it also took him well outside the city. Then he realized the assignment was more than just an insult.

Muirgel waited for him outside, and he gave her the news. She was visibly upset, but tried to act like it wasn't a death sentence.

Since today was the last day, he would be permitted in the library, he left a microdot for Jane explaining his new role. He updated his vitalibri to include how he got the map that led him down there.

He took one last look around the library and found Hamilton Bricker's vitalibri and read it. He noticed that the handwriting was different, and some of the entries about Murus had been altered to reflect service to the state. The entries after he became outcast were replaced with passages about living on the run and watching in horror as his friends died. The entries about his tranquil life on the farm and building the wall around it were redacted entirely. That confirmed that the vitalibri were just another way the Sapanites could spread their propaganda. He wondered how they would redact his vitalibri when his time came.

At the next bell, Mark started his new job as a refuse handler. He picked up his two-wheeled cart outside the nearest Office of Public Good. As he passed by the pax headquarters, he saw Sigríður in a group of pax practicing hand to hand combat. They made eye contact as he passed by, and she smiled at him.

On the first day, he collected all of the biological waste from Murus. He visited the four public outhouses and the six private ones. As he scooped the last of the sludge into his cart, he noticed that the outer wall of the septic box was made from porous stone, and potassium nitrate crystals had formed on the outer wall. He smiled to himself as he attached the shovel he had been provided onto his cart and moved along. He took his cart of sludge to the farmers growing kuja, a tomato-like plant with glowing fruit. Based upon how the farmers wrinkled up their faces when they received it, Mark was grateful he couldn't smell. He found a kuja on the side of the road that had been split open, so he gathered as many seeds as he could and put them in his pocket.

The next day, he had to collect the food waste Murus generated: stems, plant tops, tube worm husks, vegetable pomace, and containers of the used oil from the public house kitchens and take it to the tube worm farmers, but they didn't want the oil, so he sold it to the metal workers for five aluminum coins. When they asked about his gun belt, he told them he used it to keep his tunic from flying up.

On the third day, he picked up the trash from the four bins located inside the city. The trash from near the government buildings was mostly shredded paper. The trash from the trade workers was mostly rejected or broken glass and metal, and a few parts from the steam engines. The trash from the residential areas consisted of broken ceramics, rags, and used household items.

Once he had collected items from the last bin, he went to the front gate. The pax guard wished him a safe journey as he opened the gate. Mark started on the road toward the thermal vent.

He walked at a normal pace as he left the city and passed through the fields around the city, but when he got far enough away, he quickened his pace as much as the cart would allow.

He entered an area of exposed obsidian and granite that gave way to fields of pumice. He passed several hot springs and realized geothermal energy powered the mechanical looms and other steam powered equipment in Murus. One hot spring was close enough to the path for him to see the sulfur around its edges.

He stayed on the path and it led right up to the volcanic vent that he was supposed to dump the trash in. A four-foot by five-foot glass shed stood beside the trail. Some of the glass panels were missing, and the mattress inside had red stains. Parts of another cart lay near the shed. Based on what he saw, it was obvious what had happened to the previous refuse handler.

Mark walked to the edge of the vent and looked inside. The vent was a hole in the ground that measured roughly ten feet by fifteen feet. About ten feet down an outer ring was covered in garbage. The inner hole, roughly five feet in diameter, glowed with the light produced by the magma as it flowed past roughly ten feet below. The temperature around the inner ring wasn't that high since the magma was below the outer ring.

From what he knew from his college science course, the air in the vent was filled with carbon dioxide and hydrogen sulfide, but fortunately, he didn't have to breathe.

He tossed a bag of shredded paper into the vent, and it bounced on the outer ring and fell into the inner ring and burst into flame. Fire was forbidden in Subterra, so Mark mused that burning things in a volcanic vent must be a loophole in the law.

Mark dropped the remainder of his trash onto the outer ring. He had about an hour before the night bell, so he decided to explore the vent. He looked around to be sure he wasn't being observed, and jumped down onto the outer ring.

The temperature down there was a mere hundred and twenty-five degrees. He was able to walk right up to the inner vent without feeling too much heat. Only when he placed his hand directly over the inner vent did he feel the intense heat.

He searched through and sorted the debris in the outer ring. Some of the mechanical parts he found were very well made. He found a steam pressure gage that with a little work some copper wire, and a few magnets, he could turn into an electric generator. He set that aside, and he tossed in a wooden box of greasy, mechanical parts into the inner vent and watched the box burst into flame and the parts melt.

That gave him an idea. He found a ceramic pot and filled it with scrap aluminum and brass. He found a length of chain and lowered it into the magma.

While he waited for it to melt, he searched the refuse. He sorted items by category: wood, metal, ceramic, and mechanical parts that still worked. Ten minutes later, he pulled the pot back up to find the aluminum and brass had melted. He grabbed a metal pipe and mixed the two before pouring it into a makeshift mold to cool.

Since he only had a few moments left until the night bell, he jumped up out of the hole. What he saw on the surface as he rose up out of the ground would have turned his blood cold if he had been human. A moravi stood ten feet in front of him. It turned its enormous head toward him and sniffed the air. It clearly saw him but just stood there, looking him over.

Mark didn't hesitate. As soon as his feet touched the ground, he drew his revolver in a fluid motion and as soon as the sight was leveled, he fired. Deputy Calloway would have been proud. Mark saw a red splatter on the glass shed. It convulsed twice and fell. He didn't wait to be sure it was dead. He grabbed it by its feet and pulled it to the edge of the vent and pushed it inside. Then he jumped down and pushed it inside the inner vent and watched it cook for a moment.

As he pondered how moravi might taste with gravy and mashed potatoes, the night bell sounded, and Mark jumped back out of the vent and sprinted to the mattress. He fell onto it, doing his best to ignore the dried blood.

Five minutes and twelve seconds later, an airship flew over the hill behind him, hovered for a moment, put a search light on him, and then continued on toward Murus. The airship flew by again two hours later, but it didn't stop.

As Mark lay there adjusting the settings on Kak's watch, he realized that if the airship had stopped to check on him, he wasn't under constant surveillance outside the city. He also realized that the heat from the thermal vent would make getting a temperature reading from his body heat impossible.

Mark lay on the mattress until he heard the morning bell. He took one last look in the thermal vent, and decided that the job of refuse handler was going to work out after all.

He jumped back down into the vent and pulled the piece of metal he had forged out of the makeshift mold. It would need some filing, but the basic shape of a knife blade was there. He just needed to make a handle. He set the blade aside, jumped back out, and pushed his cart back down the road.

Once he was within sight of the city, he took the spent bullet and the remaining good one and put them back inside the handle. The people working the fields smiled and waved at him as he passed.

Once he was through the gate, eleven people were there to meet him. Muirgel being among them. As soon as the pax guard had finished inspecting his cart, she ran to him, gave him a hug, and wrinkled up her nose. She turned and extended her hand toward the crowd, and they each in turn put a triangular coin into it. Over her shoulder, she told him to put the cart away and go take a bath.

Mark went to the bathhouse, and since it was the middle of the day, he was alone. After he undressed, he looked on the table for the usual sponge and liquid soap, but instead he found a cake of soap that looked familiar. It was identical to the soap Jane and he made in their shop in London, right down to the icosagon logo in the middle.

Mark smiled, picked up the soap and a sponge, and got into the water. The door behind him opened, and someone got into the pool. Mark didn't turn to see who it was, but he hoped that he or she would respect his personal space. That hope was shattered when a female voice asked to borrow the soap. Mark turned and saw a woman with shoulder-length dirty blonde hair, hazel eyes, and olive skin. He recognized her as Phaenna, the woman who had sold him soup when he first arrived. He handed her the soap and the sponge, and she gestured for him to turn around.

"You know," she whispered. "You are the first refuse handler to return to the city in twenty-five bells."

"I gathered as much," Mark said.

She scrubbed his back slowly and gently.

"I have a message from Jane," she whispered softly in his ear.

"Let's hear it."

"Even unbuttoned, Emily had her uses."

Mark turned to face her. He looked deeply into her hazel eyes for any sign of the mind control a button would produce. He opened a com port to see if he could connect with her, but found nothing. He wanted to frown, but instead smiled at her. She gently rubbed his chest with the sponge.

"What does the message mean?" she asked.

"It means I can trust you," Mark lied. "Did she say anything else?"

"The handle on your cart is hollow. She needs you to bring her taba root. You will find some in the hollow tree by the hot spring."

"Is that it?"

"Yes, put the taba in the handle and park your cart next to the tree behind Muirgel's quarters."

"I have a message for Jane," Mark said.

"What is it?"

"I like the knot on the tree in the public square."

"What's that mean?"

"It means what it says," Mark said. "I like the knot on the tree in the public square."

Mark saw her glance to her right. A male pax walked past the window and stopped. She kissed him, used him, and left. He toweled off and got dressed.

As soon as he stepped out of the bathhouse, he was met by Sigríður and the pax he saw though the window. As soon as she got within arm's-length of him, she stabbed him with her stun baton. The baton released fifteen volts at four amps. Mark doubled over, and she bound his hands behind him with a leather strap.

"Our Lord Protector Kaxuth is displeased. You have failed in your task and punishment is warranted," she said.

She took his revolver from his gun belt and inspected the cylinder. She spun it around and made sure it was empty.

"Why are you carrying this?"

"It reminds me of home, and it helps to keep my skirt down."

She slapped him with the back of her hand, removed his gun belt, and bound his hands. He was taken to a room in the Office of Public Good where he was taken to a cell, stripped down, tied to a rack, and kept waiting for two hours and forty-seven minutes. Minister Batiel entered in all of her splendor. She glanced at Mark before reading from a paper.

"An inspection shows that you failed to polish the floors of the septic stations, and you improperly disposed of waste oils. You will receive five lashes with a dolor."

She turned and left. Sigríður entered three minutes later with her baton in hand that Mark realized was called a dolor. She stabbed him once in the middle of his back. Mark acted like it hurt.

"I knew if I waited long enough you would break some kind of rule, and then I would have you," she said.

"Where's Trausti?" Mark asked.

"I left him on that stupid farm you found," she said. "I followed you here."

"Why?"

"I would think that would be obvious," she said. "I want you to tell me how you got down here, so I can escape."

Chapter Ten
The Arena

In between prods with the baton, he told her the same story he told the Sapanites. They fell into the lake, drifted from air pocket to air pocket, until the current pulled them under and they ended up in the river. Each time he answered her, she shocked the rack instead of him.

She wanted to know which river led to the surface, and Mark told her he didn't know, but if he looked at a map, he may be able to figure it out. She left, and he was released twenty-three minutes later.

Muirgel was waiting for him. She had his clothes and his gun belt. She took him home, gave him three glasses of cervisia, and put him to bed.

In the morning, they ate the blue bread, and she told him in hushed tones that she had been sent to the rack three times. She hinted that he was punished more for coming back alive than for his job performance.

She questioned him about what he saw outside the city and how he survived. When she asked him if he was immersed in smoke from the vent, he got the feeling he was being interrogated. He described every aspect of the trip in detail, but omitted his trip into the vent. When she asked about the moravi, he told her that he must have been lucky. She gave him two silver coins to buy what he needed to clean the outhouses properly.

Mark declined her invitation to the bathhouse since he was just going to get filthy anyway. He bought a dustpan, wire broom, and a box of rags from a vendor in the public square. He stepped over and leaned against a tree to adjust his sandal, and left a microdot for Jane. He wondered if all these precautions were really necessary, but he also didn't want to underestimate the Sapanites. If they found out he was an android, they would dissect him.

He began his rounds and cleaned the septic boxes of each outhouse making sure to polish the floor. This time, he also scraped off the saltpeter from the outer wall. He kept it confined to the corner of his cart until he found a discarded cervisia bottle to put it in.

He returned to the vent, stopping on his way to collect the taba root. When he analyzed the taba, he knew that Jane didn't ask for it. It was the same substance that Charlotte used to end her life, and Jane's base programming prevented her from assisting with suicide. He stopped by the hot spring and filled a cervisia bottle with sulfur.

When he arrived at the vent, he tossed the trash into the hole, jumped down into the vent, and started making gunpowder. The last ingredient he needed was charcoal, and he found plenty around the sides of the vent.

He knew the ingredients had to be ground fine. Fortunately, he had a collection of metal parts, gears, and tubes to work with and he assembled a blender using the workings of a small steam turbine and the handle off a release valve. First, he ground the ingredients separately, and then came the dangerous part as he ground them together.

Once the night bell had rung, and the airship had passed, he jumped back down into the vent. He searched through the refuse for lead, but didn't find any. As he dug through a pile of metal parts, he found a rusty pipe buried in the ground. He followed it back through the lava tube to a metal door. The door was ajar, so he forced it the rest of the way open.

He found a room with a series of gages and dials on metal walls, lit by a few kuja plants that grew in small piles of dirt and emitted a faint glow. Through a window, he saw four large steam turbines sitting idle in an adjacent room. The metal consoles and chairs remained, but there were only traces of dirt where the wooden furniture had been. A door at the back of the room led to a long hallway that ended with stairs and another door. The door was marked in the Sapanite language, but he noticed that it was also marked in Latin. Mark had found a Rosetta Stone. He looked around and found that many of the switches, dials, and controls were also labeled in both Sapanite and Latin. He went to the top and forced the door open. He came out on the edge of an abandoned city. Mark checked his internal chronometer, and realized he didn't have time to explore, even though he really wanted to.

Instead of going back through the tunnel, he went back over the ridge to where he left his cart. It gave him a view of the abandoned city, and as he looked backward, he noticed that the streets were laid out in a hexagon pattern. The remains of towering structures stood in the center of the city, surrounded by smaller ones further out, but all had succumbed to time and lay in ruin. Since he wasn't looking where he was going, he didn't see the moravi until he was among them.

He turned back to see four moravi standing around him. The closest was only ten feet away. He froze. The moravi clearly saw him, but they didn't attack. They sniffed the air and looked straight at him. Mark instantly switched to battle mode and waited for an attack that never came. He stood there for three minutes and fifty-seven seconds, which is an eternity to an android in battle mode, but they ignored him. They lost interest and moved off behind him into the abandoned city like a flock of chickens looking for worms.

He went back to his cart, and found moravi tracks near his cart and the glass sleeping hut. The moravi had pecked his mattress until there was nothing but a few tufts of material scattered on the ground. The morning bell sounded, so before he started back, he used some pieces of iron as makeshift tools and swapped the hollow handle of his cart for the handle of the ruined cart.

He swallowed the contents of the bag of taba, and kept it in his esophagus, so he could regurgitate it when necessary. He wasn't sure that he was being set up, but it didn't hurt to be cautious.

When he got back to Murus, the pax guard let him through the first gate. He was held there for twenty-three minutes. He watched the pax guard pull on the handle of his cart several times. Then, the First Minister herself supervised the inspection of his cart. When that yielded nothing, he was brought before her, and she frowned at him as if she was disappointed. Still, she handed him two gold coins.

"You have completed your first week of work," she said. "The state shows its gratitude by offering compensation."

She held out a clipboard and indicated where she wanted Mark to sign. It was a list of names and occupations. He saw Jane's name listed as a weaver, but no signature. She dismissed him with a wave of her hand.

He parked his cart near Muirgel's house and went to the bathhouse. Sigríður was waiting for him. She held up a bar of soap and a wash cloth. She looked alluring in the waist deep water of the bathing pool with her long, honey blonde hair draped over her modest chest.

"Please come join me," she said.

Mark stepped into the warm water and walked over to her. He stopped when he got within arm's length. He searched her topaz blue eyes for a sign of a button, but found nothing. He didn't think Jane would use a button on her because they generate a lot of radio that the Sapanites could detect, but to be honest, he didn't know that much about the technology.

"This isn't social," she said. "I just needed to talk to you."

"So, you're not going to scrub my back?" Mark asked.

"Please, I'm taking a risk being here."

Mark took the soap and the wash cloth from her. He noticed that the soap was the greasy, inferior soap that they'd gotten when he first arrived.

"Jane has been arrested," Sigríður said.

"Okay, what happens after that?"

"She will be held until the day after tomorrow, and then she and the other prisoners will be sent to the arena."

Mark scrubbed his chest and underarms.

"What happens in the arena?" Mark asked.

"She and others will be put into a pit with a moravi. Anyone who makes it across to the gate at the far side is determined innocent and outcast."

"Really," Mark said.

He rubbed the soapy rag through his hair.

"You don't sound too upset," Sigríður said.

"Can you get a message to her?"

"No, I'm a pax, not a custodiae. It would create too many questions."

"Do you know why I was searched so carefully today?"

"They're searching everyone more thoroughly. Informants say someone is trying to bring in taba root."

"Isn't that poison?" Mark asked.

"Only if too much is taken," Sigríður said. "In small amounts it's like drinking whiskey. It helps you forget for a while."

"What's it worth?"

"I didn't come here to discuss taba root," Sigríður said firmly. "You are my only hope of getting out of here, and I need you to know I had nothing to do with Jane's arrest."

Someone walked into the bathhouse, so Mark gestured for her to turn around. He scrubbed her back with the wash cloth.

"I believe you," Mark whispered. "Can you fly one of their airships?"

She nodded yes.

"I know they are trying to kill me, so the best thing for me to do is die, but I may need your help."

She pulled away, looked at him like he was crazy, rinsed off, and left the pool. A woman with shoulder-length platinum blonde hair, beige skin, and a modest build entered the pool. The two women avoided looking at each other as they passed. She walked over to Mark and turned around.

"You can scrub my back if you like," she said.

As soon as Mark finished his bath, he passed through the public square. The microdot was still on the tree, just above the knot. So, either Jane didn't receive the message, or she didn't have time to act on it before she was arrested.

When Muirgel came back from the library, she took him to the public house near the front gate and bought him dinner and two bottles of cervisia. She questioned him again, and he told her that he fell asleep on the mattress, but when he awoke, he was on the edge of the vent and a well- placed rock had prevented him from falling in.

She asked him about the moravi, and he said he didn't see any. He saw their tracks and the ruined mattress, but he didn't see them. She questioned him about it right up to the night bell.

The next morning, they followed their usual routine. While they were eating breakfast, Mark asked if he could return one of her soup bowls, so he could have soup for lunch. She found one that she had been using to store something that resembled dried peas, emptied it out, and gave it to him.

Mark started his route, but when he got to the first outhouse, he went inside and regurgitated half of the taba root which was enough to fill the bowl. He added a microdot on the lid, and took it to the soup vendor in the public square at lunch time. Her hazel eyes widened a little when she saw him.

"I would like you to deliver this bowl with some of your finest soup to a friend of mine," Mark said.

"I don't do deliveries."

Mark slid the lid open and she looked inside.

"Except for my finest customers," she said.

"You'll get the other half when delivery of the bowl is confirmed by my friend."

She smiled, set his bowl aside, and made him a fresh bowl of soup. He took it and left.

Mark finished his route, and took the outhouse sludge out of the city. As he reached the kuja farms, pandemonium erupted. Some of the farmers ran toward him, others picked up makeshift weapons and formed a line, while others continued working. As people rushed past him, he found the compost pile and emptied his cart. A horn sounded, and he saw what was causing the chaos. Two moravi stood on the edge of the field, each feeding on a kuja farmer.

As soon as the horn had sounded, those who were still working stopped and moved toward the wall in an orderly retreat. Once everyone passed through the line, they fell back toward the river. Mark was the last one to cross the bridge. As soon as he reached the other side, the bridge retracted, and the farmers queued up to be admitted to the city. One or two of them were crying, but the rest of them acted as though they were waiting for a bus.

Mark turned to the red-haired woman who stood in line beside him.

"Does this happen often?"

"Yes," she said.

"Ever think about putting traps in the field?"

"You're the surface dweller everyone has been talking about, right?"

Mark nodded.

"When our Lord and Protector, Kaxuth, deems it necessary, that will be done, but questioning our ways is sedition. Sedition gets you sent to the arena, so please keep your ideas to yourself."

She turned away from Mark and went to stand with another group. When his turn came, his cart was searched, and he was admitted as usual. Things in Murus seemed normal. If he hadn't been outside when the attack occurred, he would have thought the farmers had just ended a little early.

He went to the bathhouse to get cleaned up. Since the field hands returned early, he had to wait in line. The soup vendor was ahead of him in line, and they made eye contact. She shook her head 'no' once and looked away. He bathed and when he got back to Muirgel's house, she was waiting for him.

"A couple of pax came to see me," she said.

"What did they want?" Mark asked. "Abby Hobson filed a sedition complaint against you. If you weren't on probation, you would have been sent to the rack."

"Who's Abby Hobson?"

"Short, red-haired woman," Muirgel said. "She turned you in to the pax at the gate. She said you were questioning how our Lord Protector handled the moravi in the field."

"I just asked about using traps," Mark said.

"I understand you meant well," she said. "But you have to understand any ideas that challenge any order given by our Lord Protector are sedition."

"So, it is best I not talk to people," Mark said.

"Yes," Muirgel said. "If you have a question about Murus, it is best that you ask me. You can tell me anything."

"I'm sorry," Mark said. "This place is going to take a lot of getting used to."

She took Mark by the hand and guided him to the bed. She sat down next to him and looked him in the eyes.

"That isn't everything they told me," Muirgel said. "The woman you came here with has been charged with sedition. She was warned twice and sent to the rack once, but she refused to comply."

"That sounds like Jane," Mark said.

"Despite being on probation, she has been deemed a disruptive influence and sent to the arena."

She held him and explained how the arena operated, and that there was a chance that Jane could escape. She told him to bury his pain and try and disassociate himself with her. If anyone asked about her, say that it was for the good of the state.

She went to her counter top, opened a cupboard, and took out two huge, blue-speckled eggs. She handed Mark a cutting board, and he finely chopped a red carrot-like vegetable and two purple celery-like vegetables.

She beat the eggs in a bowl, and then turned two spring-loaded valves that delivered a measured amount of two liquids to a chamber inside the box. Thirty-eight seconds later, the top of the box was two-hundred-and seventy-five degrees Fahrenheit. She added the chopped vegetables to the bowl, stirred, and five and a half minutes later Mark had the strangest omelet of his life. He just wished he could taste it.

Over dinner, they shared a bottle of cervisia, and she told him he was to stay in the city tomorrow and clean the library floors. The arena was scheduled to begin after midday meal, and he was expected to attend. She let him finish the bottle and they got into bed and waited for the night bell. Once Muirgel was asleep, Mark continued adjusting the dials on Kak's watch. On his 10,438th try, he found a setting that worked. The cover of the watch flashed, and he saw an image. The image was a kuja plant just outside the gate. He adjusted the outer dial and lost the image, but when he adjusted the inner dial, the image became a spot of dark water in the underground ocean. He learned to adjust the inner dial and the tiny touchpad at the bottom, and he was able to direct the field of his vision.

It took a little practice, but he found the arena, and he searched the holding cells for Jane. He found her sitting alone in her cell. Her dress was dirty, but she looked fine. She was fashioning a sling from her sandal straps and a piece of her dress. There were ten cells in the arena cellblock, and four of them were occupied.

He searched the Office of Public Good for signs of the illusive Kaxuth, and found none. He found the First Minister asleep in her massive bed. On her desk sat a device that resembled a primitive computer. The wall above the keyboard had a device that resembled a hexagonal television set. It had been left on, and images of Murus flashed across the screen. One image caught Mark's attention. A room that reminded him of a NASA control room filled with Sapanites who sat at work stations looking at images from various places in Subterra. This confirmed Mark's suspicion that the Sapanites used hidden technology to keep the human population under control. It also confirmed that the illusive Lord Kaxuth wasn't on the island, but made his will known remotely.

He found Sigríður sleeping alone in the pax dormitory outside the Office of Public Good. Her room was the size of a walk-in closet with barely enough room for a bed.

Mark put the watch away just before the morning bell. After breakfast and bathing, he went to the library with Muirgel. She gave him a mop, bucket, and soap and told him to clean the third floor. He went down to the public fountain for water, and a woman with jet black hair, jade green eyes, and ivory skin filled her bucket as well. She looked to be about four or five months pregnant.

"The delivery wasn't made, but I do have a message."

"What is it?" Mark asked.

"Fourteen-point-three when you see me," she said.

Mark nodded his thanks and once he made sure his bucket wasn't dripping, he returned to the library. As he finished scrubbing the third floor, Muirgel came in and told him it was time to leave.

They left the building together and followed the crowd toward the arena. She held his hand as they entered the arena, and he noticed that he was surrounded by pax. Two officers walked behind him and one on either side of him, so he wasn't sure if he was being escorted or arrested.

The arena reminded him of the Coliseum in Rome except for the evenly spaced kuja plants lighting up the field. There was a large gate to the outside at the far end of the field, and the field contained a maze-like structure of stone obstacles and plants that prevented someone from running directly for the gate. Mark doubted if someone on the field could even see the gate.

They sat on the hard, stone seats in the fifth row up from the arena, and Mark noticed that the pax that had followed him in were all sitting nearby. Muirgel squeezed his hand and whispered in his ear.

"You must sit and watch. You are not permitted to get up for any reason until the spectacle is over. Any interference will get you sent to the arena."

She put her arm around him and whispered.

"I know this will be difficult for you to watch, but you must not react in any way."

He turned to her and nodded. They sat in silence for the next seven minutes and eight seconds, then a wooden staircase was rolled out, and put next to a platform on the field. The First Minister walked out on to the field and climbed up the stairs. She spoke about how the spectacle protected the people of Murus by purging the influences that would bring them all to ruin. Then she read the name and the individual charges of each convict. As the charge was read, the convict was pushed onto the field.

Geina Norina, a brown-haired woman, was convicted of possession of contraband. Brigand Romola, blond haired man, was convicted of conspiracy. Jane Aaron was convicted of producing illicit goods and inciting public unrest, and Olympia Countess, a blonde woman, was convicted of sedition.

Mark noticed something on the horizon. He enhanced his vision, and saw a Sapanite airship approaching. A moravi dangled on a cable under the airship. Based on the speed, he realized it would be there in about three minutes.

He turned his attention back to Jane. She found him in the crowd, and they made eye contact. He opened a communication port at 14.3mhz, and put together an encrypted, burst transmission for her. He told her the moravi react to smell, and since she was a Gamma class android and didn't smell like a human, the moravi should ignore her. He also sent her a diagram of the field, a map to the thermal vent, and details he'd gathered about the abandoned city.

He used the microwave emitter in his right hand to send the message in a narrow pulse that lasted a tenth of a second. A second and a half later, Jane smiled and gave him a thumbs up.

She sent him an encrypted, burst transmission on the same frequency, and she asked him to retrieve her backpack, particularly the dress with the button.

The First Minister continued to prattle on about the spectacle demonstrating the compassion that the Sapanites had for their human children by protecting them from influences that were counter-productive to group harmony.

She said sacrificing a few disloyal citizens was a small price to pay for the continued safety and wellbeing of Murus. Last, she said that their names would no longer be spoken, and they would all be quickly forgotten, but the lesson of their sacrifice would be remembered because Murus would live on and the justice of the arena was above question.

No one spoke or took their eyes off the field as she left the podium, climbed down the steps, and took her place in a luxurious, red chair high up in the stands. As soon as she sat down, she gestured to the airship, and the moravi was dropped onto the field. The airship peeled off, and the moravi oriented itself on the field.

Geina screamed. The moravi turned toward the sound. Jane remained still, but the others ran. The giant bird sniffed the air and ran toward them. It passed by Jane to chase down Brigand. It only took four seconds for it to overtake him, and strike him in the back with its massive beak. Jane turned away and walked calmly toward the open gate, while the other ladies ran from obstacle to obstacle, and the moravi held Brigand down with a massive foot and pulled him apart limb by limb.

It only took the moravi a minute and fifty-four seconds to tear apart and consume Brigand, and then it turned its attention to the ladies. It sniffed the air and moved toward Olympia, who managed to evade the moravi for a minute and twenty-three seconds. Then it cornered her, and a slash from its front claws ended her.

By now, Jane was more than halfway to the gate. She walked calmly, and used the obstacles between her and the moravi to mask her movement. Since everyone's attention was on the moravi, no one noticed her until she sprinted across the open ground to the gate.

Jane reached the gate at roughly the same time the moravi had finished with Olympia. As Jane stepped though, two men confronted her. They wore uniforms similar to those of the pax, so Mark assumed they were custodiae. Since the men blocked Jane's path, it became clear that this was a game the players were not permitted to win.

A silent cheer broke out in the crowd as Jane kicked one of them in the groin hard enough to lift him off his feet, and in the same fluid motion grab his dolor and use it on the other custodiae. Then she grabbed each of them in turn and threw them onto the field before running through the gate disappearing from sight.

The moravi was attracted by the motion, and ran across the field to where the men lay recovering.

Mark noticed more than a few smiles on the faces of the crowd as the two men were dispatched and consumed. Afterward, the moravi ran through the open gate.

This left Geina on the field alone. The First Minister ordered her to be taken, but the pax refused, saying that no one may interfere with the games. Since the moravi left the arena, she declared that the games were over. The arena was evacuated, and Geina was taken into custody.

As they were herded out of the arena by the pax, Mark noticed that the mood of the crowd was silent and tense. It seemed like everyone wanted to do something, but no one wanted to be the first one to do it. Muirgel held his hand until they were home, and she didn't speak until the door to her tiny house was closed.

"That was bad," she said.

"Jane got away," Mark said. "I thought it was great."

"She defied their authority and lived. That is something the Sapanites won't tolerate. They will have to publicly demonstrate their authority. Which means, things are going to be difficult."

"Difficult, how?"

"More security checks, more investigations, and more prosecutions of anyone who challenges Sapanite authority."

She drew a breath and tears welled up in her eyes. She sat on her bed and put her hands up to her face.

"All we can do is pray," she said.

Mark's jaw dropped in surprise. As she sat on her bed, quietly reciting the Lord's Prayer. He held her, and he prayed with her until the night bell rang, and she fell asleep.

Once she was asleep, he used her body to keep his watch out of sight, just in case a Sapanite came by for another roll call. He looked around the city and found the cause for the alarm. Based on the graffiti and broken windows he saw, some of the citizens had protested Geina's arrest. Someone had written "Mors tyrannis," or death to tyrants on main entrance to the Office of Public Good. The Pax office had two broken windows, and the office itself was in disarray. Since no one was on the ground sleeping, Mark realized that it must have been a hit and run attack.

He looked inside the Office of Public Good, and he found the First Minister in her office. She wore a brass helmet that covered her head except for an opening for her eyes, nose, and mouth. She spoke to a Sapanite on a hexagonal television screen, and the conversation didn't seem to be going well for her.

The Sapanite on the screen, who Mark assumed to be Kaxuth, sat back and seemed to be considering what the first minister had said. Mark wished he had come into the conversation earlier. Kaxuth leaned forward in his chair and criticized the First Minister for being publicly cruel. By violating the justice of the arena, she destroyed the illusion of fairness and justice. Therefore, she was responsible for this rebellion. He ordered that Geina be released as an outcast and those in custody be racked and released. She was warned that if the rebellion didn't end quickly, she would face the arena.

The call ended abruptly, and the First Minister cried for three minutes. Then she went upstairs to her bedroom, undressed, took off her helmet, and got into bed.

Mark didn't know what to think. On some level he wanted to feel sorry for Lamere because she was being forced to carry out Kaxuth's wishes, but on the other hand, she had no problem killing innocent people if it meant she stayed in control.

He searched the island for Jane. He checked the volcanic vent where he dumped the trash, but didn't see her. He explored the ruined city, but he didn't see any sign of her.

He followed the river to where it emptied into the fresh-water ocean. He discovered a bend in the river with human bones along the riverbank, and realized that this was where the bodies put in the river ended up. He reversed and followed it back upstream to its origin, a large hot spring. Water from the ocean was heated and went up through a volcanic vent to where it boiled out to cool back down and became the river.

Mark searched back in the direction that the airship carrying the moravi came from, and he found the Sapanite breeding ground for the moravi. It looked like a cattle ranch, but with better fencing and protection for the humans who operated it. The layout of the ranch was a little unusual. It was surrounded by fields of red and purple vegetation and laid out in a triangle. He could see that on the first side of the ranch they raised daeodons, presumably to feed the moravi. The second side was where the moravi were allowed to mature, and the last side was where the eggs were incubated.

A modern hexagonal building with stainless steel walls and electric power stood in the center of the ranch. An airship was parked on its roof, and the building contained living and working areas for the humans who ran the ranch. A steel watchtower stood on each of the three corners of the ranch making it look like a prison.

Mark spotted movement in the water north of the ranch. He moved over that spot and found a pod of plesiosaurs feeding on a school of shrimp. He was fascinated by them, but they weren't what he was looking for.

He took another look at the river to try and determine where Jane had climbed out. He reexamined the river and found a spot where the vegetation had been disturbed. He searched in a spiral pattern from that point, and he found a well-hidden cave. Inside, Jane sat on a stone throne with a banquet table in front of her. Banquet tables formed a large square in the room, and the outcasts celebrated with music, dancing, and a lot of drinking.

Mark surmised that the walls of the cave must be shielding them from the night bell. Otherwise, they would all be asleep. He explored the cave, now that he knew Jane was okay. He found family dwellings, workshops, stores, and even a restaurant. The cave was actually a small community.

Muirgel stirred, and Mark realized that it was almost morning, or what passed for morning down there. Mark put his watch away, and waited for the morning bell. When it rang, it took Muirgel three minutes to awaken.

They didn't say much to each other as they ate the blue bread she had purchased the night before. Mark was about to say something comforting, but he saw Sigríður through the window standing under a large-leafed tree. She wasn't wearing her pax uniform, but the same tan, low cut dress that everyone else wore. Mark shoved the last of his bread into his mouth.

"I should get an early start," Mark said. "I don't want them complaining about the quality of my work."

Muirgel forced a smile.

"I'll see you tonight then," she said.

"Today is local pickup."

Mark kissed her on the cheek and went out to his cart. When he got to his cart, he pushed it in Sigríður's direction, nodded toward the closest privy, and turned toward it. Sigríður left walked quickly around the adjacent house and entered the privy just before Mark. He parked his cart near the entrance, marked the privy as closed for cleaning, grabbed his bucket, brushes, and rags, and entered.

"What's wrong?" Mark asked.

She got close enough to him to whisper.

"You're going to be arrested today," she said. "We have to go."

She went over and sat on the privy seat.

"Really," Mark said. "On what charge?"

"Growing surface plants," she said. "Now keep working in case we're being watched."

Mark shrugged and got down on his hands and knees and started dry brushing the floor.

"Didn't know that was a crime," he said.

"It wasn't until this morning," she said.

"What will happen?"

"You will be taken to the Ministry of Public Good and racked."

"Okay, not fun."

Sigríður swallowed.

"You are to be given fifty lashes," she said. "Most people can't survive more than twenty."

"So, you're saying they are going to kill me today."

She nodded.

"Well, I've been dead before."

She rolled her eyes at him.

"Do you know what happened to Jane's backpack?" Mark asked.

Sigríður bit her lip to keep from shouting.

"I just told you you're going to die today, and you're asking about your wife's clothes!"

Mark started scrubbing the area by her feet.

"You said you wanted to escape, right? Well, I can't do that if they're watching me. The only way to get them to stop watching me is to fake my death."

"What do you mean?" she asked.

"They put the bodies of the people who die here in the river, only in my case, I won't be dead."

"No one can survive fifty lashes," Sigríður said.

"It won't be fun, but I can handle it. I have some taba root to kill the pain."

Mark smiled.

"Now, do you know what happened to Jane's things?"

"She was outcast," Sigríður said. "By law her possessions will be given to the outcasts the next time they come to trade."

"How long do I have before I'm arrested?"

"The order was signed after the day bell, but it won't be executed until the pax on patrol come in for a meal break. No more than a couple of hours."

"Thanks," Mark said.

"This is insane," Sigríður said. "Our only hope is to walk out with the kuja farmers. Make our way to the edge of the field, and escape."

"What about the moravi?" Mark asked. "They just released more of them around the city."

She narrowed her eyes.

"The towers in the field aren't for spotting the moravi. They're there to prevent escape. The Sapanites control the moravi, and they send them to attack escapees and outcasts."

"How do you know?"

"I saw it myself," Mark said.

She sighed and got up.

"If I'm questioned about this meeting, I'll tell them we are having an affair."

"We don't have affairs down here," she said. "But I understand what you mean."

"Get back to where you're supposed to be, and I'll send for you when I have some sort of plan."

He gestured toward the door.

"How will you send for me?" she asked.

"When you hear thunder, I'll be close by."

"You mean gunfire?"

She gestured toward Mark's Fort Worth Special.

"Yes," Mark said.

"What's your plan?"

"I honestly don't know yet."

The conversation paused and a woman with shoulder-length, honey blonde hair, blue eyes, and a very stern looking mouth opened the door. She wore a pax uniform and kept her hand on her dolor. Mark stopped scrubbing and looked up at her.

"It's closed for cleaning, but you can use it if you really need to," Mark said.

Mark gestured toward Sigríður.

"No," she said.

She glanced around and then left. Mark was grateful that she didn't seem to notice that his bucket didn't have water in it.

Sigríður visibly relaxed when the door closed. She waited for forty seconds and then left without saying anything.

He dry-scrubbed the entire floor, wiped it down with the rags, and left. He got his shovel and went around back and scooped the waste into his cart.

He took his cart back to Muirgel's to find that she had gone to work. He got his watch, scrambled the dials, wrapped it in one of her old dresses, and put it inside a soup bowl. Then he put it, along with his gun into the backpack, along with his surface clothes and shoes, coin purse, and his vitalibri.

He weighed it with his right arm, and was happy with the result. He hoped that the bowl and the clothes would protect the watch from the impact and the water.

He turned the table on its side, upturned the chairs, pulled the covers off the bed, and opened all of the cupboards to make it look like it had been searched. When he finished, he took one last look around and then left.

He put his backpack into his cart and covered it with the tarp. After stopping at the fountain for water, he broke from his normal route of privy cleaning, and went to the one behind the Office of Public Good. It was the one closest to the river.

Mark parked his cart behind the privy and looked around. He used his infra-red sensors, and as near as he could tell, he wasn't being observed. He grabbed his backpack from the cart and in a single fluid motion, flung it over the wall. A second and a half later, he heard the faint sound of the splash.

He cleaned the privy as usual, and then he cleaned three others before he was confronted by two pax as he pushed his cart along the gravel walkway. A stocky blond pax, who stood five feet tall, but seemed to compensate for his lack of height with bulging muscles, blocked his path. Mark glanced behind him, and a second pax, a woman whose coal black hair offset her alabaster skin and dark brown eyes stepped up behind him.

"Excuse me officer," Mark said. "You're blocking my path."

"You're going to have to come with us," he said.

"Why?" Mark asked. "I've been scrubbing the . . ."

The woman stabbed him in the hip with her dolor before he could finish his sentence. The pain was intense, and Mark didn't block it because he wanted his reaction to seem genuine. He fell to his knees and started to sob, and she shocked him again, so he pretended to pass out.

They carried him to the Ministry of Public Good, stripped him down, tied him to a rack, and left him alone for thirty-nine minutes.

The First Minister entered wearing her full ceremonial robes of blue and gold. She read the charges from a sheet of elongated hexagonal, yellow paper.

"Our Lord Kaxuth has decreed that you will have been found guilty of misuse of waste materials, growing surface plants, and inciting others to rebellion. The penalty for these deeds will be fifty lashes."

She stopped reading for a moment and glanced up at Mark. He gave her the finger with his right hand, but since it was secured to the rack she didn't seem to notice. Mark knew the gesture was lost on her, but he felt like he should do something defiant.

"Should you survive the lashes, you will be sent to the arena where you will face the judgment of the moravi. Our Lord has spoken."

"Obedience is strength," Mark said.

The First Minister paused for a moment. Looked Mark in the eyes, and repeated.

"Obedience is strength."

She left and the stocky, blond man entered and began giving Mark lashes with a whip. Mark endured the first five without readjusting his pain sensors. Then he reduced the pain by five percent each lash. By the time he had received thirty lashes, he wasn't feeling anything. He opened his internal system menu, and navigated through the submenus like Jane had showed him.

Since he was an Omega class android, he was designed to pose as human and react like a human, so he had a simulated death subroutine. He activated it, and he felt his heart flutter and stop. Every muscle in his body went limp, and he emptied his bladder on the floor.

He could hear what was going on, but he couldn't see or move. The burly pax gave him three more lashes before he figured out that he wasn't reacting.

Mark heard him step over, but since he had lost all feeling and vision, he had no idea what he was doing to him. He heard the door open and close. He came back a few moments later with the First Minister. She asked if he was sure. Then he heard a knife being removed from its sheath. Mark's internal sensor registered a penetration near his right kidney. Then he heard her say that the wound wasn't bleeding, so he was dead.

The door opened and closed again, and he was left alone for three hours and twenty-two minutes. Then he was untied, carried to the river, and thrown in. He heard the splash his body made, and the sounds of the rushing water. He waited for five minutes before he restarted his systems. He got his vision back first, but he couldn't see much because he was facing the river bottom. His heart restarted, and he got control of his muscles back. He flipped over and swam around the bottom of the river.

He spent the next five hours and fifty-one minutes searching the bottom of the river for his backpack. He had his nanites repair the damage to his back and kidney as he searched. He finally found his backpack lying up against a large rock in the river. He let the current carry him down to the bend where the human remains had accumulated and he climbed out of the river, got dressed in his surface clothes, and went looking for Jane.

Chapter Eleven
The Discovery

Finding the hidden cave of the outcasts was harder than he thought. He walked around for three hours and forty-four minutes until he found the rock outcropping he saw in his watch. Then he realized that if he wanted the First Minister and the Sapanites to think he was dead, going to the outcasts may not be the best thing for him to do.

When he asked Sigríður about the taba root, she said an informant told them that someone was trying to smuggle it into the city, but Phaenna wasn't arrested. That means whoever the informant was, he or she didn't know who tried to bring it in, only that someone left a bag for him to pick up. That would mean the informant was an outcast.

Mark changed direction and walked toward the volcanic vent. He stayed off the main road and used his thermal sensors to watch for moravi. When he got to the vent, it was just as he had left it.

He jumped down into the vent, went to the control room, and unpacked. He opened the soup bowl and found that the dress and watch were still dry. The moisture-resistant paper of the vitalibri did its job, and it too had survived being in the river. Mark set it up on its spine to let it dry out.

He used the watch to check on Jane. He found her in the cave's central chamber, surrounded by outcasts like a librarian at story time. She was telling them about her escape from Murus. Once he knew Jane was okay, he finished making his knife and started making bullets.

He looked through the metal refuse for anything made of lead, but couldn't find anything. He ended up casting them out of iron with aluminum jackets. Iron wouldn't have the impact force that lead would, but it would have more penetrating ability, particularly against the moravi's Kevlar feathers.

He used his remaining bullet as a model, and even with the help of his advanced technology, and the skills he'd picked up during the Civil War, it took him three tries to make a set of bullets that worked.

Then he took a look at the steam generators. He unclogged a steam pipe and swapped parts with the broken ones to get one working. He was careful to be sure it was disconnected from the energy grid before he turned it on. Once he got it working, he sent the power to the lights in the control room, a few of which still functioned.

Once his vitalibri had dried out, he chronicled the story of his escape from Murus. In this version however, he found ten platinum coins in a privy and used them to bribe the burly pax to give him enough taba to simulate his death. Mark added details about stitching up the wound to his kidney and almost drowning in the river.

He added a description of the abandoned city with sketches of the monuments and buildings.

As he wrote the details of the city and how he hid from the moravi, he heard a noise in the volcanic vent.

He used Kak's watch, and found an airship parked near the vent. A crew of humans who wore the blue coveralls of the mainland worked to erect a new sleeping hut. They threw the pieces of the old hut and the ruined cart into the vent. Mark kept an eye on them until they had finished.

When the airship left, he used Kak's watch to follow it back to the mainland. Then, he spent the next six hours exploring the Sapanite city. The city itself was laid out in a series of triangularly shaped districts. Six triangles formed a hexagon, with three additional triangles attached to the sides for a total of nine districts. Each district was subdivided into three smaller zones. The zones were all interconnected with light rail and a series of walkways. Mark looked, but he couldn't find anything resembling an automobile. The closest thing they had to that was their airships, and he only saw a handful of those.

He learned that the state of their technology was fairly advanced. The city was powered by geothermal energy carried by a network of underground cables. They had an advanced network of computers, but no hand-held devices. Everything was wired with almost no electromagnetic noise. Since Murus was alive with overlapping data signals, Mark had to conclude that the Sapanites had radio, but chose only to use it in areas where humans lived.

The Sapanites mixed agriculture and technology to the point where there wasn't an urban center and rural farms, but an odd mix of the two. Multi-story buildings stood next to a field of purple plants and a lake of tube worms. The only exception to this was the ranches where they raised their livestock. Those were kept far away from the cities.

He crossed over the fence and looked at how the Sapanites lived, but since he didn't speak the language, or understand the customs, he had no context to know what they were doing. They had what appeared to be office space where they typed on oddly-shaped keyboards and looked at hexagonal screens, factories where they produced parts he didn't recognize, and medical centers where they treated their sick and injured with technologies alien to him.

He did notice that humans and Sapanites didn't mix. There were zones for humans and zones for Sapanites. A series of gates, fences, and walls kept the two apart.

Life inside the human areas wasn't quite as rosy as it was for the Sapanites. They worked ten-hour days, and didn't converse much during working hours. They didn't have much technology. They lived in large dormitories with electric lights, but only had state-approved media, books, and card games for entertainment.

He looked inside some of the human public buildings, but he didn't see anything useful. He found a school, took a look inside, and saw a group of a dozen children reading in the library.

The uniforms they wore were much more conservative than what the adults wore. Both the girls and the boys wore pants and pullover shirts. The shirts all had the Sapanite symbol embroidered on the right side. Some of the sleeves had some kind of rank symbols on them. From the vitalibri he had read, he knew the higher the rank the more likely a classmate had betrayed someone for a minor infraction because betrayal was rewarded. None of them made a sound as they read. It was eerie, like something out of a horror movie. The most advanced thing he saw in the human school was a manual typewriter.

Mark heard a knock at the back door. He turned off Kak's watch and went to open it. Jane stood there wearing her dress with the special button over her leather pants. Her hair had been cut, but otherwise she looked unchanged. He gave her a hug and a kiss, which she accepted reluctantly.

"You are so human," she said.

"What's up with you?" Mark asked.

"Sorry," Jane said. "Murus reminded me a little too much of Mars."

"Yes, I found the forced copulation and constant surveillance to be annoying as well."

"At least you got to get out of the city for a while. I was stuck working ten-hour shifts doing laundry, making soap, and running the weaving machines."

"Did they try to kill you?" Mark asked.

"Three times."

"Me too!"

Jane smiled and Mark laughed.

"I know it isn't funny, but somehow it is," Mark said. "Oh, did you ask me to bring you taba root?"

"What's taba root?"

Mark held out his hand and barfed up the rest of the taba, along with the blue bread, he had been keeping in his esophagus into his hand.

"No, that's disgusting," Jane said.

"It's what Charlotte used to end her life."

"No, why would I want that?"

"In smaller doses it has analgesic qualities."

"Really? Who told you that?"

"Sigríður."

"I thought you wanted to bash her face in?" Jane asked.

"I did. Things change."

"So, what have you been up to?"

"I made more bullets for my gun, and I figured out how to use Kak's watch. How about you?"

"Not much, I'm afraid. I found a series of overlapping signals for their camera network, made a few new outcast friends, but everyone down here seems to have some serious trust issues."

She leaned up against a consol.

"Why didn't you come find me as soon as you escaped?"

"I did look for you," Mark said. "But then I realized that I'm dead, and I wanted to stay that way for a while."

"What do you mean?"

Mark took the taba in his hand and dropped it onto the consol. Then he cleaned his hand with Muirgel's old dress.

"Phaenna told me to pick up a bag of taba and bring it to her, but from your message, I knew not to trust her. When I got back to Murus, my cart was searched, particularly the place where she told me to hide it. At first, I thought that Phaenna had set me up for some kind of reward, but Sigríður said all the informant knew was someone was trying to smuggle in taba."

"So, that means the informant was an outcast who knew a drop was made, but not who picked it up," Jane said.

"Exactly," Mark said. "If I showed up at the outcast cave, the First Minister would know I was alive."

"Okay," Jane asked. "What's the advantage of staying dead?"

"If I'm dead, the Sapanites aren't going to be looking for me, and I can move around more freely."

"Good point," Jane said.

"How about you?" Mark asked. "Are you going back to the outcasts?"

"I have to," Jane said. "They're starving. They only let me out because I told them I would bring back food."

"Do they have a problem eating moravi?" Mark asked.

"No," Jane asked. "Why should they?"

"Just asking?"

Mark opened up his vitalibri, skipped a few pages, and drew a map of the island. Then he drew an expanded map of the moravi ranch.

"When Trausti said the Sapanites bred the moravi to kill humans, he wasn't exaggerating."

"The question we've been avoiding is what are we going to do about it?" Jane asked.

"I'm starting to think Murus is more than a human breeding ground. It may be a testing facility to see if the Sapanites can control the humans on the surface."

"What do you mean?"

"What would happen if the Sapanites were to set up moravi ranches on the surface in remote areas, breed a few thousand of them, and release them?"

"They would find their way into populated areas and attack," Jane said. "But people would fight back."

"I'm sure they would, but the moravi would be able to increase their numbers by feeding on the surface animals, before encountering people," Mark said.

"So eventually, they would overwhelm the human resistance, and people would be forced to fall back to places like Murus," Jane said.

"Yes," Mark said. "Places the Sapanites could easily control."

"Again," Jane asked. "What are we going to do about it?"

"Right now, nothing. I want to gather as much intelligence as I can before I make a move. I would love to build some mortars and blow the moravi ranch to Hell, but I don't know how the Sapanites would react."

"I'm okay with you taking a few weeks to plan, but just remember what Grant said, 'when a general tries not to get anyone killed, he gets everyone killed.'"

"What does that mean?" Mark asked.

"If we have to sacrifice the people down here to save the ones up there, I'm okay with that."

Mark narrowed his eyes and frowned.

"You've said it yourself. It's either the death of thousands now, or the death of millions later."

"Yes," he said. "But in that situation, I was letting history take its natural course. This situation is different. I don't have a historical guide to rely on."

"Mark, I would love for there to be a solution where the humans are freed, the moravi are extinct, and everyone lives happily, but that outcome isn't too likely," Jane said.

"I see your point," Mark said. "The people of Murus are very close to open rebellion now. It wouldn't take much to push them over the edge."

"And a good rebellion would go a long way toward covering our escape."

"I still have no idea how to get us out of here," Mark said. "Do you have any thoughts on that score?"

"No," Jane said.

"I thought about putting a button on the First Minister," Mark said.

"So did I, but a button generates a lot of radio on frequencies that the Sapanites use for their surveillance, it would be detected."

"Yeah, that's what I thought."

"You know the hub for their transmission network is behind the Ministry of Public Good, right?"

"No, I didn't know that."

"Most of the radio traffic is one direction to the hub, but every once in a while, they will send a signal out to adjust a camera. I traced them back to a room in the rear of the Office of Public Good. From there the signals are sent by a hard-wire connection to the mainland."

"So, if we take out that room?"

"The Sapanites will be blind to what is going on here."

"What are you thinking, that we should plant a bomb?"

"I'm not thinking anything right now," Jane said. "I'm just saying if a rebellion of any kind is going to succeed, we have to terminate that connection."

"Have you been tapping into their feed?"

"I tried, but I couldn't make sense out of their signal matrix."

"How could you use your receiver in stealth mode?" Mark asked.

"Mark, I am a Gamma class android. I don't have stealth mode. I have to individually turn my systems off, so I can also choose to turn them back on individually."

"Do you think you can locate their cameras?" Mark asked.

"I can go through the data I've gathered and I should be able to locate most of them, why?"

"I'm hoping to find a few blind spots," Mark said.

"Well, it's been great catching up with you, but I told them I'd bring back some food," Jane said.

Mark thought about it for a moment.

"How about fish? There's plenty of material to make a net near the vent."

Jane nodded, so Mark led her out into the cave with the volcanic vent. They dug through the refuse until they found the discarded cloth remnants from the weavers. They untangled it as they gathered it. Then, they took it back to the other room and tied the strips together to form a rope.

"I think this is why the First Minister is so adamant that garbage be picked up," Mark said.

"To prevent people from making nets?"

"To prevent people from making weapons or anything that might improve their lives."

Mark gestured toward the new knife on his gun belt.

"They do seem intent upon keeping everyone miserable," Jane said.

"What got you arrested?" Mark asked.

"I made a bra without the express permission of Lord Kaxuth," Jane said.

Mark smiled and nodded.

"I was arrested for growing strawberries," Mark said.

Once they had finished knotting the rope, they began forming the net.

"How did you escape?" Jane asked.

"When I was arrested, I was taken to be racked, so I used my simulated death subroutine."

"Really," Jane said. "No trouble navigating your systems?"

"I wasn't as elegant as you would have been, but I got there."

"How were you able to keep your gun?"

"When Sigríður told me I was going to be arrested, I went back to Muirgel's house, packed my stuff, and threw my backpack into the river."

"Won't they notice your stuff is gone?"

"I made it look like the pax searched her house. Why report something to the pax, if the pax are the ones who did it?"

"I hope it works," Jane said.

"Me too."

Jane tied the last knot in the net.

"Well, thank you for this. I've got some fishing to do. I'll wait until I'm at the nearest point to the outcast cave before I start. That way the smell of the fish won't attract the moravi."

"Good thinking," Mark said.

"How did you know they hunted by smell?" Jane asked.

"I figured it out that the smell of the ash from the volcanic vent was covering my body odor. That was why they didn't attack me."

"So, your boyish need to explore once again saved your life," Jane said.

Mark smiled and walked her to the door.

"I believe the social custom is to give your departing wife a kiss," Jane said.

"That isn't too human?" Mark asked.

She grabbed his collar, pulled him in, and gave him a quick kiss. She transmitted a map of the camera locations in Murus along with a message not to do anything stupid. She turned away, and he watched her climb the stairs to the surface. Then he closed and locked the door.

He sat in the control room's center chair and spent the next three days exploring the island with Kak's watch. He looked in on Murus and found that the new waste collector was someone he had seen working as a kuja farmer. Mark wondered what she did to earn the honor of being a waste collector, but he made sure to stay out of the vent while she was there.

He decided to explore the foundations of the abandoned city, and he discovered that some of them had basements. One basement was left untouched since the city was abandoned because the stairwell leading to it was blocked. Since the basement was completely dark, he couldn't be sure what was in it. The only way he could tell that it was there at all was that he got a slightly different type of black displayed on Kak's watch when he looked at the basement than he did when he looked at the dirt around it.

Mark went to the building and found out why the basement was still sealed. The stairwell was covered by a large, granite slab. It took him five hours and fifty minutes to break up the slab with a makeshift sledge hammer and clear away enough of the debris to get inside. Fortunately, some wild kuja was growing nearby, and he was able to use it for light.

Time had not been kind to the room. He could see clusters of debris that had once been furniture and books, but now it was little more than organic offal. He walked around the room being careful not to step on any of the debris. Despite the state of the furniture, the room had clearly defined walkways.

Against the far wall, he found the remains of two humans and three Sapanites. The corpses had completely decomposed, but he saw an outline on the floor of where their bodies had been, and he found coins near where their pockets would have been.

Mark picked up five triangular, gold coins and three aluminum ones. He put them in his pocket. One of the corpses wore a watch and carried an aluminum pocket comb. Another corpse wore a ring. He collected those as well.

He continued his sweep of the room and in a pile of debris he found a granite statuette of a human woman wearing something that resembled a graduation toga. She held a scroll out in front of her as if she were reading. On the base of the statue were the words, "Korinna princeps senatus DCXXXIII".

On his way out, Mark noticed a large iron door on the wall. He pulled on the handle, and the door fell apart, releasing a small shower of gold coins. He took a look inside, and all he saw was gold and platinum coins. He took a dozen of the platinum coins from the vault, took one last look around, and left.

He went back to the control room and examined what he had found. The gold coins were similar to the ones he already had in size and shape, but the writing on the coin was different. Along the edges of the coin were written, "pax per intellectum," which translated to "peace through understanding." In the center of the coin was an image of a human woman and a Sapanite male. The Sapanite was in front with the human female standing behind. Beneath them was written "Korinna-Raxuth DCXXXIII".

Mark flipped the coin over and shouted, "holy shit!"

The coin's reverse had an image of a pyramid with the all-seeing eye at the top, exactly like the one on the reverse side of a U.S. dollar bill. Mark dropped the coin in shock. He stood there for a minute and twenty seconds processing all the ramifications this could have. Did this coin mean that everything he thought he knew about history was wrong? He re-examined all the conspiracy theories he had heard when he was alive for clues to Sapanite influence on history, but came up with nothing.

Once he calmed down, he picked the coin back up and looked at the inscription at its base. It read, "sapientia illuminat omnia," or "wisdom illuminates all."

He put the coin down and looked at the ring. It was a simple gold wedding band, so he put it down and picked up the watch. The band had decayed entirely, and the metal parts of the watch had fused together from age, but he could tell from the face that it measured a twenty-four-hour day, and the day was divided into three eight-hour segments. He put the watch down and picked up the comb. It was made from a sheet of aluminum that had been tooled with a mechanical cutting blade. The edges along the teeth still had machining marks, so it wasn't cut with a laser.

He used Kak's watch to check on Jane. She was in the outcast cave working on another fishing net. She seemed fine, so he checked on Muirgel. He found her working in the library. Her back was bandaged and bruised, so she must have been sent to the rack recently. Mark looked around for Sigríður and found her guarding the front gate of Murus. Her uniform covered most of her bruises, but he could tell that she too had been sent to the rack.

Mark decided that even a short life of freedom was better than a life of oppression, and rebellion was the only answer. He had no idea what would come after that, he only knew that the oppression here couldn't be allowed to continue. He put down the watch, picked up his vitalibri, and drew plans for the Henry rifle.

Since he'd owned a Henry rifle during the Civil War, and had disassembled and reassembled it several times, he knew each part. He had also toured the factory once, so he had an idea of how they were produced.

Making the rifles would be a huge project because he would have to make the machines that made the rifles, but he had a way to cast the parts, and steam to power the machines, and plenty of discarded pipes and valves to work with. Casting the parts would be relatively easy. He would have to make some kind of drill press to drill out the barrels and then create a way to cut the grooves to rifle them.

Mark decided that the first thing he was going to need was sand to cast the barrels and other parts. He looked through the refuse until he found enough material to make a sack. He left the control room and walked toward the beach. He stayed off the main road and used his thermal sensors to search for moravi.

He found a creek and followed it to the ocean, and what he saw there shocked him. A plesiosaur, roughly the size of a school bus, had beached itself to lay eggs, and she was surrounded by four moravi trying to get at them. She tried to fend them off with her sharp teeth, but she was out of her element and being overwhelmed.

Mark didn't hesitate. He stepped out of the creek bed, drew his gun, and shot a moravi in the chest. It recoiled, but it didn't go down. The noise attracted the attention of both the moravi and the plesiosaur. Two of the moravi turned toward Mark. He stood his ground, took careful aim, and shot the lead moravi through the head. It went down. He trained his gun on the second moravi, and fired. The moravi kept bobbing its head, so the first shot only grazed it, but the second one brought it down.

He ran across the beach, shouting at the moravi as he ran. Both the moravi and the plesiosaur stopped to stare at him. He took up a position between the moravi and the plesiosaur and fired at the closest moravi. He struck it in the throat, and it violently threw its head from side to side. Mark shot at it twice more, but both shots missed. He had to reload, so he calmly opened his pistol, emptied the cylinder, and removed bullets from his gun belt and put them into the cylinder one by one. He was so focused on reloading his gun that he didn't see the last moravi approach him on his left until the spurt of blood fell on his hands as the plesiosaur bit its head off.

He looked up to see the plesiosaur spit the moravi's head out and watched its body fall limply to the ground. He pushed the reloaded cylinder back into place and looked for the wounded moravi, but it had fled. Mark put his gun away and turned back to look at the plesiosaur. It stared back at him for six seconds. Then, it brought its head down slowly to within inches of Mark's face. The massive, six-inch long teeth looked scary, until he noticed that they meshed together to form a straining system for catching shrimp.

Mark slowly brought his hand up, and the massive creature allowed him to touch the side of its face. It felt like touching a dolphin. After two seconds of contact. It pulled its massive head up and scanned the horizon.

"Well," Mark said. "It was nice meeting you."

He dropped to his knees, filled his bag with as much sand as it would hold, hoisted it up on his shoulder, and walked away.

He'd taken only five steps when he felt a gentle tug on the back of his jacket and was lifted up and pulled back to where he stood a few moments before.

He turned around and the massive creature brought its head down to stare him in the eyes.

"So," Mark said. "I guess you don't want to part company."

It brought its massive face down and looked at Mark. Then it snapped its head to the left and nodded. Mark looked in that direction, and saw movement in the jungle beyond the beach. Two more moravi charged from the leafy, blue vegetation and crossed the sandy strip of beach toward them.

In a fluid motion, Mark drew his revolver, brought it up to his eye, leveled the sights, and fired. The first moravi was struck center mass. It shook from the shot, but it didn't go down. He aimed for the head and fired again. The next shot went between the eyes, and it fell. The second moravi was only five yards away, but Mark calmly sighted its head and gently squeezed the trigger. The shot went up under its beak and through its spine. It fell and rolled, ending up next to a piece of driftwood.

Mark exhaled, reloaded, and put his gun away. He turned back to his right to see a third moravi less than two yards away. He reached for his gun, but before he could draw it, the plesiosaur grabbed it by its head, lifted it up, shook it like a rag doll, and flung its headless corpse twenty yards out into the water. It spit its head onto the beach a few yards away. She extended her neck to its full height and looked around. Then she came down and looked Mark in the eyes.

Mark looked into her eyes and realized there was more than animal intelligence there. He took a breath, pulled off the button on the top of his shirt, and placed it on the side of her head. He restarted his systems and sent the command. The button dissolved into her skin.

She closed her eyes, convulsed twice, and then opened them again. Her jaw dropped displaying a row of amazingly sharp six-inch teeth that could bite him in half, but she didn't attack. She just froze for a second.

Mark received the message, "link established."

He accessed the transmitter and dialed it down as much as he could without compromising the signal. Then, he opened a channel to her mind and got a flood of images from her life. Images of her family, her pod, and its social interactions flashed in his mind. It took him four minutes and eleven seconds to sort it all out.

He understood that they had a complex language of clicks and tones that expressed as much information as English. He saw that they understood math, but without the ability to build, saw little use for it.

He saw some conflict and social strife between pods over feeding territory and the conservation of food supply, but for the most part, her life has been following the shrimp schools, singing, dancing, and mating.

Since the moravi came to the island, most of the females in her pod who beached to lay eggs didn't return, and only a handful of the eggs survived to return to the sea.

He saw a few memories of fishing boats and members of her pod trying to interact with the humans, but their attempts at communication were misunderstood. She feared their fishing nets, but apart from that she had no experience with humans.

"Can you hear me?" Mark sent.

"Understand me, why?" she asked.

"We needed to communicate," Mark sent.

"We speak each other?" she asked.

"Yes, we can hear each other's thoughts. I hope I didn't hurt you," Mark sent. *"But I needed to understand you."*

"Understand," she sent. *"No hurt, just fear."*

"I'm sorry if I frightened you," he sent. *"But thank you for saving my life. I didn't see that last moravi."*

"Why you attack moravi? Why you help my children?"

"The moravi are my enemy. The enemy of

my enemy is my friend," Mark sent

"Yes, friend. That why I save you when you not see moravi," she sent.

"My name is Mark Aaron. What is your name?"

"Called Seagem am I, because my eyes remind my pod of shiny rocks."

"Nice to meet you," Mark sent.

He spent the next hour and twenty-four minutes sending her images from his life. He explained his life, his current situation, and he even told her about Nessie.

"Surface world known," Seagem sent. *"Nice to see it without dying."*

"What do you mean?" Mark asked.

"Sometimes, old members of our pod want to see the Sun before they die, so travel long tunnel to the surface."

"You know how to get to the surface?" he asked.

"Of course," she sent. *"When eggs hatch and moravi all dead, I find someone take you."*

"Thank you!"

"Make moravi dead, we thank you. Must go now, skin dry out, but stay nearby watch over eggs."

She turned her massive body and waddled into the surf. Once she was in the water, she disappeared under the waves. Mark gathered the sand and shoved it into the bag. He paused for a moment to consider what just happened.

"Now, all I need is a plan," he said.

Chapter Twelve
Getting Organized

Mark spent the next week working on the Henry rifles. He ran into a problem drilling the barrels. He was using an iron drill bit to drill through iron barrels. He took a trip to the beach and mentioned it to Seagem who brought him some titanium ore and a sapphire the size of his fist that she said matched her eyes.

She told him her pod didn't believe her at first, until two of its members swam up river to a point overlooking the moravi ranch and saw it for themselves. They were now discussing what to do.

She asked about his progress, and he conveyed his plan to eliminate the moravi, and she offered the support of her pod. She introduced him to Greyrock, her mate, and to Skydancer their leader. They asked questions about how and why the Sapanites bred the moravi, and Mark answered them as honestly as he could with Seagem translating his responses.

Mark wished that Jane was there to take his picture. It wasn't every day that he got to stand in the surf on an underground ocean and converse with plesiosaurs. Once he had answered all their questions, he got back to work on the rifles.

He used the titanium to make better drill bits, and a few armor-piercing rounds for his revolver and rifle. As he attached the butt to the first rifle, Jane let herself in.

"You really should lock that door," Jane said.

"I would have to fix it first. The mechanism is fused from age," Mark said. "I'm glad you're here though, I'm going to need your help."

"I'm happy to see you too," Jane said.

Mark put the rifle down and hugged Jane.

"I'm sorry, but you don't know the week I've had."

"Enlighten me."

"I found us a ride home, but we can't get it until the moravi are extinct. So, to that end, I've been producing Henry rifles. I also found evidence that the Sapanites are linked to the Illuminati, a group who is rumored to control the destiny of mankind. How was your week?"

"Well, you were right about someone selling information to the First Minister. I've identified two undercover pax living with the outcasts."

"How did you do that?"

"I worked out how they are communicating and traced it back to them."

"Good work," Mark said. "I'm just about ready here."

"Ready for what?"

"I've been thinking about it, and I've determined that we should focus exclusively on eliminating the moravi."

"What's stopping the Sapanites from responding?"

"Compliancy," Mark said. "They've been able to keep control down here for over four hundred years. They have become so used to being unchallenged that they are totally unprepared for a large-scale uprising."

"I think you had better start at the beginning," Jane said.

Mark spent the next twenty-eight minutes explaining his plan of attack, his exploration of the Sapanite mainland, why Seagem asked for the extinction of the moravi, and what he had found in the basement in the ancient city. He showed her the artifacts, and she agreed that the society was different four-hundred years ago, but failed to see how it related to their present situation. Mark explained that this society is built upon the infrastructure of the past society, and if that infrastructure was destroyed, the Sapanites would have trouble replacing it.

"Your reasoning seems sound, and it is a strategy that will result in the fewest human causalities," Jane said.

"We attack the ranch, the communications, and then we clear the island of moravi, and without the moravi to control its citizens, Murus should free itself."

"And you were planning on accomplishing this with half a dozen rifles?"

"I was planning on making about thirty, but what do you suggest?"

"I know you don't like it, but we're going to need explosives."

"To destroy the antenna room?"

"Yes," Jane sighed. "It has to be done."

Mark picked up Kak's watch and adjusted a few dials. He showed her an image of the cable as it crossed under the river."

"When we're ready, Seagem will rip the cable apart," Mark said.

"What about the night bell?" Jane asked.

"That we may have to blow up. It's in the center of the island on top of a stone tower."

"You have another problem," Jane said. "In order for this to work, the night bell, the surveillance cable, and the ranch have to be hit at once."

"It really hinges on the night bell," Mark said. "Once it's gone, the other two can be eliminated without fear of being put down."

He held up a paper rocket.

"I made three signal rockets. Once the night bell is down, fire the rockets, and that will signal the other groups to attack."

"I'm taking out the night bell?" Jane asked.

"If you don't mind," Mark said. "I'll lead the attack on the ranch, and Seagem will rip out the cable."

"It sounds like you've got the first assault planned out very well. How can I help?"

Mark paused and took a look around.

"I'm going to need about a thousand rounds of rifle ammo. Would you like to visit the basement vault and bring back the gold and platinum and start making bullets?"

They spent the next three weeks working together. Even without using their network connections, Mark felt in-tune with Jane. They both seemed to sense when the other needed help, needed a suggestion, or just an encouraging smile. Since they didn't sleep, the days merged together into one hot, sooty, labor-intensive, task, but Mark smiled as he worked, and he even caught Jane smiling even though she denied it.

They had to take a day off every three days to be absolutely sure the refuse handler didn't become aware of their presence. They spent the day working on their vitalibri and taking turns with Kak's watch to keep an eye on the new refuse handler, the First Minister, the outcasts, and Sigríður.

Jane's first task was to fix the door's locking mechanism and make keys for each of them, then made 2,400 rounds of rifle ammo as well as cast fifty knives, and a revolver for herself. Mark perfected his first Henry rifle, and then he made twenty-six more of them. He used the last of the gun powder to make two pipe bombs. He saved a dozen of each type of coin for his collection, and then recast some of the gold leftover from making the bullets into a dozen twenty-dollar gold pieces. If they did manage to get out of Subterra, they would need money to get home.

When it was time to leave, Mark shut down the generator he was using, and he hid his and Jane's backpack inside the empty housing of one of the other broken turbines. He disassembled his steam-powered drill press and hid it, along with his tools, in the empty housing of the third turbine.

They decided to only bring their own rifles to the initial meeting with the outcasts and moved the rest of the rifles, pipe bombs, rockets, and ammo to a spot near the outcast cave.

"I was just thinking," Mark said. "It would be rude to show up empty handed."

"What do you mean?" Jane asked.

"We should bring them something to eat."

"You want to go hunting moravi?"

"It would go a long way toward proving to them we can do what we say."

"Agreed," Jane said. "Any idea where we can find some?"

"They're usually around Murus to prevent people from escaping," Mark said.

They walked in the direction of Murus, and when they got near the kuja fields, they sighted a pair of moravi. They exchanged a glance, and Mark shot the one on the right while Jane shot the one on the left.

"Do you think they saw anything from the watch towers?" Jane asked.

"I hope they heard it, I told Sigríður to meet up with us when she heard gunfire."

They slung their rifles over their shoulders and picked up the smaller of the two birds. They carried it to the outcast cave and were permitted to enter unchallenged. They put it on the floor of the central cavern, and a dozen people stood staring at it in amazement.

"Don't just stand there, start plucking," Jane said. "Save the feathers."

Mark had seen the central room dozens of times through Kak's watch, but now that he was actually there it looked different. The room was large enough to play basketball. There were three tiers of kuja plants lighting the room, and the wall on the right side had been carved into book shelves. Mark glanced at it, and he saw the original copy of Charlotte Bianchi's vitalibri. He stepped over and examined it to be sure it was the original.

"We smuggle the original copies out," a voice from behind him said.

Mark turned to see a woman who looked about forty, with brown light brown eyes, dirty blonde hair, and warm sand-like skin. She stood about five feet tall and had a modest figure. Mark turned and held out his hand.

"Hi," Mark said. "I'm Mark Aaron, Jane's husband."

Her jaw dropped a little, and she ignored his hand.

"You weren't outcast," she said. "We would have heard."

"That's true," Mark said. "The First Minister thinks I'm dead, and I'd like to keep it that way. Is there somewhere private where we can talk?"

Jane stepped over to them.

"I see you've already met."

"Not really," Mark said. "She hasn't given me her name."

"Mark," Jane said. "I would like to introduce you to Augusta Aquila, leader of the outcasts."

She turned to face Augusta who gestured for them to follow her. She took them through a few dimly lit caverns where she stopped at a heavy wooden door. She unlocked it and motioned for them to enter. Then she followed them inside and closed the door.

"It's a good thing you brought the moravi," she said. "It will keep everyone distracted for a while."

She gestured toward a long table with six chairs. Mark sat down and looked around. The room was lit by about a dozen kuja plants growing from large pots on the floor. The back wall was wood, with a door. The wall had a couple portraits of previous outcast leaders as well as a cabinet and bookshelf.

Once everyone was seated at the table, Augusta looked at Jane.

"Do you have any idea the trouble you've brought to us?" She asked.

"Oh, he excels at causing trouble, but he is usually worth it."

"Usually?" Mark said.

"When the pax find out he is here . . ."

Jane cut her off.

"It won't matter what the pax think. We're here to provide you with the weapons you need to eliminate the moravi forever."

"What?"

Mark held up his rifle. She looked at it curiously, but said nothing.

"This is a Henry rifle. It is a weapon the surface dwellers use to hunt wild animals and to kill each other in wars," Mark said.

"What does it do?" She asked.

"It employs a chemical explosion to send a heavy projectile through the air at high speed to strike a target. Usually producing a large hole," Jane said.

He emptied the rifle, and then handed it to her.

"I've made twenty-five more of these, along with enough ammunition to kill every moravi on this island three times over."

Augusta took the rifle and held it like it was a snake.

"We can provide your metal workers with detailed plans and instructions on how to make not only these, but other surface weapons as well," Jane said. "You won't have to live in fear of the moravi or the Sapanites ever again."

She put the rifle down of the table and pushed it toward Mark.

"Do you know why I'm the leader of the outcasts?" Augusta asked. She didn't wait for them to respond. "I'm the leader because I'm the oldest person here, and I didn't get to be the oldest person here by believing in every zealot who came along spreading false hope. So, you killed a moravi or two, so what? When the Sapanites find out what you are doing, they will put you down with the night bell. Then they will send an airship to kill you, and I'm not sending any of my people out to die."

"We have a plan," he said.

"The Sapanites have been our masters for hundreds of years. Whatever plan you think you have, it's been tried before," Augusta said.

"We can give you the opportunity to fight back and end this," Mark said.

"End what? A way of life that we have had for centuries? Yes, things here are harsh, but this is a prison. Things here are supposed to be harsh."

"Don't you want to be free from the moravi?" Jane asked.

As Augusta turned to face Jane, she balled her hands into fists, held them before her, for a second and released them.

"A year after I was outcast, some of the others forced their way into Murus and took food and kuja. The First Minister at the time had the Sapanites release two moravi into our cave. The carnage they caused was indescribable. I survived by crawling into a passage too small for them to reach me, and I spent a week in total darkness living off of drip water. I am not going to risk that happening again. So, please leave," Augusta said.

"You're not understanding," Mark said. "The war has already begun. It is going to come whether you want it or not."

She got up from the table and walked to the door and opened it.

"Please don't make me throw you out," she said.

She escorted them through the cave and back out to the surface. Then she ordered the guard that they were not to be readmitted. As they walked down the trail, Mark turned to Jane.

"Well, that could have gone better."

"She is terrified, and I don't blame her. Oppression is all she knows, and she is afraid of losing what she has," Jane said.

"We'll just have to do some recruiting," Mark said.

"How?" Jane asked.

"We will kill every moravi we find. As we encounter people, we will recruit them."

They moved to a point on the road where they could observe Murus and set up a base camp of sorts. Mark hoped that Sigríður heard them kill the moravi and had come to join them.

While one kept watch, the other constructed a sleeping platform similar to the ones the outcasts use to evade the moravi.

On the second day bell, Jane saw movement along the road. They went down to investigate, and found the waste handler being stalked by three moravi. She had crawled under her cart for what little protection it provided. Mark and Jane walked up the road behind her. She saw them and shouted for them to run, but they ignored her.

Mark waited until all three of them were on the road before he signaled to Jane. Jane nodded and Mark shot the one on the left and Jane the one the right, then they both shot the one in the middle.

A blonde woman emerged from under the cart and stared at them with a wide-eyed expression.

"How did you do that?" He asked.

"It's called a Henry Rifle," Mark said. "We intend to use them to kill every moravi on the island. Would you like to help?"

She brushed her shoulder-length golden-blonde hair out of her blue eyes, adjusted her dress, and looked up the road at the three dead moravi.

"No one can kill a moravi," she said.

"There are three dead ones down there that say otherwise," Mark said.

"You can teach me to do that?" she asked.

"Yes," Mark said.

"What's your name?" Jane asked.

"Thalia Briggs," she said. "I was a weaver until I was reported for using taba. Aren't you Jane?"

"Yes," Jane said.

Her eyes brightened, and she stepped closer to them. She stared at Jane and smiled.

"Everyone has been talking about you since the arena. It was supposed to be a public execution, but you not only survived, you fed a couple of collaborators to the moravi."

"They were just in my way," Jane said. "It wasn't anything personal."

"Still, you resisted. You defied them, and now you want me to help you kill moravi? When do we start?"

Mark looked at Thalia's trash cart and saw a few useful items.

"I'm going to get rid of this. I don't want them to know where you stopped."

Jane glanced at Mark over her shoulder and shrugged. Mark pushed the cart down the road as Jane and Thalia disappeared into the large-leafed foliage.

He pushed the cart off the road, and found a path through the vegetation. He dumped the cart in a creek bed about a quarter mile off the road. When he got back, Thalia was teaching Jane how to weave baskets to bring back the moravi feathers. Mark kept watch on Murus, but there was still no sign of Sigríður.

After the next night bell, Mark heard screaming from the direction of Murus. He ran toward the sound, rifle in hand, to discover a pair of moravi on the edge of the kuja field. It moved toward a man who was trying to protect two terrified young women.

Mark didn't hesitate. He shouldered his rifle and fired. The golden hollow-point went through the moravi's neck, severing its spine. Its head fell down onto its chest while the body twitched and fell over. The man saw the moravi go down and ran past it to keep himself between the remaining moravi and the women. Before the second moravi could move toward him, Mark shot it through the chest. Since it was moving when it was shot, it stumbled, rolled, and lay in a shallow ditch.

A red-haired woman, who had been running toward Murus, stopped when she heard the first gunshot. She watched Mark shoot the other moravi, then she ran toward him and motioned for others to follow her. In all, five women and two men followed Mark back into the large-leafed vegetation.

The red-haired woman the first to catch up with Mark when he joined Jane and Thalia just inside the undergrowth. She was flushed and sweaty from the excitement, but she smiled at Mark. He looked back at her and saw the deepest set of sapphire blue eyes he had ever seen. She gave him a huge hug and cried so much that Jane had to come over and pull her away from him.

Mark asked for their names, and the red-haired woman introduced herself as Gaia Norina. She introduced him to Mari Florean, a woman with dirty blonde hair and marble gray eyes, and Marilena Pepouli, who had platinum blonde hair and blue eyes. Both appeared to be about six months pregnant. A man with spiked bond hair and hazel eyes reached over Mari's shoulder to extend his hand. He introduced himself as Antonio Heilyn, and the man who had been trying to protect the women stepped around the ladies and extended his hand.

"I'm Michael McKee. Thank you for saving my life. If there is anything I can do to repay you, let me know."

"You're welcome, Michael, and there is one thing. Can I borrow your clothes?"

Chapter Thirteen
Contact with the Enemy

Jane wasn't too crazy about the idea of Mark returning to Murus, but she had to concede that stealing an airship would increase their odds of success, and Sigríður was the only one they knew who could pilot one. Unfortunately, he had killed the moravi within sight of the guard towers, and missed his opportunity. The city gates were sealed, so there was no hope of sneaking in with the kuja farmers.

They moved their camp deeper into the woods where they encountered Matthew Irm and Kate Fol, along with Jacob Richardson and Rayia Abovian.

Matthew and Jacob looked like they could be brothers, or at least half-brothers. They both stood just over six feet tall and had spiked, jet black hair, alabaster skin, and dark blue eyes.

Mark now had a dozen people under his command, and his experience as a Civil War officer came in handy. He created three, four-person squads and ordered that the squad stay together at all times. The squad would not only protect each other in combat, but it would ensure that no one left camp alone.

He drilled them with empty rifles, and taught his squads how to use overlapping fire to cover each other left, forward, right, and rear. He watched them drill, looked for leadership potential, and designated Thalia as a First Sergeant with Mathew, Michael, and Gaia, the sapphire-eyed red head, as squad leaders. Once he was certain they understood basic gun safety, he issued them ammunition.

During their first encounter with a flock of eight moravi, Mari, one of the kuja farmers Mark had rescued, froze. Mark was about to intervene when Thalia stepped over and talked the petite, blonde-haired woman through sighting and shooting her first moravi. It fell in three shots, and then she killed another.

Jane looked over at Mark and smiled. She had been opposed to naming Thalia First Sergeant, but she seemed happy to be wrong. When the shooting stopped, he reviewed the importance of staying out of each other's line of fire, drilled them on forming up, and told them to be grateful that the moravi didn't shoot back.

They marched toward the ocean, but since Mark and Jane were the only ones who knew about Seagem, no one knew why. They paused for a meal break. Mark ordered the squads to forage in the woods for things to supplement their main course of moravi. While the squads were away, Mark started a fire and cooked the moravi meat on a spit. When the squads returned with several types of fruit and roots that Mark wasn't familiar with, they were both shocked and amazed at the sight of the fire. Marilena, a platinum blonde woman with porcelain skin and dark brown eyes quickly reminded him that lighting a fire was punishable by death, but then Thalia reminded her that they had done five things that morning alone that were punishable by death, and she broke out into a contagious laughing fit that lasted seventy-six seconds.

After lunch, Marilena broke out into an Irish Celtic song that Mark had not heard before. Seventeen seconds into the song, Gaia and Mari joined in. The song was so beautiful that Mark gathered them together by a waterfall and had them sing it again from the beginning, so he could record it.

On the third night bell, Mark and Jane left the others so they could confer with Seagem and Skydancer. He asked that they attack the cable in five days, but that request was more complicated than Mark realized, since the plesiosaurs didn't measure time the same way people did. Jane solved the dilemma by putting a count-down clock in Seagem's mind.

Skydancer, through Seagem, told them that the hit and run attacks against Sapanite shipping and food production were going well. When Mark asked about casualties, Skydancer was confused at first, but then he told them that plesiosaur deaths had gone down since the war started because the pods were no longer fighting each other. Then he asked them what they wanted to end the war with the Sapanites. At first, they seemed confused, but then Skydancer stated that he wanted the breading of moravi to stop and the fish around the island replenished.

They asked how he was progressing, and Mark told them that he had swept the area around Seagem's eggs of moravi. For that, Seagem was grateful, but Skydancer wanted to know more about his plans for his overall land operation. Since they were conversing on a low power, encrypted radio signal that was being translated into plesiosaur, he had no problem telling them that he intended to divide his forces and attack the moravi ranch while Jane destroyed the night bell. Skydancer approved of Mark's plan, especially the moravi ranch part, and promised to send some plesiosaurs upriver to support him where possible. Mark thanked him, and he and Jane returned to camp.

Mark marched them around the side of the island for two days before turning them back toward the moravi ranch. Mark spotted an airship on the horizon conducting a grid search. He ordered his people under cover and reloaded his rifle with the titanium bullets, and did the same for Jane.

The airship passed over as it executed its grid search, and just when Mark thought they were in the clear, it came back for a low pass. Despite Michael's whispered order to stay hidden, Jacob started firing as the airship started to move off. It turned back toward them, and Antonio, Oriana, and Kate joined in, so Mark gave Thalia the order to fire.

Then he and Jane opened fire, and fifteen seconds later a blue steam erupted from the side of the airship and it started to wobble. It moved off toward the beach, but at the rate it was losing altitude, Mark didn't think it would make it to the moravi ranch, let alone the mainland.

As a few of them cheered, the night bell was activated early. They stumbled and fell asleep.

"Well, so much for a coordinated attack," Mark said.

"Augusta was right," Jane said. "They're going to send another airship to finish us off."

"Yeah, that went pretty much as she predicted," Mark said. "But that gives us a tactical advantage."

"What advantage?"

"They think we've been neutralized, so they won't be in a rush to come back."

"What did you have in mind?" Jane asked.

"The tower for the night bell is about two miles that way."

Mark leaned his rifle against the twisted trunk of the leafy tree next to him and pointed toward the interior of the island.

"We've been marching through the forest slowly to engage the moravi, but if I hurry, even with the rough terrain, I can be there in an hour-- two tops."

"So, you want to go attack the night bell while I do what?" Jane asked.

"Move our people to a safe place," Mark said. "The Sapanites are expecting them to be where they fell."

"Did you notice that Jabob wasn't shooting at the airship, but to give away our position?" Jane asked.

"I noticed," Mark said. "Collect his rifle, ammunition, and gear. Leave him behind when you move everyone else."

"I know you want to destroy the night bell, but I could really use your help moving our people," Jane said. "I don't want to be forced to leave someone behind."

Mark looked down and took a breath. He asked himself, what U.S. Grant would do in this situation. Grant would destroy the objective despite the losses, but he also had an army of 50,000 men.

Mark personally knew and cared about everyone under his command. When he looked back up at Jane, he saw a tiny blue lizard about a quarter of an inch long jumping from flower to flower on the leafy bush behind her. Its tail reminded him of Seagem.

"You're right, our people should come first. How about we take them back to the waterfall with the overhanging rock."

Jane picked up Thalia in a fireman's carry, and Mark picked up Gaia. They moved through the woods as fast as the terrain would allow. They found a dry, level spot, where they couldn't be observed from the air, and gently lay them on the large rocks under an overhang near the waterfall.

It took a dozen trips, but all of their people and equipment were moved back down the trail to the waterfall. They left Jacob with his head resting on his backpack in the edge of the clearing where he'd fired to alert the airship.

Now that everyone was safe, Mark kissed Jane goodbye, made sure the pipe bombs were in his backpack, and set out for the center of the island.

Since this part of the island wasn't visited much, Mark had to push his way through undergrowth. He stopped and used Kak's watch to keep an eye on what was happening at the moravi ranch. The airship that had been parked there when Mark first discovered it was still there, so the airship they shot must have been from the mainland. Mark searched for it, but he couldn't find it on the island.

He looked for an easier route to the night bell and discovered a stream that ran in the general direction he wanted to go. He pushed through the growth until he found its banks. Then he followed it upstream for forty-six minutes.

Despite having to walk through the water, the stream made his progress much easier. As he continued, he noticed pieces of oxidized metal and refined glass in the streambed. Then the undergrowth opened up to reveal the ruins of another city. He saw the remains of a granite building sticking up through the leafy plants around it.

Mark left the stream and worked his way through the ruins. The remains of the ancient streets made his walking a little easier. He finally got within sight of the night bell, and he looked for the best spot to plant his explosives.

When he got within fifty feet of the granite tower that housed the night bell, he paused to examine it. After ten seconds of observation, Mark heard a cracking sound. He looked at his feet to see the dirt and vegetation around his feet disappear. Then a second later a loud cracking sound and Mark plunged thirty-four feet down into the ruins of an ancient building.

He landed flat on his back, in near total darkness. The ancient flooring he fell through had broken his fall somewhat, but the final granite floor hurt like a bitch. The fall had caused some minor damage, but it wasn't anything his nanites couldn't handle. He had to turn his pain sensors off before he could get up again.

He looked up at the dim light supplied by the hole and surveyed the damage he caused when he fell through. The flooring above him hung in rags, and looked as if it could collapse down on him at any moment.

He looked around and discovered ruins similar to those he had found in the ancient bank. Piles of organic offal with a few surviving bits of metal. He looked for a door, and found one, but it was hopelessly blocked with dirt and debris.

He went back to where he landed and looked up through the hole. He was able to get to a point where he was within line of sight of the night bell. He saw some circular metal disks on the granite face, shouldered his rifle and fired. He emptied his rifle into the metal disk, reloaded and emptied it again. The night bell continued to broadcast.

He put the rifle down, sat down, and tried to think. Being stuck in an ancient city reminded him of New York. So, he asked himself, what would Tesla do? He thought about the noise Tesla made with his radio experiment. Then he realized the night bell was transmitting, so that meant it was drawing power. Electricity by its nature creates magnetic waves. He could detect these waves and locate the night bell's power source.

Mark took himself out of stealth mode and looked for the electromagnetic signature of the night bell's power source. It didn't take him long to find it. He had to open up a wall, but the ancient concrete had been water damaged and was easy to remove. It only took him about half an hour to expose the power cable.

He wedged the pipe bombs into the cable and surrounding metal work and lit the fuses. He ran back through the room and around the corner. Despite being forty feet away and behind a granite partition, he felt the pressure wave of the blast. It was more than enough to kill a human and he was thrown up against the partition and then onto the floor.

When he recovered, he noticed that the night bell had fallen silent. Two seconds later, he heard a cracking sound and then the room shook followed by a loud crashing sound and large chunks of debris falling from the ceiling.

Mark used Kak's watch to see what had happened. The tower that had been the night bell had fallen over on its side. It now rested at a twenty-degree angle. The person-sized hole that Mark had made when he fell had now turned into several large holes.

He adjusted the watch's dial to check on Jane. He found her where he had left her, sitting on a rock with her rifle in her lap. The others had started to wake up, and they all looked fine.

Then he looked in on the First Minister. She was in her office, speaking with Kaxuth on her hexagonal computer screen. Kaxuth told her to declare an emergency. She was to tell the citizens of

Murus that the rebels had brought the wrath of the moravi down upon the city, and they were surrounded. The night bell had been turned off to keep the citizens alert. When she asked for additional pax be sent from the mainland, Kaxuth said "no" and ended the conversation.

He wondered how many people would believe Kaxuth's story, but then he realized that propaganda rarely made sense. If it made sense, they wouldn't have to force people to believe it.

He searched the city for Sigríður, but was unable to find her. He found Muirgel with the others being herded into the center of town for the First Minister's announcement.

Mark flipped Kak's watch closed and weighed his options. He was stuck in a granite box, fifty feet underground, with little hope of rescue. Jane's first objective would be to attack the moravi ranch, not search for him. It would take at least a day before she even realized he was missing. So, it looked like he was going to be there a while.

He could see signs that this area had been periodically exposed to water, and that had taken its toll on the structure. He spent the day searching and found a few more examples of Sapanite writing with Latin below, and he was able to add about a dozen more words to his database. He found a metal object that may have once been a pen or a stylus that was well preserved, but apart from a few lumps of oxidized silver that may have once been coins and lots of corroded wiring, he didn't find anything recognizable.

He could no longer hear the electronic noise that the Sapanites used to monitor their human prisoners, so either the walls were blocking the signal, or Seagem had removed the cable early. Either way, he felt safe using his microwave emitter to see what was behind the walls. He did a quick survey of the walls and floor and found nothing. Then, he spent another six hours doing a grid search. He found a spot that looked promising, and spent twelve hours clearing away debris from a shaft that was once an ancient stairwell, only to find that the stairs had completely rusted away.

He checked Kak's watch and found that Sigríður had escaped Murus and met up with Jane. They were camped near the moravi ranch. Jane held out a blue Sapanite uniform, the ones worn by the humans on the mainland, to Sigríður. Jane told Sigríður that she had two hours to get inside the moravi ranch and steal the airship. From Sigríður's expression, she wasn't too crazy about Jane's plan, but she went behind a leafy bush and changed into the uniform as they discussed the details.

The room suddenly went from very dark to totally dark and then back to very dark. Mark readjusted Kak's watch to get a look at the surface above him. An airship hovered twenty feet above the hole he made when he fell, and four blond men were about to repel into the hole.

Mark chastised himself for not paying more attention to his surroundings. But on the other hand, airships used magnetic impellers and anti-gravity fluid to fly, which made them completely silent.

He just had time to shut the watch off, scramble the dials, and hide it under a pile of debris before they arrived. Mark contemplated resisting, but decided against it. Right now, they were at the only way out of the basement, so he put himself back into stealth mode.

Before he could smash his rifle against the marble floor, they hit him with the electromagnetic pulse that the cleaner had used on him in Fort Worth. Mark collapsed, and pretended to be asleep. They took his guns and backpack, bound his hands and feet, attached a rope to his bindings, and hauled him up into the airship like a calf being taken for branding. As soon as he was out of the marble basement, he detected the radio waves the Sapanites used.

Once he was in the airship, he was put into a chair with leg and arm restraints. Forty-three minutes later, the four blond-haired men returned to the airship, and it started moving. Five minutes and forty-five seconds later it touched down, and he was given an electric shock to wake him up. He didn't have to pretend it hurt, because it did.

They pulled him out of the seat and threw him out of the airship. He landed on a muddy field with the leafy plants that passed for grass there. A pair of well-manicured feet came into view. He looked up and saw the First Minister standing over him in all her glory.

"I thought you were dead," she said.

"I got better."

Mark tried to get up, but he felt the butt of his own rifle strike his back, forcing his face into the mud.

"Don't worry," she said. "I'll keep you alive long enough to see the end of this little rebellion you've started. Then I'll hang you upside down from the walls and let the moravi tear you apart."

Mark wanted to say something snarky, but was prevented from doing so by the mud covering his nose in mouth. He was held there for a minute and five seconds. Then he was lifted up, carried to one of the cells by the arena, and tossed inside.

He pulled himself up against one of the walls of his cell and watched the count-down clock in his mind for twenty-nine hours. He wondered how the attack against the moravi ranch went, and if Jane had turned their group toward Murus yet.

When the countdown clock he shared with Jane and Seagem showed one hour, the door opened and Muirgel came in with a bucket of soapy water, a wash cloth, change of clothes, and a couple of kuja bulbs. She tried to smile as she entered, but the stench in the cell was overpowering, and her smile contorted into an almost comical expression. She looked around for a clean spot in the cell, but only succeeded in finding a place that was less filthy.

"They send you to interrogate me?" Mark asked.

"They sent me because I'm still responsible for you, and yes, they believe I will get better answers."

She gestured for Mark to step over. Mark complied and she began to pull his muddy clothes off.

"The First Minister has sent for you to answer questions for both her and Our Lord Kaxuth. You must cooperate with them."

"Or they'll hang me upside down and let the moravi tear me apart?" Mark asked.

Mark undressed and gave her his clothes. She threw them on the floor. Then she pulled a soapy sponge out of the bucket and started cleaning his back before she answered.

"No, your fate is already sealed. You are to be executed. Somewhat horribly I would think. No, your cooperation will determine the fate of your fellow inmates. Whether they die quickly, or die slowly and painfully."

"So, I guess amnesty is off the table?" Mark asked.

"I don't know what that means," Muirgel said. "I know what you must think of me, but I'm doing this because if I don't get your cooperation, I'll be sent to the rack again."

She did her best to hide it, but Mark heard her voice crack.

"You have my cooperation," Mark said. "What would you like me to do?"

She smiled as she handed him a clean toga. He took it and put it on, and then she helped him lace and tie his sandals as they spoke.

"You are going to be bound and taken to see the First Minister and Kaxuth. They are going to ask you questions about the numbers and strengths of the rioting inmates surrounding Murus."

"Wait," he said. "There are rebels surrounding Murus?"

"You call them rebels. Our Lord Kaxuth refers to them as rioting inmates. It is very important that you never call them anything else in his presence. Otherwise, things could go badly for everyone."

"Understood," Mark said. "What else can you tell me?"

"As soon as the night bell fell silent, we were told there were moravi surrounding the city. The gates were sealed, but the moravi never came. Instead, the outcasts armed themselves and took our crops. They've taken the entire harvest."

Once she had finished, she led him out of his cell, where two pax cuffed his hands behind his back and escorted him to the Office of Public Good. He was surprised to see both the First Minister in person and Kaxuth on the hexagonal monitor.

By the time he was shoved onto the rough, wooden bench, the countdown clock showed twenty-one minutes. The First Minister adjusted something on her keyboard, and Kaxuth spoke.

"We read your vitalibri. Thank you for keeping such detailed notes. It saved us hours of interrogation, but I do have a few questions."

Mark smiled.

"Just a few?"

Both of the pax standing next to him drew their dolor and shocked Mark. Apart from slightly increasing his available power, he hardly noticed, but he pretended all the same.

"Speak only to answer questions!" the First Minister shouted.

"But I need to tell you something," Mark said.

The pax reached for their dolor again, but Kaxuth waived them off, so Mark continued.

"The terms for your surrender are that all breeding and experimentation with the moravi is ended . . ."

Kaxuth cut him off with some kind of sound Mark wasn't familiar with. It seemed like a throaty gurgle that must have been a laugh.

"You overestimate your strength. The rioters will be put down soon. I've got twelve airships on the way to Murus right now. It's over."

"I didn't realize you would send your entire fleet to deal with a few rioting inmates," Mark said.

Kaxuth's jaw dropped a little.

"How do you know . . ." Kaxuth cut himself off.

"Not everyone who you have enslaved is under your control. We have spies on the mainland," Mark lied. "The attacks will stop when you agree to leave Refvalnol Island, stop raising moravi, and replenish the fish you've taken from around the island."

The countdown clock hit zero. Mark looked out the window and saw Jane and the others had stopped on the road to Murus. They had been met by the outcasts surrounding the city, and Jane was issuing rifles to the outcasts.

He glanced down at the river, and a familiar looking tail cut across the surface of the water, but then he saw several more. Seagem brought some friends. A rock about the size of a loaf of bread flew up from the river. It smashed through the glass roof and broken glass fell all around them. It was followed by a dozen more.

The hexagonal screen went dark, and the electronic noise fell silent. Mark took himself out of stealth mode. He snapped the metal cuff holding his arms behind him, reached up, and grabbed each of the pax by the wrist. He gave them an electric shock twice the strength they had given him. They both convulsed, wet themselves, passed out, and fell onto the floor.

As he got up, another rock fell through the ceiling, smashing into the wall behind the First Minister. She screamed, and ducked under the table. Mark ignored her and went back out the hall and found a passage way to the north tower. He climbed it to the top, and from there he could see the entire field. Mark sent to Jane and Seagem.

"Good work everyone," Mark sent.

"Markman?" Seagem sent.

"I thought you might turn up here," Jane sent. *"Too bad you missed all the fun at the ranch."*

"We can all catch up later," Mark sent. *"We have a dozen incoming airships. Seagem, please stop attacking the city. It is secure for now. Deploy your friends around the city and tell them to be ready to attack the airships when I signal you."*

"Do I what say you Markman," Seagem sent. *"We no throw rocks until say you."*

"Jane," Mark sent. *"Get everyone as close to the river as possible. I want the airships to have to come to us."*

"You mean you're using us as bait to draw in the airships," Jane sent.

"Do you have a better plan?" Mark asked.

"No," Jane sent. *"Just wanted to be clear."*

"What happened to Sigríður?"

"Took off with the airship."

"We knew that was a possibility."

Jane paused her conversation with him to issue orders to Thalia. From his vantage point on the tower, he could see Thalia run off toward the squad leaders.

"Best thing we can do is to hold our fire until we are sure they are in range, then hit them with rocks and rifle fire and hope we can bring them down," Mark sent.

The gates to Murus opened, and the citizens streamed out. Some ran for the foliage on the other side of the fields while others ran toward the outcasts and Jane's position.

"What if they hit us with a night bell before they are in range?" Jane asked.

"I guess it is time to break out the tin-foil hats?" Mark sent.

Mark ran downstairs and searched rooms until he found the First Minister's private quarters. The first thing he saw when he entered was his strawberry plant in the corner with four kuja plants around it.

A rock had pierced the skylight, so the room was littered with glass. He went to the First Minister's desk and rummaged through its drawers. Among the papers and notes, he saw sketches of Murus. People eating in the restaurant, working in the field, and gathered in the Hall of Remembrance. In all of the sketches, the First Minister is among the people, not as a leader, but as one of them. He found her helmet in the bottom left drawer. Mark put it on and stepped over to the window.

As he stepped over to the window, he noticed a bookshelf was set into the wall, and it held dozens of books from the surface. Some of which had been published in the last five years.

"Jane, I found the First Minister's helmet. Ask if anyone knows where I can find more."

Through the window, Mark watched Jane signal to Thalia. She ran over to Jane, then ran to her squad leaders. Three minutes and twenty-seconds later, she ran back to Jane with Matthew Irm. Matthew left to return to his squad while Thalia ran toward a group of outcasts.

"Matthew says that if there are more helmets, they would be in a secret closet in the First Minister's office. He and his squad will meet you there."

Mark turned back and found the two pax he had put down in the meeting room. As soon as they saw him, they both turned and ran back out the door. Mark shrugged, and found the stairs down to the ground level where the First Minister's office was located. He stepped inside, and pondered how to best search for the hidden closet. Normally, he would do a passive X-ray scan, but that didn't work down here. He could use his microwave emitter as a kind of radar, but if the Sapanites could still detect radio, he would run the risk of them discovering his advanced technology. He examined the desk for hidden buttons or switches and found none. He pulled books off of the shelf and tossed them to the floor to search the shelf behind them.

Fortunately, he didn't have to ponder the question long. Matthew Irm, Kate Fol, Rayia Abovian stepped into the room. The others fanned out and Matthew walked straight to the desk. He reached under it and pressed on a panel. The bookshelf to the right of the desk popped open. Kate pushed the bookshelf aside, and it slid into the wall to reveal a closet roughly ten feet square. Mark stepped into the room. On his right there was a rack that held fifty dolor wands. In front of him, two racks held what looked like synthetic body armor, to the left of them a shelf with fifty brass helmets arranged on five shelves of ten each.

Kate pulled a suit of body armor off the rack and examined it, as Mark handed everyone a helmet.

"We don't have time for that," Mark said. "Put on a helmet, and carry as many as you can out to the field. Give a helmet to everyone with a rifle."

Mark gathered ten helmets into two stacks of five helmets each. He turned and walked out the door, followed by Matthew Irm and his squad. They calmly walked through the pathways of Murus and out the unguarded front gate. They were among the last few residents who decided to gather belongings before fleeing the city.

As they reached the bridge, Mark saw a glint of royal blue out of the corner of his eye. The First Minister stepped out of a doorway in the side of the wall. Mark and Matthew paused to confront her while the others crossed the bridge.

"You traitorous avisca," she said.

She advanced upon them, so Mark and Matthew stepped backward across the bridge to keep their distance. The people who were still trying to flee paused and stepped back at the sight of the First Minister.

"What?" Mark asked.

"Moravi poop," Matthew said to Mark. "Nice to see you too Lamere. Strange that you should say that, because if anyone is a traitorous avisca it would be you."

"You two have history?" Mark asked.

"Oh, yes," Matthew said.

As the First Minister reached the center of the bridge, she pulled Mark's revolver up pointed it at Matthew and fired. The bullet struck Matthew's right thigh, and he went down.

As she turned the gun toward Mark, Seagem's head and long neck popped up out of the river behind her. Seagem raised her head to where it was about three feet over the First Minister's and paused.

"You really want to put that gun down," Mark said.

"I should have killed you when you first arrived," she said. "But at least I get to kill you now."

As her finger began to squeeze the trigger, Seagem struck. Her mouth came down and engulfed the First Minister's head. She bit down and picked her up. The gun flew out of her hand to land on the riverbank and her royal blue gown was sprayed with blood and gore. Seagem shook the First Minister like a rag doll before tossing her corpse to the other side of the river. Her body hit the ground with an audible thud and rolled over a few times before resting against an abandoned cart.

The sight of Seagem rising from the river drew everyone's attention. Both the people fleeing through the gate, and those preparing for battle in the kuja field stopped to stare the sanguinary spectacle before them. A cheer broke out on both sides of the river that reminded Mark of the way fans cheered at the Super Bowl when someone scored.

Kate dropped her helmets and rushed to Matthew's side. Mark gestured to a few others to help her.

"Take him to the First Minister's bedroom," Mark said.

Kate nodded as she applied pressure to the wound and the others lifted Matthew up to carry him off the field.

"Thank you Seagem," Mark sent.

"Seagem protect Markman. Markman member of pod. Pod protect each other. Why people make noise when woman die?"

"She hurt many of them, so they were showing their gratitude for your help."

Seagem made a sound that resembled a tuba being played by an elephant. The people nearby covered their ears and stared at her in disbelief.

"Seagem show gratitude for Markman," she sent.

"Thank you," Mark sent.

Jane walked over to join Mark and Seagem.

"It looks like Murus is under new management," Jane said.

"Taking it was easy," Mark said. "Keeping it may prove to be more difficult."

Thalia stepped over to them and handed Mark his pistol, a rifle, and his gun belt that had fallen onto the bridge. Mark noticed that someone had embroidered three chevrons and three stripes on the front of her toga dress, and the color still hadn't returned to her face after witnessing Seagem's attack upon the First Minister.

"Sir," Thalia said. "May I ask what just happened?"

"Oh," Mark said. "I made some new friends."

"Sir?"

"The plesiosaurs have agreed to support us against the Sapanites. Please pass the word not to attack them."

"Yes sir," Thalia said. "Glad to know that."

Thalia turned to leave, but Mark stopped her.

"Make sure everyone with a rifle has a helmet. Form a line along the riverbank on both sides. Use whatever is available to provide cover to hide behind when the airships arrive. Then tell everyone to get some rest."

"Yes, sir," Thalia said.

She saluted, scooped up the helmets Kate had dropped, put one on, and left to pass the orders to the squad leaders.

"You taught her to salute?" Mark asked.

"Seemed like the thing to do," Jane said.

"Okay," Mark sent. *"This is our battle plan. We can't be sure what direction the airships will approach from, but more than likely they will fly a straight line from the mainland."*

Mark gestured in the direction of the mainland.

"That will bring them up parallel to the river. We keep everyone spread out and under cover. That will force them to get up close. When we have three or four airships in range, we hit them with rocks and bullets."

"Okay, what's next?" Jane asked.

"That's the unpredictable part. They may fall back if they lose enough airships. That would be bad because they could regroup and come back later."

"Markman," Seagem sent. *"Airship fly low over water. Want you have pod throw rocks at them?"*

"Yes, please," Mark sent. *"Each one your pod can stop is one less we have to fight here."*

Seagem disappeared back into the river, so Mark and Jane walked the riverbank and oversaw the preparations being made to hide from the airships and distribute rifles, ammunition, and food.

Thalia ran over to meet with them. Her blonde hair bounced on her shoulders as she ran. Mark had to admit that it was strange seeing a pregnant First Sergeant wearing a toga dress run up to them and salute.

"Sir, the leader of the outcasts is being held at our outer picket. She says she would like to speak with you."

"Tell them she may advance," Mark said.

Thalia looked at Mark and her jaw dropped a little.

"It's okay for her to come," Jane said.

Thalia nodded, turned, and whistled at the line. They stepped aside and let Augusta pass. She was escorted by Rayia Abovian, who watched her closely.

"You're going to get us all killed!" Augusta shouted.

She raised her arm to strike Mark, but found two knives were at her throat before she could follow through.

"Put your hand down," Rayia said quietly but firmly. "These aren't the outcast caves. You don't have any authority here."

Augusta looked to her left at Rayia, then to her right at Thalia. Each pressed a knife against her throat. She lowered her arm.

"If you ever raise a hand to my commander again, you will not live to regret it," Thalia said.

Mark nodded at them, and they put their knives away. He looked over at Jane who stood there smiling like a mom watching her daughter's school play.

"Now, how can I help you?" Mark asked.

"They will send moravi and their skyships to kill us all."

Mark turned to Thalia.

"First Sergeant, how many moravi are in this area?"

"None sir," she said. "We swept the area as we approached Murus. The moravi ranch was burned, the moravi slaughtered, and all the eggs were broken."

"Casualties?" Mark asked.

Thalia's jaw dropped a little.

"How many died?" Mark asked.

"Seven of the collaborators resisted and were shot, the rest surrendered. We suffered a few injuries from the moravi, but no deaths."

"Ranch, what does she mean by ranch?" Augusta asked.

"The Sapanites were breeding the moravi at a large farm. Training them to attack anything that smelled like a human," Jane said.

"What about the skyships?" Augusta asked.

"On their way," Mark said. "There will be a battle for Murus, but I'm confident about our chances."

Augusta opened her mouth to speak, but no sound came out. The color drained from her face, and she wet herself. Mark glanced behind him and saw Seagem rise up out of the river. Thalia and Rayia looked a little wide-eyed as well. Mark decided the best way to keep everyone calm was to be casual about the forty-foot plesiosaur behind him.

"Oh," Mark said. "I see you've met Seagem. She is a friend. She won't hurt you."

"Tell that to the First Minister," Jane said.

"Jane," Mark said. "You're not helping."

Jane gave him a toothy smile. Seagem paused and stayed about twenty-feet back. Through his connection to her, Mark could sense that she was as frightened of them as they were of her. She brought her head down level with Mark's.

"I speak Skydancer. He say that make war with airship good. He say war go well. Pods work together now. More fun than fight each other."

"Thank you, Seagem," Mark sent.

Mark turned back to Augusta as Seagem slipped back into the river.

"If you want to sit this out, you are more than welcome to take whatever food and kuja you can harvest from the fields and hide in your cave for as long as you want, but if I catch any of you providing information or support to the Sapanites, he or she will be shot as a collaborator."

Augusta had trouble focusing on Mark until Rayia nudged her in the back. Then she only nodded and backed away from them. As soon as she was a few steps away, she broke into a run.

Mark and Jane continued to walk the field to ensure that everyone was prepared. A few of them asked if they should hide inside Murus, but Mark told them to stay clear of the city. He didn't want to give the Sapanites a legitimate reason to attack it. And by spreading out along the river, he hoped to deny them a target of opportunity while forcing them to get close in an attempt to locate them.

Two hours later, Seagem raised her head out of the river.

"Markman, Skydancer say that eight airships be here soon. Pod make four airships go into water. Throwing rocks at airships fun."

"Thank you Seagem, please ask your friends to hide in the river until I give the signal."

Seagem slipped back into the water and disappeared. Mark turned to Thalia who had been walking with him awaiting orders.

"Seagem says eight airships will be here soon," Mark said. "Please pass the word. I estimate we have about thirty minutes."

"How do you know?" Thalia asked.

"Seagem just told me," Mark said.

"Okay, how does she know?"

"The plesiosaurs communicate by low frequency sound that can carry for thousands of miles under water. Since the river is noisier than the ocean, they have two other plesiosaurs in the river relaying messages to Seagem."

Thalia stared at Mark with a glassy-eyed expression. Then she shook her head from side to side and shrugged her shoulders a little.

"Okay, airships will be here in thirty minutes," she said.

She ran off to relay the information to the squad leaders and messengers. Mark found Gaia's squad under a leafy, purple tree. They had dug a hole roughly three-feet-wide and five-feet deep that they could drop into when an airship approached. A thatched cover for the hole lay nearby to cover them. It reminded Mark of some of the rifle pits he'd seen during the Civil War.

Thirty-eight minutes later, the airships arrived. Only, Mark counted nine airships, not eight. Just as he was starting to think that Skydancer couldn't count, the ninth airship broke formation and positioned itself above two airships at the rear of the formation.

Mark detected an energy burst similar to the night bell, but much weaker. The two airships below tumbled end over end until they crashed into the forest. A quiet cheer broke out among the entrenched troops, but no one broke cover.

The rogue airship repeated the maneuver and two more airships dropped from the sky. Then, the remaining airships realized they had a wolf among them, and a dogfight began. The airships darted around each other in a way that defied everything Mark thought he knew about aerial combat. The airships made right-angle turns, rose and fell, and rolled over 180 degrees, but in the end the wolf airship was struck by a night bell. It tumbled end over end and crashed in the kuja field near the edge of the leafy forest.

As the remaining airships regrouped for their ground attack. Mark turned to Gaia.

"Once we break cover, I want your squad to get to that airship. Rescue the pilot and bring him to me."

"Yes, sir," Gaia said.

The remaining four airships converged on Murus. The hovered over the city and fired their night bells. Since the city had been abandoned, Mark didn't see any effect.

One airship peeled off from the formation and flew to the edge of the kuja field and fired its night bell. Mark saw a few shapes on the edge of the field go down.

The remaining three moved down the river toward Mark's position. They fired their night bells directly over him. He saw several of the people without helmets fall. They made several high altitude passes over the kuja field and fired several times. Then two of the airships dropped down to within a hundred feet of the river.

"Seagem, Jane, attack now," Mark sent.

Mark jumped out of the hole and shouted.

"Break and attack!"

He gestured to Gaia's squad, and they jumped out of the hole and ran across the field. Then he shouldered his rifle and fired at the closest airship. Seagem and her three friends hurled rocks the size of bread loaves toward the airships at three-hundred miles an hour. Their tails made a cracking sound as they flung the rocks. The lower two airships were shredded. Parts flew in every direction, most of which ended up in the river. The airship flying high cover was struck twice. It belched blue smoke and dropped like a stone into the kuja field.

Having witnessed three airships brought down in less than a minute, the remaining airship turned toward the mainland at high speed.

A cheer broke out on both sides of the river. Then Seagem and her friends raised their heads up from the river and joined in as well, elevating the cheer to thunderous proportions.

"Thank you Seagem," Mark sent. *"You were wonderful."*

"Thank you Markman," Seagem sent. *"You save our children. Make moravi go away."*

Jane walked over to him with Thalia following close behind. Thalia stepped in front of Jane and saluted.

"Orders sir?"

"Send the squads out to the airship wreckage to search for survivors. Try not to kill anyone you don't have to. If you find anyone, put them in the Office of Pubic Good until we can figure out a way to release them."

"Not the arena?"

"No," Mark said. "I wouldn't keep a rabid dog in there."

She shrugged her shoulders, saluted, and left.

"Now what?" Jane asked.

"We won the war. Now we try to win the peace," Mark said.

Gaia, Olympia, Leonia, and Eudocia walked over to them carrying Sigríður on a stretcher made from airship parts.

"Well, look who's back," Jane said. "Did you plan this all along?"

Sigríður winced in pain. Her right arm was bleeding. She had a nasty cut on her forehead, and her left leg had a jagged piece of metal protruding from it. She scowled at Jane.

"Of course I did," she said. "I knew they would eventually send airships against you, so I hid in the foliage until I heard the order to attack."

"Why didn't you tell me?" Jane asked.

"Because my plan needed surprise to work and the only way to keep a secret in Subterra is not to tell anyone."

"Nicely done," Mark said.

"That leg is going to need surgery," Jane said.

She gestured for Gaia's squad to follow her. Mark followed them as far as the bridge to Murus. Then Seagem raised her head from the river to where it was level with Mark's on the bridge.

"Markman, podmates hungry. We go to sea," she sent. *"Call if need me."*

"Thank you, Seagem," Mark sent. *"I am very grateful to you and your pod. We couldn't have won here today without you."*

"Grateful to you, Markman," She sent. *"Fight you with Seagem to protect eggs. Tell us who enemy is. Now, we make war right way."*

She turned away and slipped back into the river. Mark looked over and noticed that a blonde woman with gray eyes and shoulder-length hair had been sketching him. Mark stepped over to her. She put down her sketch book and saluted. Mark returned the salute.

"May I see?" Mark asked.

She picked up the sketch book and held it out to him. There was a charcoal sketch of Mark conversing with Seagem on the bridge. It was very good considering she'd only had three minutes to sketch it. He flipped through and saw another of the airships being destroyed, one of Mark's meeting with Augusta, and several of the attack on the Moravi ranch.

"These are really good," Mark said.

"Thank you," she said. "People will be talking about this day for a hundred years. I wanted to capture it."

Mark sighed and handed the sketch book back to her.

"I hope you're right."

Chapter Fourteen
Going Home

As Mark stepped across the bridge, he heard someone shout, "All hail King Mark. Tamer of dragons and Lord of Murus." A crowd formed around him, and he lost sight of Thalia. The cheer was taken up by several others and repeated twice before they noticed he had put a hand up to stop it.

"I am no king," Mark said. "No one is going to be king."

He heard several shots being fired on the other side of the city.

"What is that?" Mark asked.

"We are executing the pax," a raven-haired woman said.

Mark turned to look for Thalia. He saw her on the edge of the crowd.

"First Sergeant, go get a couple of squads and patrol the city. No one is to be executed. We've had enough death today."

She saluted and ran out the front gate, and Mark addressed the crowd.

"We are all going to have to listen to our better angels until we can sort out who willingly participated in oppression and those who were forced to comply."

A tall, bald, muscular man in the back shouted, "King Mark has spoken. No more death today! Spread the word."

"I can see this is going to be a work in progress," Mark said to himself.

By the time Thalia returned with the two squads, the crowd had disbursed. Mark asked them to patrol the city, stop the executions, and to remind everyone not to waste ammunition.

He went to the First Minister's office and examined her computer. The technology behind it seemed to be equivalent to what was commercially available around the year 2000. The electronics were very fragile, but in good condition for being hundreds of years old. There was just no power.

He looked through the First Minister's books and discovered a few of them were legal statutes, but most of them were vitalibri of the previous First Ministers going back at least three-hundred years.

Jane stepped into the office and held out a locket. She opened it for him, and it had a photo of a light-haired, bearded man and a little blond boy.

"Sigríður's?" Mark asked.

"Now we know why she was so desperate to get back to the surface," Jane said.

"Think you can devise a way to keep her alive when we go through the underwater caves?"

"I have a few ideas. Fortunately, we seem to have an abundance of metal parts to work with. What will you be doing?"

"Haven't you heard?" he asked. "I'm king. I can't be bothered with a menial task like that."

He guffawed, and then smiled.

"No, just kidding. My motives for driving the Sapanites out weren't entirely altruistic. Now, I feel kind of obligated to clean up the mess I've made."

"Well, as they said in your century, good luck with that."

Through a shattered window, Mark heard music start up. It sounded like an Irish folk song. He looked out the window and saw people dancing in the streets. Bottles of cervisia were being passed around.

"Well," Jane said. "It looks like they're out of revenge mode and into party mode."

"Let them," Mark said. "They deserve a celebration."

A steady stream of people returning home after fleeing Murus kept the party going a little longer than it otherwise would have, but after nine hours, the city fell silent. The night bell may be gone, but the habit to go to bed at nine o'clock remained. A few people walked the street for a while like teenagers rebelling against bedtime, but even they eventually succumbed to exhaustion.

Mark went out to survey the wreckage of the downed airships, and found one with a working communicator. He tried to contact Kaxuth to negotiate independence for Refvalnol Island, but when he called, the Sapanites hung up on him. Jane stepped into the wrecked airship just as they ended the connection.

"I hear negotiations are going well," Jane said.

"I don't think you have a knack for sarcasm."

Mark started to get up, but Jane held up her hand.

"There are reports of a handful of moravi left on the south side of the island. I'm going to take a squad or two and go deal with them. Would you like me to recover Kak's watch along the way?"

"That would be great," Mark said.

Jane stepped over to him and held out her hand. Mark took it and shared his memories of the ancient city and where he left Kak's watch.

Jane smiled.

"While I was fighting battles and training the troops, you were stuck in a hole in the ground."

"A very treacherous hole, so be careful," Mark said.

She hugged him, playfully saluted, and left. Mark returned to the city and went to Muirgel's house. He knocked on her door, and through the glass wall, he saw her jump out of bed. The door flung open, and she threw her arms around him.

"I'm so sorry," she said. "I didn't know what to do. They put me on the rack when they found out you were still alive. I didn't want to go back to . . ."

Mark peeled her off of him. He held her hands and looked into her eyes.

"All of that is in the past," he said. "But I need your help with something."

"Of course, anything for my king."

"I'm not a king. I'm more of a military governor until I can establish a working government."

"Of course, your highness," she said.

Mark rolled his eyes and sighed.

"I have a job for you," he said. "In the First Minister's office there are vitalibri going back hundreds of years. I looked through them, and they contain a great deal of history. I want you to take them to the library, sort through them, and write a comprehensive history of Murus. Can you do that?"

"Of course, but that will take some time."

"That's fine," Mark said. "I just don't want the history being lost."

She nodded.

"Do you know where I can find Phaenna?"

"The soup merchant?"

"She is more than that, but yes."

She asked him questions about the history he wanted her to write, and then gave him directions to Phaenna's apartment, and apologized again. When she started sobbing, he pulled away from her. He glanced over his shoulder as he turned to walk down the central path and saw Thalia had joined him.

"Good morning, First Sergeant. Did you sleep well?"

"Yes sir, but I'm still not used to sleeping without the night bell."

"I would imagine it will take a little getting used to,"

She nodded and smiled.

"I thought you would have gone with Jane to exterminate the last of the moravi?" Mark asked.

"No sir. I'm your First Sergeant. My place is here."

She paused on the path for a moment to let a couple of people walk past them. They stared at Mark for a moment, but Thalia waived them on.

Once they were on their way, she turned back to Mark.

"Do you have any orders sir?"

"Not at the moment," Mark said. "But you're welcome to accompany me while I try to put together some kind of representative government."

"What is that?"

"It is a system where citizens elect someone to create rules to manage how things get done. Where the rule of law replaces the fear of death."

"Sounds wonderful. What's 'rule of law?'"

"A system where everyone has to obey the same rules and suffer the same punishment for breaking them."

"I didn't think that was possible," Thalia said.

"The trick is preventing one person or group from taking over and becoming worse than the Sapanites. We also have to set up some sort of economy and tax system to pay for public services."

They found Phaenna's apartment and Mark knocked on her door. It was strange being able to see inside her apartment, so he tried not to look.

"King Mark," she said.

"He's not king," Thalia said.

Mark held up his hand.

"Phaenna, I know that you ran a smuggling operation for the resistance."

Phaenna's hazel eyes showed no sign of fear or excitement. It was the best poker face he had ever seen. She just stared at him until the silence became awkward.

"I'm not here to arrest you. Exactly the opposite. I would like you to invite the resistance leaders to a meeting at the Office of Public Good at twelve o'clock today."

She looked at Mark, then at Thalia.

"Is he serious?" she asked.

"Appears to be," Thalia said.

"One of them is standing next to you," Phaenna said. "But I may have heard of one or two others."

Mark looked at Thalia. She shrugged her shoulders.

"I may have helped a few people resist the wishes of the Sapanites," Thalia said.

"Great," Mark said. "Keep the group to around ten people at most. I'll let you two work out the details."

He left them and when he got back down to the gravel walkway, Mark saw the artist who had sketched him on the bridge. She sat under the leafy tree in the town square. He invited her to the meeting and told her to bring her sketchbook.

He glanced toward the center of the square and realized the statue of Kaxuth was missing. It and the plaque that had been beneath it had been removed. The rusty poles around it gave Mark an idea. He stopped by the Hall of Remembrance on his way back and picked up two blank vitalibri.

He entered the Office of Public Good, and found twenty-one prisoners awaiting his judgment: eleven pax, six custodiae, and four public officials. He wasn't too surprised to learn that none of the Sapanite pilots had survived. Mark asked himself what Lincoln would do. He pardoned the prisoners and encouraged them to leave Murus as quickly as possible. He assured them that the moravi were gone, and starting a new community on the south side of the island was their best option.

Once the prisoners were out of the building, he went upstairs to check on Sigríður and Matthew. Mark found Sigríður in the First Minister's bed staring out the window. When he told her that he was going to take her back to the surface, she tried to hug him, but found it too painful.

He found Matthew in one of the adjoining bedrooms. A room he used to occupy when he was the advisor to the First Minister. They discussed the new government Mark wanted to create, and Matthew asked to participate. Kate wasn't too happy about Matthew being moved, but ended up agreeing.

Mark waited in the meeting room of the Office of Public Good for the delegates to arrive. Matthew was brought down on a stretcher. Phaenna and Thalia came next. Then a few minutes later four more people entered that he didn't know that well, so he asked them to introduce themselves.

Once the introductions were over, and Mark was convinced he had the right group of people, he explained how a representative government worked, and how it was different from a democracy. He explained the checks and balances system to prevent one part of government from taking over. Then he explained the importance of local government being able to over-rule the central government.

He provided them with a map of Refvalnol Island and asked them to divide it into districts, each with its own government. Murus would be its own district, and the capitol of the government, but it would not get a vote in national affairs to prevent its ruling body from taking over.

Once the debating started, and he was sure they knew what to do, he sat in the back corner and listened as he drew plans for an electric generator and a light bulb.

Eight days later, as the delegates were debating how many citizens were required to get a representative in the Murus ruling council and if that number should change with population growth, Jane walked in. She wore her traveling clothes from Iceland, and they looked a little dirty. She watched them argue for a moment, and smiled.

"Teaching them self-government?"

Mark looked up from the plans for a bicycle he was working on.

"Seemed like the thing to do."

Jane handed him Kak's watch. Mark put it in his pocket.

"How's it going?"

"They've got the basics, and Sigríður is well enough to travel. As soon as you can make the box to transport her in, we should be ready to leave. How did it go with you?"

"I'm happy to report that the last of the moravi are gone. They brought the last two back here to eat in some kind of celebration."

"I have wondered how moravi would taste," Mark said.

"What about the Sapanites?"

"I've tried to contact them, but it seems no one is answering."

He held up Kak's watch.

"I'll go and check on them, and, no offense, but you look like you could use a bath."

Jane smiled.

"I see you are still a master of the obvious."

Jane gave him a kiss on the cheek as she left. Mark went to the First Minister's office to check on the Sapanites. The Sapanite capitol was in a frantic state. Sapanites rushed about much the same way humans rushed about in New York City. He looked into the room where the three ruling councils met, and they were in a heated debate. Mark couldn't understand the language, but it was clear that each of the ruling councils had different ideas about what to do.

From what he was able to gather by looking at documents and listening to meetings, one group wanted to invade the island, another group wanted to use a large weapon on the island, and a third group wanted to ignore the island. All of them wanted the plesiosaur attacks to stop, but none of them had an idea of how to accomplish it.

Mark used his connection to Seagem to speak with her. He asked her what the plesiosaurs wanted to stop the war with the Sapanites. Her answer was the same as before: no more moravi, they want the island, and restock the fish they've been taking from their feeding ground.

Mark sketched a rectangular object and wrote the plesiosaur's demands on the four long sides in both Latin and Sapanite. Then he took the sketch to the metal workers who refused to produce them. Anything with the Sapanite language was forbidden, and no amount of persuasion could convince them otherwise.

Mark ended up loading a cart with scrap metal and going to the volcanic vent to make them himself. It took him three days to produce the metal bricks and give them to Seagem. Seagem didn't understand what the shiny rocks were for until Mark used his connection with her to teach her Latin. After a little debate with Skydancer, they agreed to throw the metal bricks at the Sapanite coast.

Mark returned to Murus in time to hear the debate between Gualtiero, a dark-haired man with dark-brown eyes, and Kyrie, a wispy woman with shoulder-length honey-blonde hair, regarding sales tax to pay for government. Kyre argued that the best way to prevent government corruption would be to make their jobs unpaid, thus limiting sales tax to one percent. Before he could stop himself, Mark sided with Kyre, and her rule passed with overwhelming support.

Jane came downstairs and sat down next to him after the vote. She wore a white button-down blouse and blue knee-length skirt.

"I thought you were going to let them figure it out for themselves?"

"I got carried away," Mark said. "Are we ready to leave?"

"Sigríður is well enough to travel, and I built a watertight box from the hull of one of the airships. So, yes, we're ready when you are."

"Seagem's pod delivered our terms to the Sapanites, so I'm just waiting to see what their response is."

Mark picked up the vitalibri he had been working on and opened it to a sketch of a Mason jar he had been working on. He paused and looked over at Jane.

"How were you able to keep carbon dioxide from building up and killing her?"

"Kuja," Jane said.

"Kuja?" Mark asked.

"Yes, it seems that the chemical reaction that occurs when kuja juice is mixed with air is that it removes carbon dioxide and releases oxygen."

"That's amazing," Mark said.

"I thought so."

Mark spent the rest of the week with the metal workers to create an electric generator and light bulbs.

As they were running a test on the first generator, Mark heard people shouting in the street. He stepped out of the workshop and saw an airship drop a metal tablet onto the field in the arena.

As he walked to the arena, a crowd of a dozen or so people brought the metal tablet to him. It read, "We agree to your terms." in both English and Latin. Mark read it and smiled.

He contacted Seagem and told her the war was over. She was a little disappointed, and Mark wasn't sure if it was because he was leaving or that the game had ended. Seagem told him she would find someone to take them to the surface and to meet on the beach in three days.

Mark found Jane in the Hall of Remembrance writing a science textbook. She looked up at him and smiled.

"Setting up a school?" Mark asked.

"Among other things," Jane said.

"Do they have a printing press to copy these?"

Mark gestured at the stack of vitalibri that she had turned into text books.

"I have the metal workers making one, along with a typewriter and a pencil sharpener."

"It's time to go," Mark sent
"How long?"
"Three days. I'd like to leave quietly."
"Agreed, how do we handle Sigríður?"
"We don't tell her until we leave."
"What about the box?"
"I'll take it to the beach before we leave."
"Sounds good."

Early in the morning of the third day, Mark waited outside as Jane woke Sigríður. Mark heard Sigríður's harsh language at being awakened transform into hugs as she realized she was leaving. She had a travel bag ready to go, so she and Jane emerged from the First Minister's bedroom as soon as she was dressed.

Since the pax didn't run the city anymore, the gate was left open. With the moravi gone, the walk to the beach was pleasant and uneventful. They arrived at the beach and found the box and harness exactly where Mark had left them.

"That looks like a coffin," Sigríður said.

"It does indeed," Jane said. "But it is the only way we can get you to the surface."

Jane took off her backpack and pulled out a small, glass vile. She handed it to Sigríður, while Mark set up the harness and called for Seagem.

"Drink this, and get into the box," Jane said.

Sigríður looked at the vile. Then she opened it and sniffed it.

"Taba?" she asked.

"Yes," Jane said.

"That could be poison," Sigríður said.

"It is just enough to get you to sleep. The journey through the caves will take several hours and you may not have enough air if you are conscious," Jane said.

Sigríður stared at the vile.

"I know that trust . . ."

Jane stopped mid-sentence when she saw her drink the contents of the vile.

"I can't live without my family, so I don't care if it's poison or not."

Jane smiled, helped her take her backpack off, stow it in the box, and get settled.

"When you wake up, you'll be on the surface," Jane said.

She held Sigríður's hand until she drifted off to sleep.

Twenty-one minutes later, Seagem's head popped up out of the surf. She introduced them to Ring-tail. Mark showed them the harness he had devised to carry them to the surface. He explained that the loop in the middle would fit over Ring-tail's neck, Sigríður's box was attached to one end and Mark and Jane would be attached to the other. Ring-tail approved.

Mark and Jane thanked Ring-tail for taking them to the surface, but Ring-tail said the honor was his. He wanted to go to the surface, despite the cost, and see the Sun for himself. Being able to help Markman was an additional honor.

After assuring Ring-tail, through Seagem, that they could breathe underwater, Mark and Jane sealed up Sigríður's box, carried the harness out to the water and held it open for Ring-tail. Once it was around his neck, they strapped themselves to it.

Ring-tail swam slowly until he got used to the harness. Then, he picked up speed. He didn't dive down like Mark expected, but he went into a large cave at the edge of the giant bubble that was Subterra. The trip through the caves lasted for six-hours and twenty-four minutes, that seemed like an eternity to Mark. He didn't have a way to measure it, but he felt changes in the water pressure that went from intense to extremely intense, to less intense. But finally, the pressure decreased as they emerged from another cave. Mark saw the haze of sunlight through the water. Ring-tail went toward it and when he broke the surface, Mark saw blue sky.

As soon as Ring-tail's eyes adjusted to the light, he took them to the closest shoreline. Once Mark and Jane were able to stand, they took the harness off him. He gave them a thunderous cheer, and then swam out toward the middle of the lake.

"How long do you think he has?" Jane asked.

"Those pressure changes were pretty intense, so a few hours at most, but at least he got to see the Sun. Any idea where we are?"

"None whatsoever."

They opened up the box and revived Sigríður. She opened her eyes and shielded them from the sunlight.

"I'm on the surface," she said.

"You're on the surface," Jane said. "Take it easy until the taba wears off."

She reached over and hugged Jane. Then she staggered out of the box to hug Mark.

Now that Sigríður was out of the box, Jane folded in the sides, and it became a two handled steamer trunk. They put their back packs inside, found a road, and started walking.

They passed over a hill, and they saw a sign that read, "Inverness fifteen miles." Once they got into town, they found a Woolworths on Haywick High Street, and Mark bought them a change of clothes. Then, they went to the train station, and he bought them train tickets to Aberdeen. As they sat in a pub in the middle of town called Criterion Bar, waiting for their train to arrive, a local man with a thick blond beard and deep blue eyes entered, sat down at the bar, and told anyone who would listen about seeing the monster in the loch. Mark bought him ale, and he told his story.

When they arrived at Aberdeen station, Mark gave Sigríður a hundred dollars in gold.

"This should be enough to get back to Iceland," Mark said. "I would get your family as far away as possible."

"I will," Sigríður said. "Where will you go?"

"London," Jane answered. "We have some business there. Then America."

"Good luck to you both," Sigríður said.

She hugged them, smiled, and left. As she walked away, Mark couldn't help doing an active X-ray scan of her to see if she had taken anything. She hadn't, and he felt a little embarrassed for checking.

Jane looked over at him and smiled.

"Don't feel bad," she said. "I scanned her too."

Other Books by Alfred Taylor

Full Circle: Electronic Afterlife
Full Circle: Freedom's Firewall
The Write Way to Get a Girlfriend
Full Circle: Time's Warden
Full Circle: Covert Invasion

Audio Books by Alfred Taylor

Druid Dreams and Other Stories